disgrace

book two

BETHANY-KRIS

Published by Bethany-Kris

BK

www.bethanykris.com

eISBN 13: 978-1-988197-54-8

Print ISBN 13: 978-1-988197-55-5

Cover Art © Mignon Mykel

Editor: Elizabeth Peters

For every reader who messaged me to thank me for John. This one is for you, loves.

CONTENTS

CHAPTER ONE

STIFLING WAS NOT a word Siena Calabrese used often, but at the moment, it was the one that best fit her life. Hot, stuffy mid-June air blew through the hallway of her oldest brother's brownstone. It reminded her that it wasn't only the two men looming at her back making her feel like she was roasting with suffocation. Even the muggy weather had hot, sticky hands around her small throat.

So was her life, now.

"Greta, Giulia," Siena greeted.

The two teenaged girls stepped into the brownstone with guarded eyes. As they always did. As they *should*. There was nothing in that house—but for Siena, perhaps—that could be trusted, and the girls knew it.

Every time were faced with their half-brothers, Siena highly suspected Greta and Giulia wondered about their fate. Or rather, what their fate might bring for them today.

Greta more than Giulia, likely. She was, after all, closing in on eighteen faster and faster. Giulia, on the other hand, was only fifteen. She still had a few years of safety under her belt.

Not even the girls' mother had been able to save them.

Not when it came to Kev and Darren.

"I like the red," Siena said, reaching out to play with a few strands of Greta's long, wavy hair. Her half-sister only offered a slight, yet still awkward, smile in response. "I thought you were thinking about something darker?"

Greta shrugged. "Ma liked red."

Silence saturated the hallway. Both of Siena's half-sisters refused to look up from the floor, not even after Kev cleared his throat, and Darren let out an exasperated sigh.

"Too bad she won't be able to see it," Siena said.

She was only forcing herself to talk because every part of her felt like Greta and Giulia. As though she should hide away somewhere, and avoid drawing attention to herself. That would be for the best—that was what would be the safest for her.

7

Siena couldn't do that.

Not now.

Not after everything.

It would be like throwing these two young girls to the wolves. Those wolves being their own half-brothers.

It wasn't like any of the Calabrese daughters—not Siena, being the only legitimate daughter, or her half-sisters, born to her dead father's equally dead mistress—could trust their brothers to have their best interests in mind. Kev and Darren had proved over the last few months that their interests were solely tied up in one thing, and one thing only.

Moving higher.

Ruining the Marcellos.

Taking over New York.

Siena's mind drifted over the months that had passed since her father's murder, and then John going into a facility. A little bit of February, March, April, May, and now here they were in the middle of June.

Her father was still dead.

John was still gone.

And yet ... so much had changed.

So very much was different.

Kev had taken over as the boss in lieu of their father's death. Darren was, of course, Kev's right hand man. If only that was all ...

A failed marriage arrangement. A missing half-sister. Two others, now orphaned. A war on the streets. Bodies piling up.

Siena shook those thoughts out of her head. She could not afford to get lost in them today, and certainly not right now. It didn't help that Kev and Darren were at her back damn near constantly. She couldn't move without one of them knowing about it.

Again ... so was her life.

But for these two girls?

For her little sisters, so lost without their own big sister to guide them, Siena was present. She forced herself to be present and to do what she needed to do, so they saw a smiling face, and someone they could trust.

Because fuck Kev and Darren.

They would not do to these girls what they had tried to do to their missing sister. Well ... to Greta and Giulia, Ginevra was missing. Siena knew the truth—and while right now, the younger Calabrese girls hurt, it would not last forever.

Missing did not mean dead. Someday, they would know that little fact, too.

"Are we all going to linger in the goddamn hallway all day, or have lunch?" Kev asked. "I'm starved."

Greta and Giulia kept their gazes locked on the floor. Neither of them answered their brother, but frankly, they had learned rather quickly about Kev and Darren. When the two men asked a question, they weren't actually looking for a response, but rather, an action.

They only wanted well-behaved women.

Very little else.

"Are you hungry?" Siena asked the girls.

"A little," Greta said.

Giulia dared to look past Siena, and her familiar blue eyes narrowed. "Not particularly."

Siena let a little smile slip through at the youngest girl's barely hidden contempt. "I cooked, though."

The girl's gaze darted back to Siena in a blink. "Did you?"

"Your favorite."

"Oh, well … okay."

"I'm hungry," Kev repeated.

"Then, go sit down in the damn dining room," Siena barked over her shoulder.

The warning that flashed in both her brothers' eyes was enough to tell Siena she was toeing a very thin line with them. Before her father's death, she used to get away with a hell of a lot more than she did now.

Kev and Darren barely let her breathe. Apparently, even breathing was wrong. Or rather, *Siena* breathing was wrong.

"Let's grab some food," Siena told them.

The girls nodded, and then followed in front of her when she urged the two forward. Greta and Giulia passed by Kev and Darren without saying a word. Siena didn't miss how the two sisters' lips curled a bit in their disgust at being close to their brothers.

That could happen when a person was forced to watch brothers you barely knew do things like try and force your older sister into an arranged marriage, not to mention, how they found their mother one morning.

All by Kev and Darren's hand.

Siena tried her fucking hardest to ignore the awkwardness as the siblings settled into the kitchen together. What else could she do at this point? What else could she possibly do for these two girls—both fighting invisible battles, and confused?

At least, she thought, Greta and Giulia had some freedom even if it was just an illusion. The two lived with an aunt, although the woman was largely paid and happily so by the Calabrese brothers. The sisters weren't forced to be in Kev and Darren's presence every single day of their lives. Usually once or twice a week, instead.

Siena, on the other hand …

Well, it all went back to the stifling thing again.

Her brothers were the worst.

9

She was rarely able to escape them.

It was a couple of hours later before Siena saw her half-sisters off. Shuffled into the back of a black town car driven by a Calabrese enforcer, Greta and Giulia were taken away once more. They were packed up like prized beauties to be brought out and dusted off for showing on another day.

Siena knew it.

The girls knew it.

A fucking shame, really.

"You're late, Ma," Kev grumbled.

"I had things to do, son."

"Things like what, exactly?"

"A friend called."

Kev scoffed. "Sure, Ma."

As the footsteps of her mother and older brother came closer to the kitchen, Siena tried to relax the tension in her shoulders. The anger she felt toward her mother reared its ugly head whenever the two were in a damn room together.

Today was not going to be any fucking different.

How could it?

"I really did have other things come up, Kev," her mother said.

The two were just outside the kitchen, now. Siena didn't care to eavesdrop, but that had kind of become a part of her job.

So to speak ...

"We are *trying* to put on a united front," Kev reminded Coraline. "It is the most important thing right now. I'm quite aware of how you feel about Greta and Giulia, but you need to forget about it, Ma. Put it aside for now, so we can all handle our business in this city."

"Mmm."

"What?"

"Handle business," Coraline said. "I suppose we're going to pretend that another Calabrese Capo was not killed last week, are we?"

"No one is pretending—"

"Well, we can't forget about that *united front*, Kev."

"Ma."

"I said what I said, didn't I?"

Kev let out a harsh sigh. "We have a plan—an attack coming up. A few days after the funeral. One of their warehouses on the west end that they think we don't know about. An answer to the Capo's death. Darren thought it would be appropriate that we wait until after. Respect to the man, and all that."

"Sure," Coraline said. "Your father never would have *waited*."

"I am not my father, Ma."

"Obviously."

Siena didn't even bother to look up from the dishes she was washing as her mother and brother slipped into the kitchen. Coraline moved toward the island where a plate of hot food had been left to sit out for her, and looked it over.

"Really, Siena, chicken alfredo?" her mother asked.

Siena kept her attention on her work. "It's Giulia's favorite. I was trying to make her comfortable."

Coraline made a noise under her breath.

It sounded a lot like disgust.

"It might have helped had you shown up like you were supposed to for dinner," Siena added. "They were looking forward to having an actual conversation with you, Ma."

Siena did turn around and chance a glance at her mother, then. Coraline looked like something awful had been shoved into her mouth. Horrified, displeased, and disgusted all at the same time.

The last thing this woman wanted to do was greet, be nice to, or handle anything about her husband's mistress's children.

It wasn't like it was the girls' fault. They hadn't asked to be born, or for their father to be an unfaithful bastard. Yet, here they all were.

Coraline had been perfectly fine, pleased, and pampered in her life before Matteo's death. She had not minded turning cheek to her husband's behaviors, and dalliances with women. She even pretended like she didn't know her husband's mistress had once lived in a bigger house than she did simply because she birthed him the same amount of children that Coraline had given to Matteo.

No, none of that had mattered to Coraline *before*.

Now, with Matteo dead, and the girls' mother dead, Coraline had no choice.

Despite knowing it might cross one of her brother's many lines, Siena didn't mind reminding her mother of her place at the moment. Sometimes, it was the only thing that actually worked where Coraline was concerned.

"It would not look very good for you to shun the only Calabrese *principessas della mafia*," Siena murmured, letting her finger edge along the line of the island as she spoke. "Even if those mafia princesses are illegitimate daughters born from a several decades-long affair. You know this, Ma."

Coraline scowled.

Kev passed a look between the mother and daughter, but said nothing.

"They are not the only *principessas* of this family," Coraline said, smiling in that cruel, cold way of hers. "And don't you forget that, Siena."

Dread slipped down Siena's spine.

A cold fear met it with open arms.

Siena knew all too well how open and vulnerable she was to her brothers' games. She could just as easily be used as fodder for her brothers' plans as her half-sisters.

And shit …

Maybe better her, than them.

Siena didn't show her fear, or her weakness. Not to a woman like her mother. Coraline ate that shit for breakfast.

"Maybe that's what bothers you the most, Ma," Siena said, shrugging. "That one of the illegitimate daughters will be used before I ever am—the only legitimate daughter. *Your* daughter. What a fucking shame that would be, huh?"

Coraline's gaze narrowed.

A silent threat.

A vicious promise.

"Legitimate in name and birth *only*," Coraline hissed right back. "We all know how you've betrayed this family with all you have done to us, Siena. None of us will ever forget the disgrace you are. Marrying you off to get you off our hands, or getting rid of you by some other means would be a *blessing*. Nothing more."

Kev chuckled. "She's got a point."

What a life this was.

The disgraced one.

Siena wished she cared.

• • •

The church quieted as the Calabrese family slipped inside. Siena stayed firmly behind her older brothers, yet still in front of her mother. Appearances were everything, and even how they entered a space was now a well thought out event.

Kev stayed a half of a pace ahead of Darren. A subtle, yet still clear, message about which of the two men now ran the Calabrese show. Darren never seemed to mind, as his brother's right-hand man, seeing as how he still had quite a bit of control himself.

Siena was always made to be in between her brothers and mother—a clear indicator that she was both protected, and watched. Enforcers trailed behind them all. One for each person, and sometimes more.

Somedays, it felt as though Siena couldn't breathe. Every direction she looked, someone new was watching her. Someone else would be reporting back to her brothers on her latest behaviors.

She found it easier to be compliant and complacent, but inside, she was a raging monster battling against the walls of her cage. A prison cell that no one else could see, sure, but that she was all too aware of when it came right down to it.

Siena's gaze drifted over the people already sitting down and waiting for the funeral to start. She didn't linger on one person for any length of time, and she didn't even give them a smile. What would be the point?

She was only there for show.

Much like her brothers.

At the front of the church, standing at the closed casket of a now-dead Calabrese Capo, was the family of Arty Moretti. Siena stayed back beside her mother as Kev and Darren greeted the dead man's wife first, and then his oldest daughter, and one son. Both of the man's children were adults— Siena counted that as a blessing in disguise when it came to this war between the Calabrese and Marcello families.

At least this way, the two were not young children now left without a father. They were already adults into their own lives, and would not be left feeling abandoned and alone. Or … that was her hope for them.

She suspected it still hurt them, of course. Grief was a lot like the ocean—wide, sometimes clear and sometimes murky, and always dangerous. It could swallow someone whole, and drown them in pain.

Siena stepped up to the family when her brothers moved away. As Kev and Darren moved to speak with a couple of their men gathered close by, she and her mother took to comforting the family.

It was also their job.

Another one added to the pile.

And what did they say to these poor people?

"We're so sorry."

Sorry our family has taken from you.

"We're here for you."

So long as you are here for us.

"He is with God."

And more men will soon join him.

Because that was the way of war, and that was all that could be guaranteed for these people, and their pain. More deaths would follow, and it would be all the Calabrese family's fault.

Why?

Siena's gaze drifted to her brothers again. Sure, they looked as though they fit the part of mafia *principes* turned kings in their black suits, shined shoes, slicked back hair, and straightened postures. Their cold eyes held little warmth, and their tones delivered orders with a sharp flatness that could both chill, and slice at the same time.

Matteo—during the years that he lived—had certainly trained her brothers well. They stepped into the positions they needed to without hesitation, and without batting an eye. The rest of the Calabrese organization didn't think to question the brothers when they moved up in power, and replaced others that might have been a better fit. No one said a thing when they first tried to strong-arm the Marcellos into a peaceful deal, and then turned on them when said deal went sour.

Fingers pointed.

Bullets were readied.

Blood spilled.

The city tasted like war now.

Nothing could stop them. Kev and Darren were obsessive in their desire and assurance that the Calabrese family would soon be the one running New York City with an iron fist.

Well, that's how it felt, anyway. They still had to get the little issue of the Marcellos out of the way. The Marcello family made it very clear that would not be an easy task.

Siena patted the hand of the Capo's widow, and offered her a smile. A forced smile, sure, and one that didn't reach her eyes, but who could tell? It was a funeral, after all. No one was supposed to be *happy* or *true*.

"Anything you need, I promise," Siena repeated.

The woman nodded. "Thank you, Siena. You're such a sweet girl. Your brothers must be so proud of you."

Siena smiled a little more honestly at that statement. Bitterness coated her tongue with the taste of bile, and she patted the woman's hand once more.

"You have no idea," she murmured.

As quickly as Siena had greeted the woman and her adult children, she turned away from them, and followed behind her now-moving brothers. Kev and Darren weaved through the group of men who had come to talk to them, and made for their designated seats.

Only because this was not their family's funeral, and this was not their church, did they sit in the pew directly behind the family. Unfortunately, while sitting, there was no chance for Siena to hide her displeasure or discomfort behind her brothers' backs. She was forced to take a little more care with her appearance, and the mask she put forth.

Darren looked over at her. "Did you really have to pick a purple dress?"

"It's a dark color."

"*Black* is appropriate."

"I'm fucking sick of black, Darren."

All she ever seemed to wear anymore was black.

Once this was all over—she had not forgotten what Andino Marcello told her months ago when she was ripped away from John, after all—she was never going to wear black again. Not unless someone fucking forced her into the color.

This won't be forever.

Those words rang and rang.

They echoed and echoed.

She kept them close.

What else could she do?

A few minutes before the service was supposed to start, murmurings passed between the people in the pews. Heads began to turn in the direction that the whispering started. Hot, humid heat from the outside slipped up the church's aisle.

Siena turned, too.

She wanted to see, too.

There, at the back of the church dressed in black on black and standing in a close line of at least ten men, were Marcellos.

The boss. His men. John's father.

Dante Marcello—the boss of the family—smiled and ticked a finger forward. His men moved behind him as he took a step forward, and then another. Slow, purposeful strides. A confident, uncaring stroll.

Beside Siena, her brothers and mother hissed back and forth between one another. Clearly, they had not been expecting this move.

Siena was kind of impressed.

"How fucking dare they?" Kev asked.

"Stop sitting there—do something," Darren snarled.

"What should he do?" their mother asked. "He *cannot* make a scene in this church."

No, Kev certainly couldn't.

Once again, it looked like her brothers were bowing down to the Marcellos. It seemed as though not every battle was started and finished with bullets, blood, and funerals. Some battles were won with killer smiles, and a simple show of power.

Siena was starting to believe she should keep score.

Calabrese family—zero.

The Marcellos—one.

• • •

It was almost funny how one simple action could change all kinds of circumstances. Suddenly, the enforcers that rarely left Siena alone when she was outside of her brothers' sights were now fully distracted by the show happening inside the entrance of the church.

With the funeral over, it seemed Siena's brothers had finally decided to take action with the Marcellos.

Better late than never.

Siena hung back behind the crowd—her interest in watching men verbally spar over their growing feud was nonexistent. None of this would do her or the cause she was silently fighting for any good at the end of the day.

She kept one eye on her mother as Coraline edged along the crowd. Her mother's eagle eye was fully pointed on Kev, Darren, and the Marcellos.

Siena never would have taken her mother for a woman who involved herself in mafia politics, or the business of men. And yet, there Coraline was on a daily basis. Doing exactly those things with her sons, and never thinking twice about it.

Who knew why.

The name she carried.

The man—now dead—she had married.

The legacy behind her.

The promise of one ahead of her.

Siena didn't know.

It wouldn't matter when this was over.

A form slid in beside Siena. She stiffened a bit at the man's presence, and the scent of his familiar cologne. He wouldn't typically be so bold, but it seemed like everyone around them at the moment was currently distracted.

Andino smiled a bit when Siena looked at him. "What do you have for me?"

This little game of theirs had started months ago. It started with nothing more than a single sentence in passing from Andino—*perhaps you should take up a hobby ... like yoga.* Back when there had seemed like a chance of settling this feud between their families with something like a marriage was possible, he had given her that line, and she ran with it.

Yoga it was.

It was the only time—two hours twice a week—that her brothers allowed Siena any kind of privacy and peace. The enforcers stayed outside the complex. She slipped out the back. Andino was always waiting.

John's cousin was fighting this war in a far dirtier way.

Siena respected him for it, really.

"Well?" he asked again. "What do you have for me?"

"A west end warehouse," Siena said. "An attack in a couple of days. Retribution for Arty's death. That's all I know."

Andino's face cleared of emotion, and his gaze hardened. "All right. You don't know what, or how many—"

"I would tell you if I did. You know that."

Andino's hand touched her shoulder lightly. "I know."

She glanced back at him again. "I miss him."

John.

She always missed him.

16

She hadn't seen him in months.

Andino nodded once. "I know that, too. Soon, Siena. I know he'll be getting out soon. He made the choice to stay in the facility for this long because of his own health. He *chose* stability. That's the thing about John, and being bipolar. I don't think he's ever really chosen stability before now. And with that comes taking a hard, long look at a lot of things in his life. I don't think he felt it was good for him mentally to try handling his personal business while dealing with everything outside of it, too."

"I want him to be good."

She wanted John to be healthy, and happy.

Safe.

He was not going to come out to stability, or safety.

Not now.

"He's going to be fucking great," Andino said with a grin, "as long as you're still waiting for him when he's ready to come back, then nothing else matters."

"Of course, I'll be waiting."

She loved John.

Nothing was ever going to change that.

Andino nodded. "So, hey, what's the thirtieth looking like for you?"

"Of this month?"

"Yeah."

Siena shrugged. "Yoga."

Andino chuckled. "Thought so. I'll be waiting. We should really go visit John."

"Really?"

"Yeah, girl, really."

That made everything so much better.

"Okay, go before someone sees you with me," she said, flicking her hand at him.

Andino rolled his eyes. "Trust me—they're all too stuck up their own asses to even think about you right now. You didn't seriously think this whole show was just about fucking with their heads, did you?"

"Well ..."

Yeah, kind of.

Andino smirked. "I will always find a way to get my message in, Siena, no matter how protected they think you are. Do you have a new phone?"

"Yeah, Kev changed it again last week."

"Same old, same old."

Siena nodded once. "Random wrong numbers, I know."

"This whole thing isn't forever, remember. Soon, you'll have what you want."

Not what.

Who.
She reminded herself daily that this wasn't forever.
No, it was just for right now.
Forever was going to be far more beautiful.

CHAPTER TWO

THE RED CIRCLE around July twentieth both taunted and promised Johnathan Marcello. It was just a date—a single date among many on the calendar. One of the nurses at Clearview Oaks had given him the calendar months ago when he first arrived. Each month showcased a different picture of the facility's grounds.

The older nurse had suggested that crossing off dates on the calendar would give him some sort of satisfaction. It hadn't, of course. Not until he knew his release date.

Now, every little black X in permanent marker felt like another chain coming undone from his body. And yet, the closer he got to that big red circle, the tighter the invisible rope became around his throat.

Strange how that worked.

"Nervous, John?"

He spun on his heels to find his therapist leaning in the doorway of his private room. Patients weren't allowed to have their doors closed unless the doctor was also in the room, and only if the patient was nonviolent. On a suicide watch, the door was never closed. Ever.

"Well?" Leonard pressed.

"For what?"

"Your chosen release date is coming up. Three weeks away."

John passed the calendar one more look. "I like how you posed that as if *I* chose when I could leave, when actually—"

"You did choose."

Leonard smiled when John glanced back at him.

"You made it clear you didn't think I was ready to go," John said pointedly.

The older man shrugged. "Yes, well, you weren't. Every little medication change sent you into another round, and we had trouble getting you settled with the right dose of Lithium. Never mind the actual therapy, John."

"I am, though. A little nervous, I mean."

"All normal, considering."

"I'm looking forward to it, too."

"As you should," Leonard replied. "I'm curious, though, what has you the most nervous."

John laughed under his breath. Running this fingers through his hair, he once again turned to face the calendar. Leonard had a way of pushing John into talking about things beyond the surface of what he presented to the world. The therapist had no problem with really digging into the crux of John's issues.

About life.

His family.

Being bipolar.

Out of the many, *many* therapists John had gone through in his life, Leonard was—by far—the best for him personally. Sure, he didn't always like what the older man had to say. He didn't particularly appreciate being forced to drag out old issues and dirty laundry to reexamine. That didn't mean Leonard's tactics were useless.

They weren't.

They worked.

They worked especially well for John.

What more could he ask for?

"Well?" the therapist pressed when John stayed quiet. "What has you nervous—reentering life, integrating with your family again ... *her?*"

John swallowed hard.

Her.

Siena.

John chuckled. "Not her. Never her."

Leonard returned John's smile. "You haven't seen the woman in ... well, almost four months, now. You sound very sure of that statement, though."

He was.

It wasn't like he had a reason to be.

He also didn't have a reason not to be.

John shrugged. "It's not her."

"The rest, then?"

"It's a mixture of the rest, I think."

Leonard closed the door behind him, and stepped further into the room. He waved a hand at John, and then gestured toward the seating area next to the windows. So was the therapist's way when it came to a session. He liked to make John sit, while he remained standing, or pacing. Sometimes Leonard would also sit, but it wasn't particularly often.

John's private room was more like a very expensive, yet also clinical-feeling, bachelor pad. He had his own small kitchen with a two-person table. A double bed, and private bathroom. A sitting area with bookshelves and a flat screen television. The walls showcased photographs of mountains and colorful flowers set in clear frames. The floor was a marble stone that somehow never felt too cold in the mornings.

If anything, it was comfortable. Clean, which he appreciated. Simplistic in design, and catered to his private needs. He had a private phone line to make calls out if he needed to or wanted to, but other than a few calls to his mother, he had not used the phone a lot. After all, he was here to get better, and to focus on himself. Besides, the person he wanted to talk to the most—Siena—he had not been able to. For whatever reason, her old number was dead. No one had given him a reason why.

John had been able to make his room at Clearview Oaks feel somewhat like home in different ways.

John opted to sit in one of the white leather recliners next to the window. Leonard leaned against the wall beside the flat screen, and gazed out the window. Next to the backdrop of crisp white walls, the therapist blended in with his stark white hair and jacket.

"Let's talk, John," Leonard said.

"You are aware I know why you like to stand and pace while I stay sitting, right?"

Leonard's gray eyes cut to John with amusement dancing in his thick, lifted brows. "Oh, do tell."

"When you sit, then I can zone out. I know exactly where you are, and I feel safer to focus my attention elsewhere. The wall, or the clock. Maybe a picture. My hands. Whatever it is, then I don't have to keep an eye on you because you're no longer moving around and keeping my attention on you."

"Keep going."

"When you move, the kind of man I am, means I have to keep an eye on you constantly. I can't let you move behind me, or too close to my side. I need to see your hands, and what they're doing. It takes up a great deal of the focus in my brain, and that makes my mouth vulnerable to letting things slip. If I *can* zone out, I am far less likely to talk. Or if I do, it's … as you say, surface things."

"What people see, not what really *is*."

John nodded. "Although, if you would sit, I would talk, too. For you."

The man's smile softened a bit. "Would you?"

"I would, Leonard."

"I thought so," Leonard replied as he moved to take a seat across from John. "And well done on figuring that strategy of mine out. It only took you … a few months."

"A couple," John shot back. "I knew about a month in."

Leonard chuckled, and wagged a finger at John. "Talk, now."

"It's different."

"What is?"

"Here, to there. Being *inside* here, and then going back into the outside. One of the first things you told me was that I had to choose stability. Not just for now, or for a while, or even for a few years. I had to choose stability for the rest of my life."

Which meant meds, even when they made him feel like shit. It meant choosing to get up every single day and take medications regardless of how he felt about it until a better medication could be chosen. It also meant never excusing himself because of being bipolar, but accepting and being honest about it. It meant being honest to those in his life about what was happening inside his mind, and keeping himself accountable.

Stability was a choice.

Because he could just as easily choose to refuse meds, to self-medicate, or to live his life in a constant spiral of hypomania, full blown mania, and depression. A vicious cycle that would continue to hurt him, and those around him.

John chose stability.

He didn't expect it to always be easy.

"Because in here is routine," John said, glancing out the window. "Here, I know exactly what time the lights are going to come on, and when I can go outside. I know which channels will be on the television, and what the menu looks like for the next week. I know which meds are coming, and which ones need to change. I just … know everything."

"Your life is also pretty structured outside of here, too," Leonard reminded him. "You have made a great effort to set up personal routines that you like to follow, from what time you get up in the morning, to how you clean your house. You're not leaving an environment like this and walking into pure chaos, John."

John nodded because the man was right. "Sure."

"But you have the factor of the unknown out there that we don't provide in here."

"Exactly."

"I understand why that's a little unsettling."

"It might help if they told me more," he said.

John didn't say who, specifically, but the therapist understood what he meant. The only people who came to visit him—his choice, not others— were his father, and Andino. His uncle, Giovanni, had come once as well, and got the bottle of booze he brought along confiscated. It was, by far, one of the most amusing days since John entered the facility.

Still, when the men of his family came, they didn't talk about business. They never told John what was happening outside of these walls, or what he could expect once he left the facility. It was a little unsettling because he wasn't quite sure what that meant.

Were they hiding something from him?

What was it, if they were?

Leonard also knew some of the private details of John's life that he didn't share with outsiders. Or rather, the illegal side of John's life being that he was a made man, and fully engrained in the way of Cosa Nostra.

It certainly helped for these talks.

John didn't need to skip details, or dance around them in some way. He was able to be honest with his therapist, and because he too knew things about Leonard's personal life, he did not feel as if it might get him in trouble simply to talk.

All good things.

"I think they intend for you to focus on yourself, and not … the business," Leonard murmured.

"Funny."

"What is?"

"I've been focusing on the business a lot lately."

"Because you don't know what's happening?"

"Mostly."

Leonard nodded once. "You're going to do fine, John. Regardless if you leave here and it is sunshine, rainbows, and puppies, or if it is hellfire, chaos, and anarchy. The unknown can only really threaten your stability if you allow it to dig in a bit too much, if you get what I mean."

"I do."

"Good." Leonard stood, and brushed invisible lint from his pant legs. "I also have another proposition for you before I give you some good news."

John smirked. "How about you give me the good news first?"

"Nice try. I make the rules."

Asshole.

"What is the proposition?" John asked.

"You need a therapist when you leave here."

John stiffened.

This was not a topic he wanted to discuss because it was a sore spot for him. He didn't like the idea of leaving Clearview Oaks only to need to find a new therapist to see. He was not about to trust someone after the last debacle.

"I can physically *feel* how much discomfort this is causing you," Leonard said.

"Yeah, well, what can you do," John said through gritted teeth. "Nothing, apparently."

"I would take your file on as a patient outside of this facility. Twice weekly. One weekday, and one day on the weekend."

The tension in John's body bled out slowly. "Would you?"

"Sometimes," Leonard said, "it is more about the patient finding the right doctor, than it is about anything else."

"Twice weekly, then."

"Do you want the good news, now?"

John nodded, and stood from the chair. "I almost forgot about it with the whole new therapist thing, actually. What is it?"

"You'll have visitors tomorrow. Your cousin—Andino—and a couple of people he's bringing along. Ladies, apparently, if the information he provided is to be trusted. Unlike his father, Andino doesn't tend to be disruptive when he comes here."

John only laughed. "My uncle, Giovanni, makes it his first and only goal to have fun."

"This is not the place for fun."

"Mmm."

"You didn't ask who Andino is bringing, by the way," Leonard said over his shoulder as he left the room.

Fuck.

He hadn't.

Too late now.

• • •

"John, my man. You're looking good."

He heard his cousin's greeting, and felt Andino's firm hug, but John's gaze was locked on the dark-haired beauty standing just a few feet away. After all, it was kind of fucking impossible for him to pay attention to anything when the love of his life was once again gracing his presence. She was the only thing that ever mattered.

Siena wore the brightest smile that matched the flower printed summer dress accentuating all of her curves and height. A dress that showed off all kinds of leg, and the four inch heels on her feet. She had let her long, dark hair down in soft waves. One of his favorite styles on her because he could wrap his fingers in the silky strands, and get lost. She'd painted her lips a striking red, and those blue eyes of hers never left him once.

Damn.

What had Andino just said?

John didn't know.

His attention was somewhere else entirely.

"What?" he asked Andino.

His cousin only laughed, and the man's green eyes looked John over. In his usual suit and shined shoes, Andino made John miss the fact he hadn't worn proper Armani in months. Instead, he'd dressed down with jeans and T-shirts.

"Shit, you didn't hear a word I just said, huh?" Andino asked.

John's gaze drifted to a very patient, quiet Siena. "Not really, no. Sorry, man."

Andino clapped John's cheek with a gentle pat as he chuckled. "Nah, it's okay. You've got a good reason to be off your game today. I guess they didn't fill you in on who I was bringing along to visit, or what?"

"Leonard has his odd ways."

"Sure, sure."

"It's good, though."

So good.

John wasn't the type who appreciated surprises, but this was far more than fine. Surprises were unknowns that he couldn't prepare for, and he much preferred to prepare for an unknown. This, though? He didn't mind this surprise *at all*.

"Anyway," Andino said, turning to stand beside John. His cousin gestured in front of them. "I said, I hope you don't mind that I brought someone else to properly meet you. I mean, I know this place is supposed to be sacred for you, and all. Focusing on you, but I might not get another time to do this before you come home."

Yes.

The woman standing at Siena's side.

Haven.

John had noticed the woman, of course, but his mind always tended to focus in on the most important things first, and then everything else second. Siena was, by far, the most important thing standing on the walkway in that moment when it came to John and his life. And shit, he had been counting down the days until he would get to see Siena again. Not that he had known today would be the day.

No offence to Haven.

Or Andino.

John said none of those things out loud.

"You don't mind, do you?" Andino asked again.

John shook his head. "No, man. Of course, not."

"Good. I want you to meet the girl I'm going to marry, you know. Properly fucking meet her, John. Not hear things about her from someone else, or see her in passing. Actually meet her *with* me. Take some time to sit down and have a real conversation with her. I talk about you all the time, and she's a little out of the loop about me and you. Kind of a big fucking deal to me, and everything."

John's brow rose high as he took in his cousin a second time. Andino never looked more nervous than he had in that moment. His cousin scrubbed a hand over his unshaven jaw, and his gaze kept darting back to Haven like he didn't want to take his eyes off her for even one damn minute.

Huh.

John knew that look.

He had that look.

Every time he looked at Siena, that was.

It was kind of strange for John to see his cousin so off-balance in this way. And *marriage?* Genuine, honest to God, going to settle down *marriage?*

John never thought he would see the day. Not where Andino was concerned, anyway. His cousin just wasn't the type to settle down into a monogamous relationship where something like forever and love might get thrown in the conversation. Not to mention, Andino was usually the guy who liked to poke fun at a man who did get his dick tied into a knot over a woman.

This was a whole one-eighty.

So yeah, John did a double-take.

"Seriously?"

Andino nodded. "Yeah, man."

"I thought … I mean, the family didn't have a high opinion of her a few months ago, and all. I thought they had made it clear she wasn't acceptable, or some shit. You kind of gave me the impression you didn't know what the hell you were doing about them, her, or the rest."

"It's not about them."

Fact.

He knew that all too well. Sometimes when it came to their family, the best thing a man could do on the personal side of his life was shut the fuck down. Keep everything closed up tight. Make it clear nothing was open for discussion.

John didn't know if that's what Andino had done when it came to Haven, or not. It also really didn't fucking matter.

Good for Andino.

Whatever it took to get what the man wanted.

John laughed, and clapped his cousin on the shoulder. Dragging Andino in for a quick, tight one-armed hug, the two men's laughter colored up the front yard of the facility. Andino hugged John back with a firm hold.

Some of John's unease about leaving the facility started to drift away in those few seconds. Despite how his disorder often colored up his impressions and perceptions of his family, he still found himself reminded time and time again of their loyalty and love for him.

No, he didn't mind at all that Andino brought his girl along. He appreciated it, really. He would make sure to take time and speak with Haven while she was there because it was what she, and Andino, deserved.

Besides, the woman had to be something interesting to catch Andino Marcello's eye, and steal his fucking heart.

But for now ...

"Give me some time with Siena," John said quietly as he pulled away from his cousin. "It's been too long."

Andino stepped aside. "You got it, John."

All John needed to do was hold his hand out in Siena's direction, and she instantly darted forward to catch it with her own. The second her warm palm fitted in his, and her fingers wove around his own, John's world tilted back to its proper axis once more.

Strange how that worked.

It had been months since he looked at her—*talked* to her—and yet it took only one single touch from her to settle him. His restless heart calmed, and his tight chest relaxed. Everything that was right and good in his world was currently holding his hand. It was just a gesture. A small act of affection, but it was everything and more to John, too.

Siena's blue eyes met his, and her sweet smile grew a little more. Her olive-toned skin flushed with a happy pink when he bent down and caught her lips in a quick kiss. Maybe he should have asked if that was okay with her, but the way she kissed him back said it was just fucking fine, anyway.

He had a million and one things to ask.

About her.

Them.

The outside.

The families.

Business.

The war she had alluded to the last time she was there with him.

So damn much.

And yet, all John wanted to do was kiss her. He only wanted to drag Siena closer, wrap his arms around her, and breathe her in. All her familiar warmth, scent, and love. All of her.

The world ceased to exist.

Nothing else mattered.

Unfortunately, the facility had goddamn policies about public displays of affection, and that forced John to pull away from the kiss far sooner than he wanted to. Siena only grinned and kissed the pad of his thumb when he stroked her bottom lip.

"Damn, I missed you," he said.

Through thick, lowered lashes, she watched him. "Did you?"

"Every day."

"Every *single* day?"

John smirked. "First thing on my mind in the morning."

"What about at night?"

"Last thing I think about before I go to sleep, *bella*."

Siena's love colored her happiness. John knew his wasn't always as easy to see because he made a great effort to keep those vulnerable parts of himself well hidden from the world. It had become such a habit that he worried now whether or not the people who deserved to see his love could actually see it.

People like Siena.

She had her ways of reminding him everything was just fine. Her palm came up to cup the side of his face, and her thumb stroked his cheekbone.

"I missed you, too."

"Walk with me," he demanded.

Siena nodded, and tucked in close to his side as they moved off the main walkway, and headed onto the cobblestone path that led all over the facility's private, protected grounds. John took a quick look over his shoulder, and found Andino was still standing side by side with Haven. His cousin hugged the woman in close, and kissed the top of her head when she laughed about something.

Yeah, John most definitely knew that look his cousin sported.

Siena's quiet little hum brought John's attention right back to her. Glittering eyes looked him over, and she reached up to stroke his face once more with her fingertips. "I wish I had more time today."

John tried not to frown, and failed. "Andino didn't say anything about you leaving."

"I only have a couple of hours before I have to be back. Yoga ends at two, so."

"Yeah, still doing that, huh?"

Siena let out a hard breath, and looked away from him when she spoke again. "It's the only way I can get out of my brothers' sights for more than five minutes. Or hell, one of the enforcers they're always sticking me with."

He didn't like the sound of that.

Not at all.

"So what, they haven't figured out that you sneak away when you're supposed to be at yoga, yet?" he asked.

"No." Siena shrugged. "But I've only done it when I need to do something, or meet someone."

"Meet someone?"

"Andino, mostly. Sometimes it's someone else."

"Meet them for what?" he pressed.

"Not important."

John tugged on his girl's hand, and the action made her look at him. "It is important, *amore*. Why are you meeting people behind your brothers' backs, and what's happening that people aren't telling me about?"

"A lot."

"Like what?"

Siena glanced over her shoulder, and back down the path. They had gone far enough that neither of them could see Andino or Haven any longer. John doubted his cousin would leave him alone for very long, especially not if the visit wasn't meant to last.

"Andino doesn't want me—"

"Fuck what he wants," John said. "It's *me* asking right now."

Siena looked down at the path. "There's a lot of stuff that's happened over the past little while since you came here. At first, the families tried to avoid a feud between them with more peaceful means. When all that went to shit, the violence really got started."

"You said war before."

"That's the impression I got from my brothers."

"But was it?" he asked.

Siena shook her head. "Not like it is now. It's bad now."

Fuck.

"No one's mentioned this to me when they visit," he said.

Siena cleared her throat. "You have to focus on *you*."

"I'm aware, but—"

Quick as a blink, Siena had turned on her heel, and stopped John from walking any further on the pathway. Her hands came up to press against his chest, and her fingernails dug in just enough to make him suck in a sharp breath.

She tipped her head up, and pressed a fast kiss to his lips. Just like that, everything he was worrying about was gone in an instant.

The girl had many talents.

Distracting him was just one.

"I promised Andino I wouldn't tell you," Siena whispered against his lips. "Please just focus on you for the time you have left here, John."

"I am," he assured her.

His hands cupped her face, and he kept her close enough that she was forced to keep her eyes on only him. Nothing else but him.

He needed to see her, too.

"They mean well," she said. "You have to trust them."

He heard her.

He understood.

It still was hard.

CHAPTER THREE

SIENA STEPPED out of the cool complex into humid July air. It made the lingering wetness from the quick shower she had taken to get rid of the workout sweat stick to her skin. The smell of chlorine from the complex's pool vanished with every breath of fresh air she took in.

The day was beautiful, and the streets were quiet. A clear sky, and a bright sun that suggested no rain was on the horizon, despite the humidity. Siena couldn't complain about that. Nobody wanted rain in the summer.

Then, as quickly as her happiness came, it fled just as easily at the sight of the man waiting for her next to a running Mercedes.

No, not her enforcer.

Her brother.

Darren pulled the aviator sunglasses he wore away from his face as Siena took the steps of the complex slowly. The longer she didn't have to be in his presence, or talk to him, the better. He gave the simple black dress she wore a curious look, and his gaze narrowed on the bag she carried. She was barely within reach of her brother before he snatched the bag from her shoulder, and opened it up.

What the hell?

"Hey," Siena snapped. "Give me that back, Darren."

"In a sec."

He didn't even look up at her as he dug through her bag. His hands pulled out her personal effects without any care at all. All that was in there were her workout clothes, a bathing suit if she felt like using the pool when she came to the complex, the cell phone her brothers provided, and her wallet.

Nothing more.

Nothing less.

Still, he kept looking like he expected to find something.

He wouldn't.

Siena was not dumb.

"Why are these clothes damp?" Darren asked.

"Because working out makes people *sweaty*," Siena said. "Which you know, gets on the fucking clothes you wear while you work out."

Not that her brother would know anything about exercising. The older Darren got, the rounder he became in his middle. Pear-shaped when it came to his body, while his hair was thinning at the top of his head. Sometimes, if she turned too fast, she was struck by how much he looked like their father.

She figured that was probably a lot of Darren's problem where his health was concerned. He had been spoiled too long by their father. He had become accustomed to eating whatever he wanted, and never cared for his body. He much preferred to sit behind a desk like their father had taught him to do, and issue orders, instead of doing something himself.

So far, Kev had avoided behaving that way, too. He was still quite a spoiled, demanding man, however.

"That's disgusting."

Darren made a face, and handed the bag back to her as though the item had suddenly turned diseased. *Screw him.* Siena snatched it from his grasp with a dirty look, and slung the bag over her shoulder.

"What in the hell was that all about?" she demanded. "I don't go through your stuff like I have any business doing so."

Darren gave the complex a look, and then his sharp gaze cut back to Siena just as fast. She didn't like the way his eyes glinted with something unknown. She couldn't trust her brothers with a goddamn inch, to be honest.

"It's strange—that's all," he said. "Every time you come here, your enforcer says you come out wearing the same shit you go in with. Problem is, Kev and I both know you pack clothes to work out in every time you go."

Siena barely hid her frown.

Her brothers were looking into her business, and that spelled bad news. It made her uncomfortable as hell to think that either one of her brothers were starting to get suspicious about anything she did. Especially if that meant they might take away her one opportunity for her to actually get away from them.

She had to think … and *fast*.

"Do you want to wear the same clothes you work out in for the rest of the day?" Siena asked. Pulling her bag from her shoulder, she offered it to her brother. "Here, take it again and smell the clothes in there. Do you think sweat smells like fucking roses, or what? Jesus Christ. Get a grip, Darren."

Darren made that same disgusted face, and refused to take the bag. "I get it, Siena. Chill your hormones out, all right."

She wasn't one hundred percent satisfied that she had got her brother to believe that she wasn't doing anything at the complex but working out. For now, it would have to do. Unless she got another goddamn idea, or they forced her hand.

"Just yoga today?" Darren asked as he opened the door to the car.

Siena passed her brother a look as she slid into the passenger seat. "Today, yeah."

"You didn't see anyone you recognized in there, or whatever?"

Jesus.

"No, not today."

Siena tried to close the car door, but her brother held strong. He leaned down to stare Siena right in the face as he spoke again.

"Have you seen anybody you recognize here since you started coming to the place?"

"Just my enforcers."

Lies.

Siena had never been much of a liar, but she had become especially good at it over the last few months. Maybe she was just as bad as her family—maybe she owned her last name the same way her brothers did.

The thing was, Siena wasn't doing it for the Calabrese name. She wasn't doing anything of this for her brothers, or even for her dead father.

No, she was doing this for someone else entirely.

For her.

For John.

For them.

"You're sure?" Darren pressed.

Siena tried to find what her brother was reaching for as she searched his eyes, but came up with nothing. For as good as she was with hiding things, so were Darren and Kev. It was a little unsettling when she didn't know what their game was. Besides, it was far easier for her to beat her brothers at their own game when she knew what was coming.

Even if that meant cheating a little …

Her last meeting with Andino had been the previous week when they visited John at Clearview Oaks. She had barely managed to get back to the complex in time once they left, as she dragged her feet too much while they were there. She hadn't wanted to leave John when she didn't know the next time she was going to be able to see him. In fact, she was so late getting back that her enforcer had just entered the building to come search for her as she passed by the receptionist's desk.

Sure, the guy hadn't seen her coming in through the back entrances. She had been a little sweaty from running through the back parking lot, and the building to get to the front. Her hair had been mussed, and her face clear of makeup when she scrubbed it all off during the drive back.

Nothing was out of place. Nothing for the enforcer to mention. It had still been a little too close for comfort.

Maybe that's what had Darren's suspicions up.

Who fucking knew?

"I'm sure, Darren," she said. "Now close the damn door. It's hot outside."

She barely even got to finish her sentence before her brother did just that. Siena moved her fingers out of the way in the last second to avoid getting them jammed. She shot him a dirty look through the window, but Darren only smiled in response.

Fucking asshole.

All too soon, Darren slipped into the driver's seat, and without even looking over his shoulder, pulled out onto the road. He kept quiet for a long while, and hell, that only made Siena even more unsettled. Like he was trying to think about what he wanted to say, or something.

Everything about her life, and her brothers, was now a very carefully thought out process. Nothing was said without it meaning something, and they very rarely told her things unless it was to demand something, or announce something.

Shit.

She wished they would talk to her less, actually.

"Someone mentioned they might have seen Andino Marcello around this part of Brooklyn a couple of times," Darren said. "Kev wanted me to ask if you had seen the fool, too. You know what he drives, right? Black Mercedes, kind of like this one."

Actually, Andino drove two vehicles. One was a white Porsche, and another was a black Mercedes SUV. And it was nicer than her brother's.

Siena swallowed hard. "No, I haven't."

And by *someone*, she suspected her brother meant one of her enforcers. She didn't bother to ask if that was actually the case, though. Too many questions from her, and it would drive Darren's suspicions even higher. She didn't need that trouble right now.

Siena kept her gaze on the sidewalks and people they passed by. Many of the shops were taking down their Fourth of July decorations as the holiday had now passed. It gave her a chance to keep her attention on anything but her brother.

Maybe then, he would get the hint.

She wasn't up to chat.

Darren never did care. "We've got to keep a better eye on them, that's all."

Well, that piqued her interest.

"The Marcellos?"

"Yeah."

"Why?"

Darren shrugged. "Things are happening in that family, that's all. It's important we keep up with it, and act appropriately to it."

"Things like what?"

She was pressing too hard.

She seemed too curious.

Darren was too focused on the road to notice, it seemed. That, or whatever he was caught up with regarding the Marcello family had him distracted. "I guess the Marcellos announced Andino's engagement to some chick—let everybody know at their Fourth of July party. Shit, they're not even waiting, really."

"I don't understand."

He passed her a look. "To get *married*, Siena. They're not waiting to get married since they just announced it and all. Fuck, keep up. You're not usually this dumb."

Ouch.

She let that insult roll off her shoulders.

"When are they getting married?"

"On the twentieth."

Wait ...

"Of *this* month?" she asked.

Darren nodded. "Yep."

"And they just announced it?"

"Like I said, they're not waiting. Sounds to me like someone wants to move little Andino up in the family, and he needs to position himself appropriately for it."

"He's not really little, is he?"

More like a fucking linebacker.

Darren scoffed. "You know what I mean."

"I don't know what any of that—him getting married, or whatever—has to do with us, though."

Her brother smiled. "No, I wouldn't expect you to, Siena. You're only a woman."

Only a woman.

That insult was not as easy to ignore, but she forced herself to, anyway. Someday, her brothers would think twice before thinking because she was only a woman, she could not hurt them. Hell, they should have already realized it.

Look what happened to their father. Sure, that hadn't been her, but she hadn't stopped John from killing Matteo, either. She didn't even apologize for not trying to stop him from doing it. She didn't even cry at Matteo's funeral.

Her father didn't need her tears. He wouldn't want them.

She had always been *just a woman* to him, too.

Besides, she had something better to consider at the moment. Andino getting married so soon likely meant he had a lot on his plate, and that was probably why he hadn't shown up to talk with her today at the complex. Sometimes, that happened.

Andino was Johnathan's best friend, and vice versa. There was no way in hell Andino would get married without John being there, too.

Siena knew, then. She had a date to count down to for when John would finally be out again. They were one step closer to finishing this forever.

Her forever was almost there …

• • •

For the first time in longer than Siena cared to remember, she sat alone in the church pew.

Well, not *totally* alone.

Just down the way on her right side sat her mother. On her left, a few seats away, sat her enforcer. Her mother's attention never left the priest speaking at the altar, while the enforcer seemed more interested in the phone in his hands than on the service.

Siena took the few moments she had to check the screen of her phone without the enforcer or her mother looking over her damn shoulder. She didn't get that chance very often. The date on the home screen stared back at her.

July twentieth.

She had counted down the days. She had paid way too much attention to the calendar on her wall every single day she woke up, and then again before she went to sleep.

The day was finally here.

John was getting *out.*

Siena only knew for sure that he was getting out today because of a *wrong number* call from someone. The call came to her cell phone like it always did when Andino sent a message. Some random person asked for the wrong name, Siena would apologize and say it was the wrong number. Then, the person on the other end of the call would quickly deliver whatever message needed to be said before she hung up without a second thought.

That way, should anyone be near her when she picked up the wrong number call, no one would think anything was amiss. And should someone else pick up her phone when the call came in, like Kev had done once, they would only have the person on the other end apologizing for calling the wrong number.

Today, the message had been clear.

Three o'clock. Waldorf, Manhattan. Room 403. Room key will be waiting at the desk.

Siena knew that time coincided with Andino's wedding. The location for the event hadn't been given when it was announced in the society rags, but the date and time had been mentioned. Not to mention, Kev and Darren had gotten information, too.

Siena eavesdropped far more than was safe.

She was kind of betting her life on it, at the moment.

This morning, however, no one had been around to hear her wrong number call. No one had been around since the night before when Kev and Darren each packed a bag, and slipped out of the house. They didn't tell her anything about where they were going except to say they wouldn't be back until the next day or sometime after, and her enforcer would be close by.

They also made it clear she was to attend church with her mother.

Well …

Siena was here.

So was her mother.

She couldn't promise to stay, though. Not when she knew John was just within her reach, and so was the taste of freedom. Even if that bit of freedom wouldn't last for long.

It didn't matter.

The opportunity was too good to pass up.

Siena passed another look at her enforcer as she slipped the phone back into her purse. The man's attention was still firmly stuck on the phone in his hand. It looked like he was playing a game of some sort.

She swore she could hear the clock ticking down in the back of her mind. It was getting louder by the second.

Taunting her, even.

Goddamn.

She forced her attention back to the priest. His sermon on faith and love to one's family was entirely lost on her. Or perhaps, she just didn't have the right family at the moment to give those things to.

Soon, the service was over. People stood from the pews, and Siena followed suit. She had been at least able to drive herself to church in her Lexus, which was one less thing for her to figure out at the moment.

She only needed to get away …

"You should come over for dinner," her mother said behind her.

Siena stiffened. "Not tonight, Ma."

Turning, she faced Coraline. Her mother reached out to fix a stray curl, but Siena quickly stepped out of Coraline's reach. She was not interested in entertaining the woman's false affections. Besides, her mother's love was dependent on how well-behaved and loyal Siena was to their family.

"I do miss spending time with you," her mother said.

Siena nodded, and smiled. "I'm sure you do, Ma. Tonight, I have other plans."

"Like what? I know your brothers are out of town. You must be bored in Kev's brownstone all by yourself. Surely, you're not entertaining ..." Coraline trailed off, and nodded in the direction of the waiting enforcer. "Neither of your brothers need *that* kind of trouble, Siena."

God, no.

She didn't even hide how disgusting the idea made her feel.

"No, not that, Ma," Siena muttered. "I just meant I wanted a quiet night. Me, my book, and maybe some wine."

Those were most definitely not her plans, but as long as it got her mother off her back ...

Coraline's bitterness was back in a blink. "Well, don't say I didn't *try*."

"I would never, Ma."

Because she didn't try.

Neither did Siena.

This was just another game.

Siena allowed her mother to kiss her cheeks, and offered the same in return. She watched her mother step out of the pew and into the aisle before she turned to face the waiting enforcer. The man looked like he was ready to leave.

She had news for him.

"I need to speak with my priest for a few minutes," she told him.

The enforcer—a young twenty-something whose name she hadn't even been given—scowled. "Didn't you listen to him enough today?"

"You're not a very good Catholic, are you?"

"I go to church."

"Do you make use of confession?"

The man coughed. "Well, no ..."

"I do. Excuse me."

She heard the enforcer's sigh echo out from behind her, but all she could do was smile. Shooting a look over her shoulder, Siena found the enforcer had sat back down in the pew, and dragged his phone out to look at it once again. He wasn't even paying any attention to her at all.

Good.

That's exactly what she wanted.

In their life, very few things were held sacred. And for her, a woman who had disabused her family, and misused their trust, even less things were sacred for her.

Certainly not privacy.

Except, of course, when it came to confession.

Siena would disappear out one of the back doors, and be long gone in her Lexus before the enforcer even realized what was happening. He likely wouldn't know she was gone until he figured out how long he had been sitting there waiting for her.

Besides, confession could take a long time.

The phone in her pocket burned a hole as she headed past the last few people. A part of her wanted to pull out of the phone, and make one single call. She knew Andino's number—she could let him know that she would be there today.

The smarter part of her brain knew that probably wasn't a good idea. Her brothers crawled through her phone history on a regular basis. She couldn't even delete shit without them finding out. She didn't need that kind of trouble when they got back.

She left the damn phone where it was.

Their priest didn't have a particularly large congregation, but it was a decent size. He often allowed confession to be open after every Sunday service, just in case someone in the church wanted to make use of it.

He held confession in the back of the church, behind the altar. A private room set up with rich tapestries, and two chairs facing one another. Sometimes, it made confession a little awkward when a person was forced to look someone in the face when they admitted to some of their deepest, darkest sins.

The comfort of the room often helped, though. It certainly didn't look like the old confessional booths in movies. Actually, Siena didn't think she had ever used one of those kinds of confessionals.

None of that mattered.

She wasn't going to be attending confession at all.

At least, not today.

She was banking on the fact that the enforcer was rather new to watching her, and quite young in the grand scheme of things. She hoped that those facts would keep him from calling her brothers to let them know she had skipped out on him, if only because he was one of the many men in their family who had a healthy fear where Kev and Darren were concerned.

He wouldn't want to get in trouble.

Not for *her*.

Siena slipped into the back hallway that led to the offices, and the private room used for confession. The priest was already greeting a man standing outside the private room, and gestured for the man to go in.

He didn't even see Siena.

He didn't see her take a sharp right, and head out the exit, either.

Siena glanced down at the peach-colored dress and matching pumps she wore. Even the peach hat on her head was Sunday services appropriate. And wedding appropriate, although she wasn't sure if she would even be attending the wedding.

That invisible clock in the back of her mind only stopped ticking down when she slipped inside her Lexus, and turned on the ignition. She was no longer counting days or minutes or seconds to when she would see John again.

To when he would be *out* again.

She was finally in the fucking homestretch. Even just a few days of not seeing him was far too long.

Whatever trouble might find her for this …

So worth it.

CHAPTER FOUR

LEONARD SAT beside Johnathan on the bench just outside the entrance doors of Clearview Oaks. Up above, the sky was a pale blue, and cloudless.

Despite the beautiful day, the humid heat was enough to make John wish he was not wearing jeans at the moment. The thick material stuck to his skin, and made him hotter. He pulled out the collar of his T-shirt, and waved it a bit to create the illusion of cold air.

His attention to the weather did not escape his therapist's notice.

"Quite hot out," Leonard noted.

"It's been like this for a while. Going through a spell, I think."

"Better hot, than cold."

John nodded. "Truth."

Leonard passed a look at the brown paper bag resting beside John's thigh. "It didn't take you very long to pack up your things, did it?"

A smile passed between the two men. Even John couldn't help but chuckle when Leonard shook his head.

"I didn't come in with very much," John admitted. "I had everything packed before breakfast this morning, actually."

"And I suppose you didn't ask for anyone to bring you very much while you were here, either," Leonard said. "At least, you never asked me to make that request on your behalf to someone in your family."

"No."

"Shame."

John cocked a brow. "What is?"

"Sometimes packing up your things and leaving a facility can be just as cathartic as anything you find comforting—or even, a great satisfaction. Something you completed. Or even, a goal you achieved. A challenge in your life that you bested, and your reward, so to speak, is packing up your things."

"It still felt … rewarding."

Maybe that wasn't exactly the right word to use, but it was all John felt like offering at the moment. Packing up his few things to leave Clearview had felt a lot like when he left prison almost a year ago. Different circumstances, sure, but the emotions and how he felt them were still very much the same in a lot of ways.

Relief as he pulled the few photographs off the wall, and anxiety as he exited out of the bars that had kept him locked up for years. Anticipation, too, at the idea of freedom, but knowing he wasn't quite sure what to do with it.

This time had been months.

It also wasn't prison.

Yet, those same emotions plagued him. Those same worries about the *outside*, life, and even his family were forefront in his mind. Like little needles sticking in his brain, and staying like that for far longer than he wanted them to.

No matter what he did, he could not remove that strange sensation. At the same time, he wasn't sure that he wanted to, either. Although uncomfortable, it was still comforting in its familiarity.

No, Clearview hadn't been a prison. Leaving the place was still very much a variable unknown to John.

Funny how it still felt the same.

Leonard pulled out a form from the inside pocket of his white lab coat, and waved it in the air to catch John's attention. "Your probation is all set again. Of course, we had to pull some strings when you were first admitted as to not break your probation."

"Yeah, thanks again for that."

"No thanks needed."

Leonard handed over the form, and John opened it up. Looking the document over, it seemed that Leonard had finally been listed as John's official registered therapist for the unforeseeable future. Well, for after his release from Clearview.

The form listed approximate appointment dates, and Leonard's signature was heavy and bold on the bottom of the paper. A sign of the doctor's agreement to follow the letter of the law where John's probation was concerned, and report him to the probation office should he stop attending his appointments.

"Would you really report me?" John asked. "If I didn't show up to my appointments, I mean."

Leonard chuckled. "Should I, John?"

He looked over at the therapist. The man simply raised a thick, white eyebrow in response, waiting for John's answer. Leonard was too good at this shit, but frankly, John was more grateful to this man than anyone could possibly know.

"Thank you for giving my parents an answer all those years ago," John murmured. "I imagine it can't be easy to tell someone that their kid is—"

41

"Not crazy. Not in need of a cure to be *curable*. Don't say those things."

"I wasn't."

"Then what?"

John smirked. "I was just going to say bipolar, actually."

Leonard nodded, and the man's gaze turned pensive for a moment. "I know you may have felt like I sentenced you to something you did not want back then, John, but I hope in a way that you found relief in having the right answer, too."

"I did—it took a while."

"Sometimes it does for those with bipolar."

"But thank you."

Leonard waved a hand high, and settled back into the bench. "No thanks needed."

"You didn't answer my question, by the way. I'm emotionally unstable sometimes, but not dumb or stupid."

The older man laughed hard and loud, and his sharp gaze cut to John in a flash. "Which question—whether I would report you or not for missing appointments with me?"

"Yes."

"Well, you didn't answer *me*, John. Should I report you?"

John really didn't have to think about his answer. It wasn't an easy answer, sure. The thing was, nothing about his life or his disorder was easy. It couldn't be, and it was never going to be. That was something he was taking away from this place, and because of the man sitting beside him. Yet another thing to be grateful for.

For some reason, John had a sneaking suspicion that there was going to be a lot to be grateful for over his lifetime where Leonard was concerned. At least, during the period that Leonard was his therapist.

"I'm choosing stability," John said after a moment.

"You are."

"And so yes," he added, "you should report me."

Leonard reached over and clapped John firmly on the shoulder. He wasn't really the touchy-feely-type, but he was getting better at it. He had learned that sometimes a hand on his shoulder was meant to praise him, and not simply break through his personal space barriers.

He had spent almost five months at Clearview Oaks. For some people, that would seem like a ridiculously long amount of time simply to reset, recharge, and get their shit figured out. At first, it had seemed like a long time to John, too.

Sometimes, mental health couldn't be fixed with new meds, a couple of chats, and a pat on the back. Sometimes, mental health was so much more than the disorder a person lived with, and the outlook it gave them.

Mental health could not be timed.

It could not be wished it away.

It took patience.

John had needed this.

Damn, how he *needed* this.

"Seems your drive has arrived," Leonard said.

John's gaze drifted from Leonard's smile, to the black Mercedes pulling up next to the Clearview welcome sign. He had thought a lot about who might come to pick him up, but that was not the person he considered. "Huh."

"Not who you were expecting, I suspect?"

"Actually, I can't say I'm surprised," John admitted as the man exited the car, and came to stand on the other side. "Unexpected, yes, but not surprised. I thought my uncle, Gio. Or maybe even Andino."

Leonard chuckled as he stood from the bench. "Mmm, I am sure both of those people fought tooth and nail to be the one here today."

"Likely."

"Someone else fought harder, clearly."

Leonard waved a hand at the waiting man.

Lucian waved back in kind.

"Nice to see you again, old friend," Leonard called.

"And you, Leo," John's father replied.

Leonard looked down at John. "Don't keep people waiting for you—it's rude."

Goddamn.

John got his ass up, and took the hand that Leonard offered to shake. "Thanks."

"I will see you next week, John. Bright and early. Be there."

"Of course."

• • •

John's father had barely pulled the Mercedes out onto the road, before his hand reached for his son. Lucian's palm cupped John's cheek, and then slid around to grab the back of his neck. John blinked, and he was pulled closer to his father.

Lucian never looked away from the road when he laughed, gave John a quick pat on the neck, and brought him close enough that their temples touched.

"You look good," his father said when he finally let him go.

John smiled. "You think?"

"Happy, John."

"I am."

Or, as happy as he could be. Sometimes, happiness meant feeling settled and stable. It did not have to be overwhelming joy and pride. Happiness was as simple as feeling and being good inside his head.

It was the little things, after all.

"I thought Andino might come today," John admitted.

Lucian waved a hand before placing it back to the leather-wrapped steering wheel. "He's a little busy, that's all. Everyone is, but they all bickered for hours about who was going to come and get you."

"Hell, I could have taken a cab home."

"Not my son."

That was all his father said.

Maybe, it was all Lucian *had* to say.

John still heard the meaning beneath the simple words. "Thanks for coming to get me, Papa."

Lucian shot John a look, and nodded once. "I'm always going to be here to get you when you need me to, my boy."

"My birthday is in ten days—I'll be thirty-one."

He didn't finish his statement. He figured he didn't really have to.

Lucian only shrugged. "Always my boy—my *only* boy, John."

"I suppose Ma wants to see me."

"Among others," Lucian agreed. "We have to make a trip to Tuxedo Park, before we head into the city. Manhattan, specifically."

Damn.

John just wanted to relax.

"*Have* to?"

"It's a big day," Lucian murmured, shooting his son a grin.

"What does that mean?"

His father cleared his throat. "Well, a lot has happened, John."

"And that's why we're going to drive all over New York today?"

"Kind of."

"Papa."

Lucian chuckled at the tone of John's voice. "You sound just like Antony when you do that. Your grandfather would be proud as hell."

"I bet. What aren't you telling me?"

"A lot, and nothing at all. Where do you want to start?"

John looked over his shoulder, and noted a freshly pressed tux resting in a see-through garment bag. A peach-colored vest, tie, and pocket square was also inside the bag. "Let's start with why there's a tux in the back."

"It's for you to wear."

John's brow dipped low. "With a vest and tie that looks like it belongs in a wedding?"

"That's because it does." Lucian reached over, and pulled out a small box from the glove compartment, and handed it over to John. A ring box, it seemed. He opened it up to find a set of rings inside—one female, and one male. "You're going to need this, too. Keep a hold of it, and don't lose it. It's really your only job today."

John blinked. "What the fuck?"

Lucian laughed darkly. "Yeah, that's a good start. You're Andino's best man. You need a tux, and it's your job to keep an eye on the rings, and hand them over when the priest asks for them. You'll stand at the altar where you're told to stand, and leave when you're told to leave. There's really not much else to it—Andino and Haven did not want a lot of fanfare for this day, and we didn't exactly have a lot of time to work with."

His father passed him a look, quickly adding, "They are being married at Antony and Cecelia's estate, and the dinner and party will follow at the Waldorf Astoria in Manhattan. You see, we're having trouble keeping out of sight lately. We don't want to stay gathered—at least, not the whole family—in one place for too long where we might be attacked in some way. And so, we are having the wedding with a very limited amount of guests in our private home, and the larger party where people are less likely to attack in a very public setting."

Lucian ticked a finger into the air, saying, "Of course, still *highly* protected."

"Wait, Andi's getting married today?"

"I said that, yes."

"*Today.*"

"Yes, John."

"He didn't tell me—"

Lucian's gaze cut to John's, quieting him instantly. "He asked her the day they came to visit you, and only announced it to us a couple of days later. They did not want to wait to be married, and everyone has agreed to this. Andino did, however, want to wait for you."

John looked down at the rings again. "A best man, huh?"

"You're not really surprised, are you?"

"Fuck no."

Lucian let out another one of his hard laughs, and then reached for his son again. John let his father bring him close, touch their temples together, and pat his neck with affection he had denied his father for years.

Then, John had another thought.

His mind had been so caught up in the revelation about Andino getting married today that he hadn't stopped to think at all about the other information his father offered to him. The mention of moving the family from place to place because of protection. How they were planning in order to prevent an attack that they believed might come.

"It's the Calabrese, isn't it?" John asked quietly.

"How about today, we—"

"How about you just answer me, Papa?"

Lucian nodded with a dry chuckle. "All right. Yes, it is the Calabrese."

"How bad is it?"

Sure, Siena had given John a bit to go on, but that's all it had been. A little bit of info—a tease, if you will. Something to make him stay up at night and ponder, but not enough to chew on and really understand what was happening.

He needed more.

He needed it now.

"Dante wanted this feud between our families to be settled peacefully," Lucian said.

"Someone mentioned that to me already. I'm not sure what methods he used for that, though."

"An attempt to arrange a marriage, actually."

John stiffened in his seat, and his gaze flew to his father. "What?"

"You heard me,"

He didn't like what that implied. There was really only *one* Calabrese woman worthy of marrying into the Marcello family, or rather, one woman that Dante would consider worthy in the grand scheme.

Siena.

"He didn't—"

"It was not your woman," Lucian muttered. "Relax."

John did not realize how stiff his body had become in those few seconds, or how firmly he had gritted his teeth until relief flowed through his body. Sweet like sugar, the sensation washed through his bloodstream. His molars ached when they released from the tight clench. He found crescent shaped marks on the insides of his palms from how tightly he clenched his fists together, too.

Jesus Christ.

"It was not Siena," Lucian repeated. "And the details do not matter, honestly. What matters is that the deal failed, and the violence escalated from there. We had in good faith information about an attack that would happen on one of our warehouses, but it did not happen."

"That's a good thing, then."

"It is, except when one does not go through, it is usually because another bigger, better one is coming. The only major event we have going on as a family right now is—"

"Andi's wedding."

Lucian nodded. "Exactly, son. Mind you, we have been very careful about releasing details regarding the wedding. The main event is not an open invitation to *famiglia*. The party afterward at the Astoria is, but it's very public, there will be a large crowd."

"And you said it's well protected."

"That, too, yes."

"But you're still concerned."

"We all are," Lucian said quietly. "These are dangerous days, John."

And for what?

Because of him.

John still didn't regret what he did when he killed Matteo Calabrese. He would never regret any of that, but he hadn't wanted this. He didn't want his family to suffer again because of him.

"I'm sorry."

"You have absolutely nothing to be sorry for, and this is only a passing moment in all of our lives. We have lived through worse, and we will live through this. There is always something beautiful waiting at the end. What is it you want when you get to the end, John?"

Well ...

"Siena," he admitted. "But that's a little fucking impossible, isn't it?"

Lucian looked over at John. "Keep your fucking chin up, and your eyes on the prize, John. Marcellos don't look down."

"Not unless we're looking down on somebody, right?"

Lucian's chuckles echoed once more. "Right, my boy. Chin up."

● ● ●

"You couldn't fucking let me in on the little secret, or what?"

John's question—his tone coated with amusement—quieted the whole room of men. The one person he had directed his question to was the first person to find him and Lucian standing in the doorway waiting.

Andino grinned widely. "John."

"Hey, cousin."

"About fucking time you showed up. I was starting to get nervous."

John smiled. "I might have lost the rings, so, yeah."

"You didn't."

"No, I damn well didn't."

John flashed the box in question. Slung around his arm was the garment bag with his tux safely hidden inside. He still had to get dressed, but he had a few other things to take care of first. Like his family—Andino, mostly.

"Come here," Andino said.

John crossed the room, and took the tight hug his cousin offered. Andino smacked John on the back twice, and then let him go with another one of those signature grins. His cousin patted his cheek, and nodded.

Quietly, Andino said, "I really didn't want to do this day without you, man."

"Yeah, I kind of got that. Congrats, huh?"

"Hold off on that. We still need to get Haven to the altar, and everything."

Chuckles lit up the room, reminding John once again that they still had a bit of an audience. He didn't mind—it was just his family, after all.

His grandfather was the first to approach them. Antony took his time looking John over, and then the older man clicked his tongue. His weathered face cracked with age when he smiled, and shook his head.

"You're not properly dressed, Johnathan."

John held up the garment bag. "Working on it, Grandpapa."

"Work faster. We're all a little late today."

"He's not lying," Giovanni said as he stepped in beside his son to clap Andino on the back. He gave John the same attention. "Good to see you home, *nipote*."

"Glad to be back," John replied in kind.

"I bet."

And then, the one man John might have been dreading speaking to just a little bit stepped closer. His uncle, Dante. The boss of their family—the patriarch who John had, without a doubt, disobeyed, disrespected, and more before he entered Clearview.

He didn't know what to expect from Dante.

He didn't know what to say.

Dante only smiled.

Not a cold smile, either.

"Boss," John said.

Dante's grin deepened a bit. "Not for long, John."

John's gaze darted to Andino, who only smirked. No, he supposed someone else was getting ready to take Dante's place, now.

It was appropriate.

All reigns eventually came to an end.

Even a Marcello King's.

"I certainly hope you're ready for this day, and what comes after," Dante said, eyeing John with a careful eye. "Are you?"

He didn't know what the hell his uncle meant.

He didn't care, either.

"Of course, I am," John replied.

Dante nodded, and reached out a hand. John took it, only to then find himself dragged into a quick, tight hug from his uncle. Dante let him go, and smiled again in that way that reminded John of when he was a young boy, and idolized his uncle to the ends of the earth and back.

"You have ten minutes to get dressed," Dante told him with a smack to his cheek. "Hurry the fuck up—nobody here wants to make Andino wait longer than he already has for this girl of his. Isn't that right?"

Laughter colored up the room.

Everybody agreed.

John made quick work of getting dressed in a separate private room, and had only took one step out before his mother damn near tackled him in a hug. Well, his mother, grandmother, and both aunts. Lips found his cheeks for kisses that were then quickly wiped off to avoid lipstick stains, hands patted his cheeks with sweet affection, and Italian words filled his ears.

Nipote.

Bambino.

"Let me breathe, *donnas*," John heard himself say with a chuckle.

The women didn't really let him do anything.

John didn't really mind.

Soon, though, his aunts and grandmother dispersed to leave John alone with his mother. Jordyn checked him over, ran her fingers through his hair to slick the longer length of the high fade back further, and smiled in a way only a mother could when she was staring at her child. Those blue eyes of hers lit up with love, and John smiled back.

"Hey, Ma."

Jordyn let out a happy noise. "I missed you, my boy."

"I know, Ma. I didn't mean to scare you."

"Never, John. I only worry. You've certainly made my life interesting when things seem boring, though. Big day today, huh? You kind of ended up thrown in the middle of the whole shebang."

John shrugged. "I don't mind."

"Not when it comes to Andino, right?"

"Right."

"Come on," Jordyn said, tangling her arm in with his. "I will walk you to your spot. It's my job to make sure you know what to do today."

John didn't mind indulging his mother—she loved him so very much, after all. He chatted away with her as she walked him through the large Marcello mansion, and to the main ballroom where the chairs and decorations filled the room. Outside would probably have been nice for a wedding, considering the weather, but he didn't even ask why they hadn't bothered.

He already knew.

It was open.

It made them targets.

Protection be damned.

Jordyn led John to his position at the front, and he gave his mother a quick kiss on her cheek before she darted off. Probably to find one of his sisters—who he had not seen in months—or his father.

It wasn't too long after that before Andino took his place beside John. The priest was there, too. Likely paid off considering the man was marrying

49

them outside of a church, and on a very short timeline that did not allow for couple's counseling.

Funny how the church worked.

When the music started, Andino said to John, "Watch this, man."

John waited.

He watched.

Dante Marcello walked Haven down the aisle.

It was as good of a show as any. For the few guests invited, it meant a hell of a lot without ever saying a damn thing. The woman—regardless of heritage or bloodline, or history—was a Marcello. Accepted, brought in, and protected.

Respected.

John could only think of one person he wished would get the same respect: Siena.

• • •

"Walk a little slower, would you," his father joked.

John laughed as the two navigated the halls of the Waldorf hotel. "I'm supposed to be downstairs, all right. The party isn't even over yet, Dad."

Lucian shrugged. "For you, it is. At least, down there."

"What?"

His father didn't answer. A floor later, and Lucian handed over a room key. It matched the number on the door that the two stood in front of.

"What, are you putting me to bed like a fucking kid, or something?"

Lucian smirked. "Or *something*."

"I should be downstairs with Andino."

"Sure, but we all kind of pulled some strings hoping this would work out for you today, and it was just our luck that it did." Then, his father reached out and smacked John's cheek lightly. "Or shit, maybe it was *your* luck, huh?"

"I thought they used to call you Lucky."

"It's been passed down," Lucian replied. "From me, to you. And you'll pass it on, too."

Well, John didn't know about that. He wasn't sure if he was every going to pass anything on to children from his blood, but this wasn't the time for that discussion, either.

Lucian tipped his head toward the door. "Go ahead. We'll all be here tomorrow. Breakfast with your mother and sisters. They'll like that."

He didn't know about his *sisters*, really. His mother would like it, for sure.

"You really fucking took me from the party to put me to bed, didn't you?"

Lucian only grinned. "Just open the fucking door."

John gave his father a look, but did as he was told. He slid the keycard through the slot, heard the lock beep, and then the tumblers roll. Pulling the handle down, the door opened easily under his hand.

He expected the room to be dark.

It was lit up.

He expected the room to be empty.

She stood there waiting.

Siena.

"John," Siena greeted with one of her sweet smiles.

He was just ... stuck.

Speechless.

Stupid.

Happy.

Awed.

All day, he had listened to whispers from his family about the Calabrese family, and the war raging between their organizations in the city. He heard them call them snakes, and untrustworthy. He listened as they made more plans to get rid of them entirely. There was no love lost between the Marcellos, and the Calabrese organization.

This war was apparently one of the bloodiest, and messiest the city had seen in a long while. There was not one person in John's family who had any issue with saying openly and proudly how wonderful it would be once the Calabrese legacy was gone forever. Not to mention, how great it would be for the Marcellos to be the ones to do it.

Poetic justice after all the history, and bad blood.

And yet ...

Here she stood.

In front of him.

Everything his family hated right now. Everything they were working to destroy, and to remove from their lives forever.

Except, his father had alluded to everyone working together to have Siena here for him. As though they were working with her in some way. As though, perhaps, they trusted her in some way. At least, enough to bring her here.

For him.

John really wanted to know what in the hell was up, and what he had missed out on, but not right now.

Right now ...

"Your mother kept her company for a while today," Lucian said, "and I figured she had probably had enough of being alone, and missing out. She can't come downstairs, of course. We wouldn't want our best asset at the moment being photographed with the rest of us, now would we?"

"No, we definitely wouldn't," Siena said.

John still had not found the right words to say.

His father didn't seem to mind. With a clap of his hand to John's shoulder, Lucian gave his son another smile, and a nod.

"Enjoy your evening, son."

CHAPTER FIVE

SIENA CAUGHT sight of the smile Lucian directed her way one last time before John stepped into the room, and colored up her vision entirely. Nothing else mattered nearly as much as he did when he was in her presence.

"You should close the door," she told him, grinning a little.

John still seemed a bit stunned at seeing her there. Not that she blamed him. "I should, shouldn't I?"

Siena nodded. "Yeah. I mean, who knows what's going to happen now that you're finally up here. We wouldn't want to give the rest of the floor a show, right?"

His tongue snuck from his mouth to touch his top lip as he grinned in the most salacious way. A smile that spoke entirely of sex and sin, and how dangerous this man could be for her body and heart.

Goddamn.

She loved him.

Still.

So much.

John reached back, and swung the door closed without ever taking his eyes away from Siena. Like maybe he thought if he blinked, she might suddenly disappear on him. It was almost comical.

"Look at that," she said.

John's eyebrow quirked up. "Hmm, what?"

Siena waved a hand between them. "We match."

He looked damn good in the fitted tux he wore. It hugged all of his strong lines, showcased his broad shoulders, and only added to the tall, dark, and handsome thing he had going on. The peach vest, tie, and pocket square as accents to his tux perfectly matched the color of the dress she had picked for church that morning.

John's gaze traveled over Siena's body, unashamed. He didn't even try to hide the way he lingered on her legs, and then his gaze skipped back up to her face just as fast. "I suppose we do match. Was that part of the plan, too?"

"What plan?"

"You being here."

"That was the only plan," she said. "And really, I don't even think they knew if this would work out, John. Sometimes, I get a message to try and be somewhere at a certain time, and I just can't make it work, so I don't go. It happens. Today could have been one of those."

"Except it wasn't. You're here."

"I am."

Siena offered him another brilliant smile, but John only stood there, still as stone, and staring at her in that way of his. A way that put her entirely off balance, and yet grounded her at the same time. She didn't want to move, yet she wanted more than anything to reach out and drag him closer to her.

"I'll have to leave in the morning. Early, likely. I have to be at one of Kev's restaurants tomorrow, so the enforcer will need to see me leaving the house like he always does. I can't risk staying any longer than that."

John nodded. "And where are your brothers that they're not looking for you tonight? I assume that's why you were able to get away today. Or was it just the right circumstance kind of thing?"

Siena laughed, although the sound came out a bit hollow. "It's always when the right circumstances happen, John. I live with Kev, now. Occasionally, they let me go back to my apartment to grab some things, but someone is always with me."

He frowned. "Oh."

"My life revolves around them—it's not new, though. My life was always about what they wanted or needed me to do, and the small illusion of freedom that I had before was just that, and nothing more. An illusion."

John's jaw ticked—a sure sign of his irritation. "Circumstances were right today, then?"

"Something like that. I don't know where my brothers are at the moment. Out of town for a couple of days. That's all they told me when they left last night."

"Out of town," he echoed.

Siena shrugged. "I was at church when I got the chance to sneak away, and so I took it. My newest enforcer hasn't been on the job long, and I don't suspect he'll want to get himself in trouble by telling one of my brothers that I got away from him. I assume he likes being alive, and all that. Kev has killed enforcers for far less—the fear in them is real. Small blessings, you know."

There was a question burning brightly in John's eyes as he looked her over once again. He came a little closer, and then closer still. Until finally, he was close enough for her to reach out and touch him.

So, she did just that.

Her fingers stroked the strong line of his jaw, and then her hand cupped his neck. She felt the way his pulse quickened under her touch, and how his muscles jumped when her fingertips pressed a little harder into his skin. The slight bit of stubble tickled her palm, and she smiled at him when his hand came up to cover hers.

"Tell me," he murmured, "are you working for my family?"

Siena stilled, and John's hand tightened around hers. "And if I was?"

"What are you doing for them, Siena?"

"It's complicated right now."

"Why is that?" he asked.

"Because I'm not really sure what I'm doing at the moment, I only know what my end goal is."

Him.

Nothing else.

Just him.

John cleared his throat. "Are you just feeding them information?"

Siena used her other hand to reach up, and tap a single finger against his lips. "Let's talk about all of this tomorrow, okay. Not tonight. You can order me breakfast, and feed me, and then I will tell you all the things I haven't been able to."

John didn't agree, or disagree.

She took that as a good sign.

"Hey," she whispered.

John came closer again, wrapping his arms around her. "Hey."

"I know you don't like surprises."

"This was a good one. I'll deal with this one."

"But any others in careful moderation, huh?"

John chuckled. "Exactly that, *bella donna.*"

"Did you have fun today—Andino got married, right?"

"He did, and it was busy, but good."

"I bet something looked good," she teased, toying with his lapels, and then the peach-colored tie. "Too bad I missed it."

"You didn't miss it, babe. I'm here."

Siena smiled widely as she looked up at him. "You are."

The very second those words left her lips, John closed the small bit of distance left between them. His lips crashed against hers, and took her damn breath away. Their two short meetings over the past few months had been careful, and not at all affectionate in the physical sense. She got the impression that the facility did not approve of that sort of thing.

John was making up for it tenfold in that moment. His tongue struck out against the seam of her lips, and teased her without ever saying a word. She granted him access to her mouth with a grin, and a little sigh. His tongue slipped in to war with hers, while his hands slid up her sides, and then cupped her neck.

He drew her closer.

So much closer.

His body fit against hers perfectly. The world just didn't exist anymore when they were like that. All she could see was dark hazel drinking her in, and that was just fucking fine.

She didn't need anything else.

All too soon, John pulled away. He dropped quick, soft kisses along the seam of her lips, across her cheekbones, over her chin, one to her forehead, and then another to the tip of her nose. Siena's smile only grew more and more until her cheeks hurt.

She hummed a happy, soft sound under her breath.

John kissed her mouth once more.

"I love you," he murmured.

Siena nodded. "I know, John. I love you, too."

His lips skimmed her cheek, and ghosted along the shell of her ear. She heard his words whisper along her skin as she buried her face against his chest.

"Do you hear that?" he asked.

She listened.

All she could hear was his heart beat.

"I hear you," she replied.

John pulled her back a little, tipped her head up, and winked down at her. "No, the music. Can you hear it?"

Siena gave him a look, but indulged his question. She quieted, and listened hard for this music he spoke of. Sure enough, in their stillness and silence, the softest hum carried through the walls and floors.

A slow, lovely beat.

"Someone is waltzing," Siena said.

John smiled charmingly, slid one arm around her waist, and captured her hand with his. "Dance with me?"

Siena laughed. "That's what you want to do right now?"

"Right now, yeah. So, dance with me?"

How could she deny him?

"Lead away, John."

Siena found herself drifting across the large floor of the hotel room. Swaying softy together as John drew her closer, and she pressed her forehead against his. The way his smile deepened made her own grow wider. He kissed her lips, and then her cheek.

She could barely hear the music now.

Not overtop her racing heart.

Siena didn't mind.

"Who taught you how to dance?" she asked.

John laughed a husky sound. "My mother, and then my grandmother, and then my aunt, and finally my other aunt."

Siena's giggles echoed. "What, it took that many for you to get it?"

"No, none of them thought the other one knew what they were doing. My family is both large, and strange sometimes."

"I think they're wonderful."

John blinked, and the two of them stilled in their dance. "Yeah, they kind of are, huh?"

"They love you very much, John."

"I know."

Siena leaned up, and pressed a kiss to John's lips. She intended for it to only be a quick kiss, but he pressed his hand against her lower back with a firm touch, and wouldn't let her go. She didn't mind at all, and soon, their kiss had once again deepened into something far hotter than how it had first started.

"I don't want to dance anymore," she whispered against his lips.

John's smile turned sinful. "Me, either."

His skillful hands made quick work of unzipping her dress from the back. Never once did his lips leave hers, and if they did, it was only long enough to kiss her chin, or down the column of her throat. She loved the way the taste of him lingered on her tongue. A heavy, heady unique-to-him scent and flavor that always left her a little wet between her thighs, and hot on her skin.

Cool air hit Siena's body as John dragged her dress down. His warm palms slid over her curves, and he finally pulled back from their kiss long enough to let his gaze wander over the black lace panty and bra set she wore.

While his attention was on her, she started undoing his jacket, and vest. John let her pull the items off, along with his tie. She was working on the buttons of his dress shirt when, without warning, he dropped to his knees.

He didn't give her much time to think, or react. No, he simply grabbed the waist of the lace panties, and yanked them down her thighs with a hard tug. The material pulled against her skin, making her release a sharp breath.

John's husky chuckles echoed.

Siena looked down.

She only saw the flash of his hazel gaze, and that was it. Suddenly, his face was buried between her thighs, his tongue was assaulting her clit in the best way, and the rest of her thought process was gone.

Just like that.

Poof.

It was like time hadn't separated them. Space hadn't been between them. The seconds, hours, days, and months away no longer mattered. He knew her body, and just how to love it in the right way to get her hot, shaking, and falling over that blissful edge in barely any time at all.

Siena gasped when John's mouth left her sex. She wanted to refuse, and pull him right back, but his quick, dark order came too fast for her to speak.

"Open up more for me," she heard him demand. "Now, babe."

Two sharp taps of his hands to her inner thighs had her legs opening wider. He was back between her body in a flash—his tongue on her clit again, but this time, his fingers joined the effort. Two inside her pussy fucked her hard, and then widening to stretch her open as he drew them back out of her sex.

She could hear how fucking wet she was.

She could smell her own sex.

Her noises echoed.

Sweet, breathless sounds.

"Come on, come on," he growled against her inner thigh. "Give me that honey of yours, Siena."

Jesus.

She came so hard.

It took away her sight for a brief second.

Her breath, too.

It was glorious.

Siena had only blinked, and John was rising from the floor. His hands trailed over the backs of her naked legs, her thighs, and ass. He let her step out of the panties that had bunched into a useless pile at her heels. The second the garment was gone, his hands pressed at her back and ass again, and she found herself lifted from the floor.

The room spun.

John was all she saw.

Siena's back hit the bed, and his hands did that goddamn wandering thing again. Stroking her skin, and memorizing her with touch. Her back arched as his weight came over hers. A substantial weight that left her feeling breathless and oh, so high.

She fumbled with his belt, and the pants until he could pull them down, and kick them off. Soon, his shirt was gone too, and then the white boxer-briefs. He pulled at the hook of her bra connecting the two cups together, and freed it from her body. Nothing was between them but skin, and the hardness of his cock pressing into her thigh.

John's lips were at her throat again. His teeth nipped into her pulse point, and his tongue tasted her skin. His words crawled over her in the best way—soft, yet harsh at the same time. Like the promise of a hard fuck that would leave her sore, but so satisfied, too.

"Get those fucking legs open for me, *donna*," he said.

His voice was a rumble.

Thick and dark.

Siena widened for him, and he fit between her perfectly. Just like he always had. She only felt his hand between her thighs for a brief second, and then the head of his cock was at her slid. Rubbing, smearing her juices, and teasing her.

Begging was easy.

With him, it was too easy.

"Please fuck me," she whispered. "Oh, my God."

She missed him.

Too much.

It couldn't be healthy.

She didn't care.

John's hands found her hips, his fingers dug in hard enough to leave marks behind, and she sucked in a sharp breath. The waiting was a killer— the knowledge that it was coming, but not yet there was enough to drive her crazy.

And then he was.

If that first thrust was heaven, the ones that followed were unaltered sin. A bliss like no other. He stretched her wide, his cock filled her full, and her nerves sang.

He fucked her crazy.

Until her lungs ached from panting so hard, and her lips were numb from his kisses. His teeth left imprints behind, and her skin heated beyond compare.

Siena's fingernails dragged lines over the flexing muscles of John's back with each push and pull of his body into hers. Deeper, and harder he came. Hitting the right spot every single fucking time, and then dragging every inch of his cock against it as he left her once again.

She couldn't get enough.

Not of this man.

Or of them.

It was never going to be enough.

"More," she demanded.

He gave her that, too.

• • •

Warm sunlight danced over Siena's naked shoulders, but the sensation was nothing compared to John's kisses dotting down her spine. He kissed all the way down, and then back up again, only stopping at her neck.

"Get up," he murmured against her skin.

"But it's so comfortable."

"It's morning, Siena."

"Quite aware, John."

And if she woke up, she would have to face the day. Or rather, face reality. Which meant leaving the comfort of this bed where she had spent all night relearning and loving a man she had been separated from for far too long.

It would mean leaving him again.

Who knew for how long?

It meant going back home.

Siena didn't want to do any of that at the moment—never, really—so she stayed firmly stuck on her stomach, and refused to even roll over for John when he demanded it. She should have known better, though.

John was not a patient man.

Soon, she found herself flipped over. The soft white sheets tangled in her legs as she laughed breathlessly, and her vision swam. John hovered over her with one of his sinful, signature grins that made her want to get down on her knees for him.

"That was mean," she told him.

John only shrugged. "I told you to get up."

"But I don't *want to.*"

"I ordered food."

He said it as though he were dangling an offer he knew she couldn't refuse. Her stomach just had to go and growl at his declaration, as if it had heard him make the offer, too. She didn't even bother to try and look sheepish when he raised a brow at her.

"Will you feed it to me in bed?" she asked.

John's smile softened. "Whatever you want, babe."

"Remember that."

"But it is time to get up. I didn't forget what you told me last night, and the last thing we need or want is you getting into trouble with your brothers. You have to get back home, right?"

Fuck.

"Why did you have to go and ruin the moment with that nonsense?"

John frowned. "I don't live in delusions, Siena."

"Sometimes, reality is not a fun place to be."

He didn't reply, simply pushed off the bed, and turned his back to her. She felt bad, then—it hadn't been him who ruined their moment at all. It was her, and her shitty morning attitude.

"Sorry," Siena muttered.

John looked over his shoulder, and winked. "No worries. Get up. Let's have a few minutes before you do have to go. I would have let you sleep, but then you would have needed to run as soon as you woke up."

"Ah, so this was more for you than it was for me. I see what you did there."

John only laughed.

As much as she didn't want to move, Siena forced herself out of the bed. She found her discarded clothes from the night before, and carried them into the bathroom. She winked on the way past John. The man had no shame—naked and staring at her like he was.

She made quick work of using the bathroom, washing her face, and pulling her hair back into a simple, messy bun. She was stuck using her finger to brush her teeth with the small tube of toothpaste the hotel provided, but whatever, as it did the trick for now.

Slipping the clothes back on from yesterday, she was grateful nothing had been too wrinkled or ruined in their haste the night before. She smoothed down the front of the dress, and then zipped up the back, too.

Siena wasn't really a high-maintenance woman when it came to her appearance, and that came in handy for the moment. Her half-assed hairstyle worked, and she did just fine without makeup for the most part.

John held out her small clutch as she left the bathroom. "Didn't know if you needed something in it."

"Just my phone."

Which she had turned off the night before.

Siena decided she should probably turn it on, and check if she had missed any calls. The phone came to life under her hand as John went to the door when a knock echoed. She checked her phone over while he directed the man in with the cart of food.

"Well, shit," Siena muttered.

John was at her side, and pressing a soft kiss to her temple once they were alone again. "What, something bad?"

"No, actually."

She showed him the phone.

"No calls from my brothers," she explained.

John cocked a brow. "So?"

"So, the enforcer did what I thought."

"He didn't call them."

Siena nodded, and grinned. "Nope."

"Any calls from the enforcer?"

"A text," Siena replied.

She hadn't even bothered to open it, but she did when John prompted her to.

Where the fuck are you?

And then another, later that night saying, *I will be outside the brownstone at nine when you should be leaving. You better fucking be there, Siena. I am not getting my ass killed for your stupidity.*

"He doesn't seem happy," John mused.

Siena laughed. "No, I guess not."

She typed out a reply for the enforcer. Nothing to excuse herself, or explain where she went. *I'll see you at nine.*

No reply came.

Siena looked at John. "Lucky me."

He kissed her temple again. "Something like that."

Well, either way ...

"This was worth it," she said.

John nodded. "Yeah, but it still makes me fucking edgy, babe."

So was their life, apparently.

At least, for now.

Siena wanted to get her mind, and John's, far away from all of that nonsense. Well, for as long as they possibly could, anyway.

"Let's eat," she said.

John let her go with a grin, and moved toward the cart of waiting food that was still covered on silver platters. "There's a spread, so whatever you want. You made the orders, and I will feed you like I promised."

She preened. "You better."

"*No!*"

"Cella, it's—"

"*No.*"

John's head whipped in the direction of the door, but no one came busting through despite the shouting that suddenly filled the hallway outside. Still, he left their food, and grabbed his clothes hanging off the back of the chair. Pulling on the items, he moved for the door, and opened it up just in time for the yelling to get louder. More voices joined the chorus.

Siena heard pain.

Disbelief.

Grief.

Anger.

"Not my husband—not my *husband!*" Cella screamed. "You're lying, Daddy. Why would you lie to me like that?"

John's gaze cut back to Siena, and then just as fast, he disappeared out into the hall. She should have stayed where she was—after all, a lot of his family didn't actually know that she was even there to begin with. The whole point was for her to stay low, and leave out the back quietly where she wouldn't be seen.

Siena didn't stay in the room.

She left instead.

"I'm sorry," Lucian said, the words coming out repeated and sadder with every one. "I'm so sorry, Cella."

The young, dark-haired woman—one of John's sisters—fought with her father in the middle of the hallway. Her fists slammed into his chest when he tried to hug her, and tears stained her face as sobs ripped past her lips. People surrounded them. Confusion echoed as questions were asked.

Still, Siena heard the explanation given to John when he finally found someone who knew what in the hell was happening.

"William had taken the baby to grab some things from their place—I guess they forgot a bag," Jordyn told her son. "Cella was sleeping, and he told Lucian he didn't want to wake her, so he took the baby, too. His car was run off the road, and shot up. We got the call a little while ago."

"Is she—"

"We don't know about the baby," Jordyn interjected.

"And William?" John asked.

"*Why, Daddy?*"

Cella's pain coated the hallway. So thick, and heavy. Like a blanket of agony that no one could escape. Siena didn't think John really needed his question answered, not when all he needed to do was look at his sister, and hear her cries.

"I'm sorry, *bambina*, I'm so sorry."

Lucian finally got his daughter in a bear hug that she couldn't escape. Jordyn must have felt safer to move closer, and so people parted to let her through. Siena heard people murmur about the hospital, and needing to go.

Someone else mentioned waking Andino, and his new wife.

What a morning after that would be.

A beautiful wedding, and a horror in the morning.

"Was it them?" someone asked.

"It was, wasn't it? The Calabrese."

"No one's claimed it—but we suspect, yeah," Giovanni Marcello said, confirming Siena's worst fears to the questioning family.

She realized then that perhaps her brothers did have a motive for leaving the city. Something they had put into motion that she had not known about beforehand. She wondered if William had been personally picked as a hit, or if he had simply been an opportunity given the circumstances.

Those were not answers she had.

Siena wasn't able to think on it for long.

"Why is *she* here?" Cella demanded.

Siena snapped back at the venom in the woman's tone. Cella—younger than Siena, maybe, or possibly the same age—stared at her with growing hatred in tear-filled eyes. She didn't blame the woman, but it still hurt.

She stepped back.

John stepped in front of her. "Cella, she didn't do anything."

"Why is she here?"

This time, it was a scream.

A stabbing accusation.

"You just had to fucking go and get in bed with that fucking family full of snakes, John," his sister shouted. Despite being pulled down the hallway by her parents, Cella continued on. Her rage spilled out—hurt and confusion following. "You don't *care* what it means, do you? You don't even *know*—"

"Cella, that's enough," Lucian snarled.

Sobbing echoed, and then the girl was gone, along with her parents. A few people followed them, mentioning the hospital again.

Siena was left standing in the middle of the hallway, feeling oh, so fucking cold and unsure. It wasn't like Cella had been wrong, though she directed her words at the wrong person. John had not deserved those statements and accusations.

It was not his choices that did this.

It was not his family who took from her.

"Hey, babe. It's okay."

John was there in front of her before Siena had even blinked. His hand came up and touched her face with the softest stroke, but a line of tears still fell. She didn't bother to wipe them away. He did it for her.

"It's okay," he repeated.

She didn't think it was.

Not at all.

"She should have known," someone said. "Isn't she the one fucking feeding the boss information?"

Siena looked at the man who spoke, but she didn't recognize him. "I didn't know."

Giovanni—Andino's father—stepped in front of the man to block him. "Nothing at all, Siena? They didn't say anything? You didn't hear anything about something like this?"

She shook her head.

Nothing.

She knew nothing.

She fucked up.

"I'm sorry," she mumbled. "I'm sorry."

CHAPTER SIX

JOHN WAS PULLED away from Siena by his uncle. Giovanni cut through the people gathered in the hallway with a low curse, and a shake of his head. It wasn't hard to figure out that his uncle was pissed, especially when Gio waved at the men following him to get inside one of the hotel rooms. Once they were all inside, he then slammed the door hard enough that John thought the wood might have cracked.

A couple of more men slipped into the room not long after the door had closed. Once most everyone was there—barring a couple of important people—gazes drifted between one another. It was almost as though they were silently asking who wanted to speak first.

John didn't know what to say.

He didn't have all the details.

Instantly, all the men started talking at once. The Marcello Capos that had been invited to the dinner and party portion of Andino's wedding, and had stayed overnight like the family did, made a catacomb of noise inside the hotel room.

John tried to take everything in.

"Has someone told the boss?"

"Dante is awake, and aware," Gio answered. "He has something else to handle with someone else, and then we will all sit down with the boss and figure something out after we chat here. Not before."

"What about Andino?"

Gio's gaze cut to the man who had asked that question. "Someone has gone to wake him up, as well. I should have been the one to do it, but here I am instead. I don't expect him to be very pleased, all things considered."

"Shitty way to wake up from your wedding night."

Wasn't that the fucking truth?

John figured his cousin was—in some ways—ready for this sort of thing. Andino would have to be, considering he was making big steps to take over their uncle's position as the boss. No man went into that job with rose tinted glasses on. Trouble always came when you least expected it to, and even when you did expect it.

Andino had to be ready for that.

That didn't mean a man wanted to have to deal with this kind of thing on what should be one of the happiest days of their life. Some shit just shouldn't be touched in their life—women, children, and so forth. Only fucking cowards attacked made men and their families during vulnerable times like weddings, births, or even Christenings.

Those days were supposed to be sacred.

Nothing was sacred anymore.

Then, another voice joined the chorus. An older Capo—closer to John's father's age, who flat out refused to concede his position to a younger man. Sometimes, that shit happened, but it didn't always make for good business.

Nathan was the man's name.

"We're supposed to believe that the Calabrese woman being here in the morning after what they did to us today is nothing more than coincidence?" Nathan asked.

Gio's gaze darted from a suddenly stone-still John, to Nathan. "Well—"

"You honestly think she doesn't know what the fuck happened, or that it was going to happen? I heard there was some kind of behind the scenes action with someone inside the Calabrese family, but I didn't realize we were using a fucking *woman* to get it."

John opted to speak up, then. He really didn't need to, and God fucking knew they didn't need more problems at the moment, considering everything. It probably would have been a smarter idea for him to just keep quiet, and let Giovanni handle the questions and explanations for the men.

He couldn't do that, though.

Not when Siena's name was brought into it. Not if it meant letting someone drag her through the mud, or stain her with accusations she wasn't warranted, and could not defend. That kind of shit was not okay, and he would never allow it.

"Do you have a fucking problem with Siena Calabrese?" John asked Nathan.

The older man stood a little straighter in his bathrobe and cotton sleep pants. Nathan was the type that figured his age gave him some kind of edge, or even a heavier respect, than those younger than him in the family. Bullshit. The least he could have done was thrown on a fucking shirt before leaving his room, but here they were.

"Yes, I damn well do," Nathan replied.

"And what is it?"

"Her last name, for starters."

John scoffed. "So she's good to feed you information, but the second someone knows it's her, she's not good enough, huh?"

"I didn't know it was her."

"Fact remains the same, Nathan. If you're going to run off at the mouth about Siena, I suggest you do so where I cannot hear, or where she is ready and capable of defending herself. Otherwise, I'm going to make you apologize to her for acting like a goddamn prick, and I can promise that you will not like the way I fucking do it. Got it?"

"It is a little concerning that she's here," another man put in.

"She was here for me," John snapped over his shoulder. "She didn't leave my room all day yesterday, or last night. She was kept company by several people while she waited for me. And if you have a fucking problem with who I involve myself with, then you can bring that issue to *me*."

"John makes a valid point," Giovanni said, stepping in between the men. "And right now, the important topic is not who is involved with who, but what we need to do next to lock this family down, and protect anyone who needs protection."

"And what, ignore the fact he's sleeping with one of the goddamn snakes?" Nathan asked.

Jesus.

John had done *so well*.

He hadn't let his anger or frustration overwhelm him for a long damn while. His new med regime really helped with the sometimes heavy swings of emotions that he experienced. At the very least, it gave him some time to think shit over before he outright reacted to something. But sometimes, shit just could not be helped.

This was one of those times.

Rage swelled through John like a fucking tsunami coming to destroy hallowed ground. Rage was often his favorite emotion as it was the easiest to understand, and to feel. It certainly wasn't the easiest to control, but he wasn't concerned about that at the moment. He had other things to handle.

He swung around, despite seeing the warning flash in his uncle's eyes, and took aim at the idiot who smirked at him.

Good.

Wiping that off would be greatly satisfying.

John reared back, and let his fist crash into the face of the Capo. He didn't hold back for a second, and he put every bit of his weight behind the punch. He swore Nathan's nose broke under the impact as the man's bones flattened with a sickening crunch damn near instantly. That sound was quite satisfying, really.

Blood poured.

Someone swore.

Someone else moved closer.

"John," he heard his uncle warn.

John didn't need anybody to step in. He knew exactly what he was doing, he was perfectly in control, and he had this shit handled.

He had *himself* handled.

John pulled back, stood straight once more, and fixed his fucking jacket. Another time—another day in his life or another person he disliked a little bit more than Nathan—and he might have beat the guy to a bloody pulp because he couldn't fucking control himself, and it would have felt divine.

Today was not that day.

John only needed the one hit to make his fucking point clear. He looked over Nathan as the man covered his broken, bleeding nose with one hand, and nodded when the Capo glanced up at him. Bleeding and holding onto his face, Nathan muttered a garbled apology when John cocked his brow at the man.

He hadn't even needed to ask.

The Capo just knew.

So was their life.

Pointing a finger at him, John said, "And you fucking remember how this shit went down the next time you put Siena's name in your goddamn mouth, too."

Turning fast on his heel, John looked to his uncle. What had been concern and a warning in Gio's eyes before was now only a slight amusement, and shit, maybe even pride. It was hard to tell with Gio sometimes. His mind was all over the place, and really, he was usually the first man in their family to step out of line when it came to rules and whatever else.

John figured he was good to go. And even if he wasn't, that one punch had been worth it, all things considered.

"We don't assault other made men," Gio said quietly.

"Let him act that way toward your wife, then."

Gio raised a brow. "Siena is not your wife, John. Therein lies the difference, and you're quite aware of that."

Yet.

She was not his wife yet.

John didn't say that out loud, only shrugged. "I said what I said."

"Can we finish our discussion, now?"

"Sure," John murmured, "but somebody might want to get Nathan a towel. He's ruining the rug, and that's a damn shame."

• • •

"They said nothing to you?" Dante asked. "Nothing at all?"

John's defensiveness edged a little higher at the sound of his uncle questioning Siena. It wasn't that Dante Marcello was a bad man—he wasn't. In fact, the current patriarch of their family was known to be incredibly kind and giving to those he allowed beyond his hard outer shell.

To someone on the outside of their family, however, Dante was also known to hold nothing back. He could be cold, and extremely callous. He had no qualms with removing what he perceived to be threats against his family and organization.

Maybe it was the way Dante had treated Siena months ago that left a bad taste in John's mouth now. He was not willing to allow anyone to treat her with anything less than absolute respect, including his uncle.

John leaned in the doorway that separated the main living quarters of his hotel room with the small kitchen section. Dante and Siena sat at the small two-person table. His uncle drank a coffee. Siena picked at food on her plate.

Dante's gaze caught John's, but he chose not to move. He simply wanted his uncle to know that he was there, and *listening*. That was the most important thing

"Nothing," Siena said. "They left last night, like I said. Darren came over, and Kev had a bag packed. They said they might be gone a couple of days. I hadn't heard anything before that to suspect something."

"You didn't think you had any reason to tell us they left?"

"No."

Dante sighed, and leaned back in his chair. "And you've gotten no calls from them since you've been here?"

"No," she repeated.

"If this happens again—where they up and go without explanation—I will need you to let someone know however you can. I know it's a little …"

"Dangerous, yeah," Siena filled in.

Dante nodded. "I know, but it's important."

John took a single step into the room, drawing their attention his way. Siena tried to smile, but he could plainly see it did not reach her eyes like it usually would. He didn't like that at all, and he didn't like some of the shit he was hearing.

"Someone needs to explain to me what in the hell is going on with her," John said.

Dante cleared his throat, and his gaze drifted between Siena, and John before he finally spoke again. "You know I'm not required to give you any sort of—"

"You will tell me, or someone else will. Clearly, she's feeding information to the Marcellos. I got that fucking much at least. But I thought it was just Andino, or maybe even my father after he was the one who let me know she was here last night. But now you're mixed up in this scheme, too? What switch got flipped when I was away, huh? What changed your mind?"

Dante chuckled dryly. "There was no *switch*, John. I have always done whatever I needed to do for this family and organization. That's never changed in all my years."

Fair enough.

John still felt uneasy about a lot of things.

"I still need some answers," John said.

Dante's gaze fell on something—or someone—behind John. The man nodded, and then stood from the table. He looked to Siena at the same time Andino slipped in beside John. His cousin had gotten rid of the tux he wore the night before, and replaced it with dark wash jeans, and a white T-shirt.

Andino didn't particularly look pleased to be there, but John couldn't exactly blame him for that, either. The man should have been spending his morning with his new bride. Like any man would want to do.

"Siena, why don't I introduce you to my wife," Dante said. "You've met Catrina before, but I think you'll appreciate her a little more with a personal conversation."

John didn't want Siena going anywhere. "She can stay—"

"We should talk," Andino interjected. "Just you and I, John. Let her go with Dante."

Andino's statement offered no room for argument, and also, hinted at something he didn't fully explain, either. John thought back to the day before, and how a simple gesture of Dante walking Haven down the aisle for Andino would have been seen as a big deal.

"It could help her case a lot," Andino added quieter, "just to be seen with the boss. Having others trust her is of the utmost importance right now, man."

John nodded. "All right."

He didn't let Siena by without pulling her in close enough for a quick kiss to her temple, though. Her smile grew the longer he held her there, and she gave him a nod before disappearing out of the small kitchen behind Dante.

"Talk," John demanded once he was alone with his cousin. "And give me something worth chewing on while you're at it."

Andino folded his arms over his chest. "You know, I could be fucking my wife—"

"You'll get back to that. Talk."

"On your one question—Siena has been feeding us info for months now. Shortly after you went in, actually, I had the chance to give her some direction. She took my advice, and I used it to my advantage."

"How so?"

"She goes to yoga a couple of times a week. I either meet her inside, or she slips outside and fills me in on things."

"You said us, but that sounds like just you."

"Your father was involved behind the scenes, but he stepped in. My dad, too."

"And Dante?"

"Came in later," Andino said, smirking. "You know, when I didn't give him a fucking choice. It's like this—Dante wants me to take over this family, and I am going to do that. But I will do so on my terms, and how I want to do it. He didn't want a war with the Calabrese, and I am never going to bow down to those fuckers for anything. Not after what they did to us decades ago, and not after what they did to you. I wouldn't betray you like that either, frankly."

Andino shrugged, adding, "I'm going to remove them from this city altogether. Her information, when she has some to give, helps a great deal."

John cleared his throat. "So what, you take over their organization, too?"

"That's not important right now."

"I think it is. You're putting Siena in a lot of fucking danger, Andino."

"No, John, she is."

John straightened on the spot. "I beg your fucking pardon?"

Andino shook his head. "She is the one putting herself in danger. I neither need her for information now, nor to end this when the time is right. She's helped me more than enough, and got me what I needed the most—for a real war to be started in this city. For a reason to get rid of them once and for all."

"You used her to start a fucking war?"

His cousin laughed in that dark, dry way again. "John, you helped, too, but she's the one who pushed them over the edge with me. And now, she is also the one who has chosen to continue on when she knows she could step back now. She is doing this because she has something to gain, too. *You*, man. Or did you forget about that?"

"Andi—"

"She's doing this for you, John. No one is ever going to manipulate you again. No one is ever going to get to you after this. She won't let them."

"I still don't fucking appreciate you using Siena as a means to further yourself in this city, Andino."

His cousin stared hard at him for a long while before Andino dropped his arms to his sides, and pushed away from the kitchen doorway. He shook his head, and gave a little sigh.

"You know what, John, you don't get it. That's fine. There will be a hell of a lot of days ahead of us yet for me to get this through your thick skull. Today, though? Today I have other shit to handle—a new wife, and a dead cousin-in-law. A war to finish, and *win*. Either get with the fucking program, or shove off."

Andino didn't give John the chance to reply before he left the room. John heard the hotel room's door slam shut a couple of seconds later.

So, that's how it was going to be?

John wished he could be surprised, but he really wasn't.

Instead of following after Andino to demand more answers, or tear his cousin a new one, John opted to take a seat at the small table, and fucking relax. The entire morning had been too much—from one damn thing to another.

He hadn't got the chance to breathe.

He needed to think.

Too much stimulation was not a good thing for John, and he recognized that for what it meant when it came to himself. He did not need to be adding more shit to his already overactive emotional state and mind.

John was so lost in his own thoughts that he didn't hear the hotel room open and close. He didn't even realize he was no longer alone until Siena's arms wrapped around him from behind. She hugged him tight—so fucking tight.

He needed that.

He needed her.

Siena's lips pressed to the top of his head, she hugged his neck even tighter, and then she kissed his temple, too. A sweet, yet lingering kiss.

And all was right again.

"I have to go," she told him.

John nodded.

He knew that, too.

Didn't like it, though.

"Yeah, I know, babe."

"We'll figure something out," Siena whispered against his skin. "Us, and the rest of this stuff. We will figure it out, John."

He didn't know when he was going to see her again, or how long that would be. He didn't know *how* he was going to see her again, considering how controlled her life seemed to be under her brothers' demands, now.

It was a mess.

John didn't say any of that out loud, though.

Not while she was there.

Not while she hugged him.

Everything—for a moment, anyway—was perfect.

• • •

"John?"

"In the kitchen, Ma."

John popped open the blister packaging for his pills. Leonard opted to have John's prescriptions filled as a daily intake, and not a whole bottle that left John managing his meds for months.

Jordyn slipped into the kitchen, and offered her son a smile. It didn't reach her eyes, but he wasn't surprised.

Too much shit had happened over the last day.

"Come to fill me in?" John asked. "On Cella, and whatever?"

That's the only reason his mother would be there. Their family had been taking care of shit, and dealing with the mess the Calabrese attack left behind. John had taken the day after the wedding to settle back into his rented Queens home. He reminded himself to thank his father for keeping up the rent, and having someone come in to clean the place.

He tossed his pills back with water.

"Yeah, I'm here to fill you in. Your father was going to come, but Gio showed up, and Tiffany needs someone to look after her."

"Cella can't look after the baby, or what?"

"Not in her state."

"How is she?"

Jordyn cleared her throat before taking a seat at the table. "Heavily medicated tonight."

John winced. "That bad, then."

"That bad," his mother echoed. "You know, when I first married your father, I thought we would have some day in our lives to enjoy ... well, life. Things would slow down, and we would not be so on the go, so to speak. Not everything would be bullets, blood, and *famiglia*."

He gave his mother a look. "Bit naive of you, don't you think?"

Jordyn shrugged one shoulder. "I did not say that I don't absolutely love our life because I do, John. I simply meant I hoped there would be a time when for once, Lucian and I could focus on being a family, and not *the* family."

"Made man for life, Ma."

"So it seems."

"Tiffany is good, then?" he asked.

Jordyn nodded, and smiled a bit as John came to sit beside her at the table. "Yeah, she's good. A couple of scratches from the glass, but nothing too bad. Nothing that can't heal."

"Unlike her father."

His mother frowned. "Yes, unlike William."

"If you need any help with the baby, or Cella, just let me—"

"Actually, that's one thing I needed to chat with you about."

John leaned back in the chair, and stared at his mother, waiting. "Go on."

"Cella is ... still very angry, John. She needs someone—something—

73

to blame right now, and she's shooting for the easiest targets she can find."

"Me, you mean."

Jordyn blew out a shaky breath. "She doesn't mean the things she says, and she's so confused with how she feels."

"Of course." John shrugged. "Her husband is dead—a violent death. She's left with a young baby to take care of alone. Hell, she married a man unaffiliated to the mob, and even that wasn't enough to keep her from being punished for this life. I get it, Ma, really. I'll keep my distance, and let her grieve. I don't need to be showing up and making her uncomfortable or anything. Don't worry about it."

"You don't have—"

"It's *fine*," he said firmly. "Really."

Jordyn smiled, and nodded once. Reaching over, she patted the top of John's hand with her own. "Someday, your sisters will see the man you are now, is not the boy you used to be, John. It's been hard for them to separate their emotions from all the things that happened while they were growing up. Give them time, okay?"

John shook his head. "I don't think they'll ever be one hundred percent good with me, Ma. And that's okay—I get that, too. I wasn't good to them, and you can't shake that kind of shit off. It's a long history to work through, and they might never work through it. I don't expect anything from my sisters."

"I do, though," his mom said.

John smiled, leaned over, and cupped his mother's cheek. She smiled at the affectionate touch, and he felt guilty that he had not asked for his mother to visit him more during his time away. She loved him so much— she always had.

"I know you do, Ma, but don't push them to do something that they can't. I understand, and that's what's most important."

Jordyn sniffed, and patted her hand over top John's gently. "I'm happy you're home again."

"Me, too."

"I'm proud of you, John."

"You're always proud of me, Ma."

Jordyn laughed. "You still need reminders."

He did.

He loved her for that, too.

CHAPTER SEVEN

"KEV AND DARREN aren't going to be following us around all day?" Greta asked.

Siena gave the older of her two half-sisters an amused look. "You know, it would benefit you greatly to tone down the attitude when you use one of their names. Not because you *have* to like them, but because a little respect will go a long way with those two."

Greta cocked a brow. "But I don't respect them."

"Yeah, I got that. Me, either."

"I don't get your point, then."

Siena grabbed her bag from inside the hall closet, and skipped over a light cardigan or jacket. It was still boiling hot, even at the end of July. She didn't need to be adding extra layers at the moment.

Turning to face the seventeen-year-old, Siena said, "But you like having a little bit of freedom, don't you?"

"You call being taken from my school, and shoved into a private school freedom? Or losing my mom, and being forced to live with my aunt freedom? How about the fact I can't even go to the movies with friends because one of them is a *guy*? That's not freedom, Siena."

No, it wasn't.

Not *normal* freedom, anyway.

That was part of the whole problem neither of her two half-sisters realized. Nothing about their life was normal, and it was a damn shame, really. They had grown up almost entirely removed from the life Siena had lived as a *principessa della mafia*.

Maybe that had been because their mother demanded it from Matteo—that he already had one legitimate family to use to further his mafia agenda. Or, it could have been because her dead father didn't believe his illegitimate daughters would do anything for him in the grand scheme of things.

Siena really didn't know.

Frankly, none of that mattered, either.

Not now.

"Matteo is dead," Siena said.

Greta flinched. "I *know*."

It was strange to Siena in a way to see someone—other than her mother and brothers—grieve over her father's death. It seemed, somehow, that her half-sisters had a different opinion from hers on the man who helped to give them life.

They loved Matteo.

They talked fondly about him.

Siena couldn't say the same.

"And your mom, too," Siena added. "She's also dead."

"Do you think I don't know all of this?"

Greta's angry tone was matched only by the red flush covering her cheeks. Siena had hit a nerve, but that was exactly her point.

Someone had not properly sat these girls down, and explained what their life was going to be like from here on out if they didn't hurry up, and *do something*. What that something was, however, depended on the girl.

"Exactly," Siena murmured, staring her half-sister in the eyes, and refusing to look away. "They are dead, and so everything that they promised you for your life will no longer happen. You want to go to college, Greta? Will it further the family—will it further Kev or Darren somehow?"

"Well—"

"Or better yet, will college or something else make you a better house wife when they find a man to marry you to like they tried to do with Ginevra?"

Greta's mouth slammed shut.

Siena nodded. "Yeah, you get it, huh?"

"Will they really do that to us?" Giulia asked from behind Siena.

It was the first time the girl had spoken since the two had been dropped off for their day with Siena. Something was keeping the two very quiet, and sometimes, she could drag out of them what that something was. Today had not really been one of those days. The girls didn't seem interested in talking—unless Greta's attitude could be considered talking.

Siena turned to face the fifteen-year-old. "If it furthers their agenda, and they think they can get away with it, then do not put it past them."

"I don't see how respecting them will—"

"Because, Greta," Siena interjected, tossing a look over her shoulder, "if you think the more you irritate them will make them want to keep you around, or give you anything that you want, you are sorely mistaken. And until they're gone, your best bet, is to give them what they want."

"Until they're gone, huh?"

Siena cleared her throat.

Shit.

That had been a slip of the tongue.

"Pretend you didn't hear that," Siena said. "Now, are we going out, or not? I thought you two wanted to go swimming at Jacob Riis Beach, and then grab some gelato?"

Greta didn't move, and instead, put her hands on her hips. Siena had never met the girl's mother, but goddamn, when she did that, Greta looked just like Matteo. Tall, formidable, and un-fucking-moveable. Even the look in her eye was the very same. Like she was daring Siena to come closer, and try to move her.

Good luck Kev and Darren when you go toe-to-toe with this one, she thought. Her brothers deserved the trouble, anyway.

"You were the only one with Ginevra on the day she was supposed to get married," Greta said.

"So?" Siena asked.

"Kev and Darren were *very* mad at you."

"Listen, they're always very mad at me, okay? Depending on the day, they don't even look at me. There's a reason they call me the stain on this family."

Greta's gaze narrowed. "They only really started that after Ginevra went missing. They say she's dead. Is she?"

Siena cleared her throat again.

Dammit.

It felt like a giant knot was forming there, and she couldn't get it out. The uncomfortable sensation only grew the longer she tried to come up with an acceptable response for Greta. Nothing was ever simple, or easy.

This answer couldn't be, either.

"A lot of things happened on Ginevra's wedding day," Siena tried to say. "And a lot of things happened after. You have to consider—"

"Is she alive, or not?"

"I can't tell you that," Siena said.

"Why not?"

Greta might as well have stomped her foot, too.

"Because it wouldn't be safe for me to," Siena explained.

"I won't tell, and neither will—"

"It's not you or Giulia that I am worried about. It's Ginevra. Do you know what would happen if she suddenly wasn't missing anymore?" Siena asked.

Greta blinked. "No. What?"

"Let's just say you should be grateful that Kev and Darren's anger and hate is focused on me now. Being called the shame of this family is moderate and pleasant compared to what they would do if your older sister suddenly showed back up. So, she won't. Not today, anyway."

"Someday, maybe?" Greta whispered.

"Maybe."

Giulia frowned as she pushed past Siena, and her sister. "Okay, can we go now?"

"Yeah," Siena said, never taking her gaze off Greta, "we can go."

Outside at the bottom of the steps, was the enforcer who Siena had skipped out on the week before when she went to see John. The man still wasn't very pleased with her, but as far as she could tell, he had not yet run to her brothers about what she did.

Actually, Kev and Darren still hadn't come home from wherever they went.

Like cowards, they were hiding out. Likely hoping that the Marcellos would have gotten all of their violence and retribution for Cella's husband's death out of their system, or something like that.

Problem was, this couldn't end so easily. It was going to continue. It would grow. So was the way of war.

"Where to?" the enforcer asked, moving to open the back door of his black town car.

Siena gave the man a look. "I will be driving *my* car, thank you."

She didn't get to use her Lexus very often, anymore.

"Your brothers prefer—"

"I am taking my car," Siena said. "And when Kev and Darren get home, I will go back to riding with you. Okay?"

The enforcer's jaw tightened before he muttered, "Your ass, I guess."

The most her brothers would do was yell. Siena cared little about that. Yelling she could handle, and besides, their focus was elsewhere at the moment.

Plus, they weren't even home.

"Could we get gelato first?" Giulia asked as she slid into the backseat. "Before the beach?"

Siena nodded. "Actually, that sounds great."

Greta glared at the enforcer before she slipped into the car, too. Siena smirked to herself, and closed the door to the Lexus, shutting the girls in.

Poor kid.

Greta just couldn't help herself. She was a lot like Siena in that way. Hopefully, it never came back to bite her.

It wasn't long before Siena had navigated the streets of Brooklyn, grabbed them all some gelato, and headed for Jacob Riis Beach. The three sisters sat in the parking lot of the beach with the doors of the Lexus thrown wide open while warm wind blew through the vehicle.

Silent, mostly.

They people watched. Kids squealing, and parents chasing. Water flying, and music blasting.

It was both nice, and sad.

For a moment, they could pretend to be normal people, doing normal things. And yet, they were far removed from all of that.

This was just another illusion.

One soon to be shattered.

"Are you jealous that we got a good dad?" Giulia asked suddenly.

Siena looked back at the younger of the two sisters. "You mean, about Matteo?"

Beside her in the passenger seat, Greta stuck a spoonful of gelato in her mouth. The older girl looked both interested and kind of worried what Siena's response might be.

Giuia shrugged. "Yeah, I mean, I see what your face does when we say something nice about Daddy, and stuff."

Siena didn't realize her face *did something* at all.

She wasn't surprised, though.

"No," she said after a moment, "I'm not jealous. Happy, if anything."

"Happy seems strange," Greta muttered around her spoon.

"I can't be happy that he was a good father to you two? That you have fond memories of him, and loved him?" Siena smiled faintly, and peered back out the windshield at the playing children, and relaxing people. "I am happy that you will have good memories of him to carry you through life. I can't say that I have the same—I wouldn't wish my memories of him on you two at all."

"Oh."

Giulia's quiet response was only echoed by silence. Really, Siena no longer had anything to say about it. Not Matteo, or her life as his daughter. She meant what she had said about her half-sisters lives with him, though.

Out of the corner of her eye, Siena saw the enforcer approaching the car.

"What?" she asked him. "Jesus, we only got here a few minutes ago."

"We have to go," the guy said, offering no room for argument, "right now."

"But—"

"Now, Siena. Your brothers' homes are burning to the fucking ground. We don't have time to argue. Leave the Lexus here—someone will come get it later. I've been ordered to deliver the girls to their aunt, and take you to your mother's place."

Siena straightened in the driver's seat. She heard everything that the enforcer said, but only one thing really stood out the most. "*Both* of their homes?"

"Guess so."

"Burning?"

"Looks like it," the man uttered.

Well, fuck.

Where was she supposed to live, then? Oh, was Siena supposed to care that the Marcellos finally attacked back at her brothers after what they did to them?

Because she didn't.

• • •

Siena stood on the side of the street, and watched as workers began the process of cleaning away the mess left behind from the fire at Kev's brownstone. Two days after the blaze, and the smoldering and smoking bits had finally been completely extinguished.

The heat hadn't helped.

Neither had the lack of rain.

Large dumpsters had been brought in to contain the rubble and ashes covering the space between two other brownstones. It would take them a couple weeks to clean up, or so they said, and then once the investigation was finished on the fire, Kev could rebuild if he wanted.

Siena didn't know if that was her brother's plan, or not.

At least the fire department had been able to save the homes connected to Kev's. They contained the blaze enough that very little damage had been done to the main walls connecting the other brownstones, and the supports needed to rebuild.

The firefighters had made it their main focus to save the other buildings once they realized the fire was containable to the one brownstone.

Kev's place, however, was gone entirely.

Nothing but a pile left behind.

The workers placed a large tarp along the bit of charred grass, and then began dressing in their safety gear. Apparently, they would place anything they found in the rubble on the tarp for Kev to look over. Anything that might have made it through the blaze.

By the looks of it, nothing did.

All of it was gone.

A few feet away, Kev and Darren hissed between one another. As usual, their conversation was not quiet enough to keep their words just between them. They still didn't know the meaning of fucking privacy.

Not that she was surprised.

"Look at it," Kev snarled.

"Well, there's not really much to look at, Kev," Darren replied.

"Oh, you got fucking jokes today, huh?"

Darren sighed. "My place is gone, too, man. What do you want me to say? We put a hit out on one of their people, it went through, and then what? You expected them to sit back, and do fuck all about it?"

"Well, no—"

"This is what they did," Darren interjected, his voice a rough murmur.

"Now, we answer back, or figure something else out."

"Something else, huh?"

"What do you want to do, Kev? Focus on a place that means nothing to you? What did you have in there other than some documents, guns, and clothes? It's not like you had anything you gave a shit about in there. Rebuild, or go buy somewhere else."

"That's not the point!"

"Well, if you want to get into semantics about all of this, and whose fault it really is that our places got burned down, let's start with you, brother."

Kev glared. "Me?"

"Yeah, you."

"Why the fuck *me*?"

"You were the one who said it would be best if we dropped low for a while after the whole hit thing, you know what I mean? Maybe if we hadn't ducked out for a week, this wouldn't have happened. We would have been more present here, and whatever else. Kind of hard to burn a place down when you've got someone going in and out of it all the time, or somebody watching it. I mean, you didn't really do that, and neither did I."

"There was somebody here—*Siena*."

Two gazes drifted in Siena's direction. She quickly looked away as if to make her brothers think she was not paying any mind to their conversation at all.

She still needed to feed Andino and the rest of the Marcellos whatever information she could, after all. Kev and Darren were constantly predictable in the way they never looked at her—they never even considered she was smart enough, or had enough guts to be the one fucking them over.

Their mistake.

Her gain.

Darren stared hard at the empty space where Kev's brownstone had once stood tall and proud. A sharp red brick against the brown bricks of the other homes on the block. It was more than just things lost, sure, but Siena wondered if that was only part of her brother's problem.

Maybe Kev was starting to realize he had bitten off far more than he could chew where the Marcellos were concerned. Or hell, maybe not.

"Maybe we've gone about this the wrong way with them," Darren said.

"Who?"

"The Marcellos—who the fuck else?"

Kev scrubbed a hand down his jaw. "I'm listening."

"I mean, their control over this city has always been the fact they have connections, and so much territory. Not to mention, *men*. The largest Cosa Nostra family in North America, right?"

81

"What's your fucking point?"

Ouch.

Even she could hear the jealous tone in Kev's voice.

"Don't get pissy at me," Darren said. "I'm just saying. Anyway, we've got at them from the front, so to speak. We've attacked them, and caused violence on their streets. Brought attention to them, and whatever else. Figured it might make them take a step back, or reconsider their usual way of handling these kinds of issues."

"And it did none of that," Kev muttered.

"Nope."

"So, what is your grand fucking plan now?"

"Well, that wasn't *my* plan to begin with. It was yours—it didn't work really well for us."

"Keep taking those shots at me, man."

Darren rolled his eyes. "I mean, let's go at them from a different direction. From behind, in a way. Make it hard for them to do business. Rough up the streets where their Capos have control. Step in between their contacts keeping things under control."

For a long while, silence stretched on between the two brothers.

Then, Kev spoke. "I like it."

"Thought you would."

"You know, I got word someone saw Johnathan Marcello around here shortly before the fire started," Kev said.

Darren cleared his throat. Out of the corner of Siena's eye, she saw Darren look in her direction before going back to the conversation at hand.

"That so?" he asked.

"Apparently."

"Anything else?"

"So far, the investigator agrees an accelerant was used, and they've called it an arson."

"Just like my place," Darren muttered.

"But hey, we know who probably did it," Kev said.

"Yeah, I guess so."

"We'll get him."

"Among many," Darren agreed. "For now, though, where do we *live*?"

Kev laughed dryly. "Well, Ma wants me over there. You, too."

"For a while, that's fine. But you know how it is."

"That won't work with Siena, though," Kev put in. "She's the one handling Greta and Giulia, you know what I mean?"

"Ma won't have Dad's bastards going in and out of her house all the time. She puts on a good show, sure, but—"

"She'll only take so much."

"You could just say fuck the girls for now," Darren offered. "Focus on everything else."

"I need them compliant, just in case."

"Sure, sure."

"Siena's enforcer said she did well while we were gone—never acted out of line."

Siena smiled at that—faintly so it couldn't be seen. All the while, she never looked away from the men cleaning up the mess that was once her brother's home.

Good things were coming her way.

She could tell.

"She's still got her apartment, too," Kev added quietly. "A couple of months there with an enforcer looking after her won't be a big deal. I even got the guy to check on the building—there's an apartment available two doors down from hers."

"You're going to send her back to her place?" Darren asked, incredulity coloring his tone. "After everything she did with Johnathan, and even after Ginevra?"

"We don't know that she helped Ginevra—"

"Suspecting is more than enough in this case, Kev! You're fucking crazy to let her out of your sight, and you know it."

"I have to," Kev grumbled, "for now, anyway."

Siena smiled wider.

That time, she hid it by looking up at the bright sky.

Good things *had* come for her.

• • •

Siena's fingers ached from typing all day, and her neck and shoulders felt like rocks from sitting in an uncomfortable computer chair for hours upon hours. The last thing she wanted to do was climb stairs, but freedom was just a few steps away.

Her apartment, that was.

She had been back at her old place for a couple of days. Nothing was better than closing the front door to her apartment, and knowing that her brothers wouldn't be hanging around a corner or something.

Sure, it left her out of the loop.

She didn't have information to pass on.

You win some, you lose some.

Siena still kind of considered this winning. At least for her.

She ignored the ache in her feet as she climbed the stairwell, and opened the hallway door leading down the row of apartments on her floor. Behind her, the enforcer still tasked with looking after her followed close behind.

He didn't speak.

He rarely did.

At her door, Siena pulled out her key, and stuck it in the lock. Like always, the enforcer opted to wait behind her until she had opened up the door, and slipped inside the apartment. She caught sight of his nod before he headed further down the hall.

The guy had gotten that extra apartment, after all.

Siena never left her place without the enforcer waiting outside her door. He drove her to and from work, and to wherever else she needed to go.

Now, with her brothers back, the guy didn't let her have an inch. Likely because he knew Siena would turn around and take a mile back from him.

Smart.

Siena locked the front door behind her, kicked off her heels, and reveled in the cold floors pressing against her aching soles. She dropped her bag in the corner, and picked up the contemporary romance paperback she had left sitting on the stand on her way out that morning

Thumbing through the pages of the book, she went back to the spot she had left her bookmark. The heroine was getting ready for a date with a guy she despised, but felt she had no other choice given her circumstances.

Siena was so focused on her book, that she damn near rammed head-first into the tall form standing in the middle of her living room.

She knew it was him before she looked up.

Before he even spoke, she *knew*.

"John," Siena whispered.

Her eyes found his, and John smiled sinfully.

"I see you're distracted again," he said.

Familiarity comforted her.

Love wrapped around her.

Hope held her.

Still, Siena's gaze darted over her shoulder to the door. "How in the hell did you get in here?"

John shrugged. "Used the back door when someone was coming in, and picked your lock. I'm buying you a new one, by the way. No one else has a key, right?"

"The enforcer who watches after me."

His gaze narrowed. "Yeah, I saw that prick, too. Is he fucking decent to you?"

"He's okay."

She wasn't lying.

John nodded. "Can you change out his key?"

"Probably. Sometimes he's leaves them sitting in the cup holder when he runs into a place."

"Good enough for me."

Siena shook her head. "What are you doing here, John?"

His grin deepened. "Do you not want me here, babe?"

How could he possibly think that?

"Of course, I do, but it's danger—"

John interrupted her protests by grabbing her wrist, and yanking her in to him. Her book fell to the floor the second his lips crashed against hers. The kiss was enough to quiet her worries, make her wet between her thighs, and remind her of all the reasons why she loved this dark-in-his-soul man.

"They saw you," she whispered against his lips.

John hummed a low note. "Saw me, what?"

"Around Kev's place the day it was burned down."

He stiffened.

Siena shrugged. "Was it you?"

"Yes—someone else, too. But they were there to keep a look out."

"Because of what they did to Cella's husband?"

John shook his head, and kissed her lips again. "Nope—maybe partly. But mostly, no."

"Then, why?"

"Did you think I was just going to wait until I could see you from afar by chance again?" John laughed darkly, and kissed the tip of her nose. His affection was a bright contrast to how cold his voice and words were when he spoke. "No fucking way, *bella*. I am all in on this. Us, I mean. I tip hands to *my* favor, not the other way around. I needed a way to get you out from under their thumbs a little bit—now you are. See what I did there?"

Siena blinked.

John grinned.

Well, damn.

CHAPTER EIGHT

"I HAVE A surprise for you," John said.

Siena blinked up at him, happy and sweet in the next breath. "For what?"

"It's not much."

"I don't care. It's from you. Anything from you is wonderful, John."

He had no doubt she was telling the truth. He could see it in her eyes, and feel it in the way her fingers curved around his wrists to hold on tight.

John had come to figure out that Siena was somewhat of a cornerstone in his life—long term, and short term. He had regaled himself to the belief that everything he did for them now was so that they *could* have a future. He also got through the darker moments in his days by thinking about her.

She got him to the next breath. A thought about her smile made him wake up in the morning. Memories of them got him looking forward to the next week.

So, yeah.

Long term.

And short term.

Siena was all of it for John.

"It's in the kitchen," he told her.

Siena pressed her palm into John's, and wrapped their fingers tightly together. With a soft laugh, she pulled him along to the kitchen. She came to a sudden, full stop when the item on the island counter caught her eye.

"You didn't—"

"Thought I forgot, did you?" he interrupted her.

Grinning, John pressed a kiss to Siena's temple.

"Never, babe," he added.

Siena let out a little sigh, and her gaze drifted from him, to the item on the counter. A single cupcake, decorated in white frosting, and sprinkled with edible sparkles. The one candle inserted into the top flickered with a flame—he had lit it when he heard the lock jiggle in the door.

"Did anyone tell you yet today?" he asked.

Siena shook her head, and wetness gathered along her bottom lashes. "No, but I suppose it's not very important in the grand scheme of things."

Jesus.

Why would she ever think that?

Or *feel* that way?

"Siena, everything about you is *most* important—especially to me, *dolcezza*. Every part of you will always be important to me. You know that, don't you?"

Her hand came up to cup his cheek, and her thumb stoked his skin with a soft touch. It was enough to chase away the chaos that had been John's mind lately. So much had been piling up, and he took just a few minutes away from it all today, so he could be with Siena.

She took the rest away, too.

God, he loved this woman.

"Thank you," she said.

John slid a hand around the back of Siena's neck, and pulled her in for another quick, hard kiss. Her grin formed against his mouth, and he whispered, "Happy birthday, my sweet *donna*. Do you want me to sing it for you, too? I will."

Her fingertips patted his cheek. "I believe you, but you don't have to."

"Blow out your candle, then. Before wax gets all over your cupcake."

Siena laughed, and John let go of her. She reached for the cupcake, and pulled it from the counter. Holding it in front of her, she eyed him over the flickering flame. He could see the question burning brightly in her blue eyes.

"What, love?"

"So, I guess we're just going to act like yours doesn't matter, then."

John cocked a brow. "My what?"

"Birthday. A couple of days ago, right? Thirty-one."

"It's another day, and I spent half of it sitting on a sofa talking to a therapist."

"I bet your mom made you cake, though."

John flashed a smile. "She did, too."

Siena frowned.

He couldn't have that.

Stepping closer, he slid a hand along the curve of her waist, and pulled her a little bit closer to him. She kept the flickering candle at a safe distance as to not burn either of them while she looked up at him.

"What is it?"

"Sorry I missed your birthday," she said.

John kissed the tip of her nose. "It's fine—next year."

"Will we have a next year?"

"I'll make sure of it."

Siena's little smile came back. "Will you help me blow out the candle?"

She offered the cupcake between them with a little shake that made the flame flicker dangerously. Like an offer he couldn't refuse, not that he would refuse her anything.

"Anything you want, babe," John said. "Do we make a wish, too?"

"Is that too juvenile for you?"

"Not if you want it."

"A wish, then." Siena held the cupcake higher. "On three."

"One, two …"

"Three," she said.

The two of them blew out the candle together, and John made his wish. He didn't say it out loud, and he didn't even *think* it, really. Looking at Siena, he figured his wish was kind of obvious, anyway.

All he ever wanted now was her.

"This was great," Siena said as she pulled the paper from the bottom of the cupcake. Setting it and the candle aside, she pulled a chunk out of the cupcake, and offered it to John. He took the bite with a wink. "Thank you, really."

She swept a dollop of the frosting onto her finger, and sucked it between her lips.

Jesus Christ.

That one action was enough to kill him.

John tried to keep the huskiness out of his tone when he said, "Don't even mention it. This was so little compared to what I would have done in different circumstances."

"This was *perfect.*"

She sucked another dollop of icing off her finger.

"Siena."

"Hmm?"

She looked up at him.

Innocent and blue-eyed in a blink.

Goddamn her.

"You need to stop sucking on your finger like that, *donna.*"

"But it's good frosting."

She swept her finger through the top of the cupcake again, and offered it to John. Not even thinking about it, he took her finger into his mouth, and let his tongue do the work of cleaning off the digit. He felt the shiver race through Siena as her gaze met his.

"Yeah, okay," she said. "I get it."

"Good," John murmured when he released her finger.

And then she did it *again!*

Siena pulled her finger from between her pink, wet lips with a grin. She knew exactly what she had done, and John's control was all but gone.

He snatched that cupcake from her hand, and ignored her shriek of disappointment.

She wouldn't be disappointed for long, after all.

John swiped his own finger through what was left of the frosting at the same time he pulled Siena up onto the island counter. Her legs opened for him, and let him fit in between. A perfect fit, really.

It never failed to amaze him.

His gaze was stuck on her pretty little pout, and how sexy her lips looked in that moment. All pink, and wet from her tongue sweeping along the seam.

"You know, the only time your lips look better than they do right now is when they're wrapped around my cock," he told her.

Siena sucked in a sharp breath, and her gaze darted up to his. "Is that so?"

"Very much so, yeah."

"Maybe we can do that later."

"I think you could clean me off once I'm done with you."

Her smile turned sexy.

So fucking sexy.

God.

This woman made him *crazy*.

John took that bit of frosting on the tip of his finger, and smeared it along Siena's bottom lip. He didn't even give her the chance to clean it off before his mouth was on hers. He used his lips, teeth, and tongue to take away the frosting. His teeth nipped into her bottom lip, and pulled gently. She rocked her hips as he pressed closer, and it only made his growing erection grind into her center.

His tongue felt numb from their kiss, and her taste. Sweet from the sugar, and goddamn hot from her.

Siena's tongue battled with John's. Her fingernails cut into his jaw line when she pulled him impossibly closer. Shit, all he could think about now was getting his cock buried nine inches into the heaven that was between Siena's thighs.

It had been too long.

He couldn't wait—patience was not his friend, and it had never been.

Yanking up the skirt of her dress, and never breaking their kiss, John pulled Siena's thong down her legs. The forgotten material fell somewhere to the floor as Siena's lips left his, and trailed down his throat.

One kiss.

Then another.

His breath caught in his throat when her lips sucked at his jaw. The breath came out in a rush when her teeth cut into the same spot.

"Fuck," he groaned.

"We're getting there," she promised. "You should probably hurry up, John."

Laughing, John grabbed Siena by her throat, and tipped her head back. He stared into deep blue, and watched how her pupils blew wide from his rough handling. She was loving this—she always seemed to love whatever he did to her.

To the outside, Siena was sweet and innocent. Her appearance, with her gentle smiles and wide eyes, made people think she was nothing more than a doe-eyed woman. Harmless, entirely honest, and pure.

Those people didn't know a damn thing.

Not about Siena, anyway.

This girl was sin.

His sin.

John liked that just fine.

"I make the demands," he told her, "and not you."

"Sometimes me, too," she said, pouting.

John kissed her pout just because he could. "Sometimes you too, yeah."

He had to give her something, after all.

His hand snaked between her thighs—wet, hot flesh met his fingertips when he stroked her pussy. Bare and soft, he knew she had been waxed recently. He loved when nothing was between them. Loved the feel of her entirely naked against him.

He let two of his fingers sweep through her sex again, taking wetness from her slit up to her clit. One circle around the throbbing nub, and then a second, and Siena's legs trembled against the pressure. She was staring down to watch John play with her pussy, but he couldn't have that.

A slight tap of his hand against her sex made her gaze fly upward.

"Eyes on me right now," he said.

Siena blew out a breath. "But I want to—"

"Eyes on *me*."

He punctuated that statement by letting his two fingers slip inside her sex. Instantly, he curled his fingertips into her G-spot hard. His thumb slipped up, and rubbed at her clit at the same time.

It didn't take long before her fast, short breaths turned into low, sexy cries. Her legs trembled more, and her inner walls clenched firmly around his fingers.

"Right there, huh?"

Siena's gaze never left his. "Right there, yeah."

Her orgasm came on fast. Her pupils expanded again just before she came, and her legs widened a little bit more. Her lips made that perfect O shape, and he caught her mouth in another kiss to swallow all her sounds.

He loved her sounds, sure.

He still didn't want to draw attention to them.

Siena's hands fumbled with John's jeans as he kissed down the column of her throat. Salt and sex met his tongue. Her heart thundered under his teeth at her pulse point. He didn't help her at all because she had things covered.

Soon enough, his length was in her tight little palm, and she was stroking him awake even more. Not that he needed it—his dick was already painfully hard, but her firm tugs gave him a little bit of relief.

Not nearly enough.

He needed to be inside her for that.

"Don't you want me to fuck you?" he asked in her ear.

Siena shivered.

John chuckled.

"Don't you want to come again, Siena?"

He didn't need to tease her more. She fit him between her thighs, and her warm wetness coated the head of his cock while she stroked his dick through her slit.

Once.

Then twice.

She brought him down to her entrance again, and John flexed his hips forward. She was so damn wet that she took all of him in with no hesitation at all. Her cunt soaked him, tightened around him, and took away his ability to breathe for too many seconds.

It was still fucking wonderful.

"Jesus Christ," he grunted into her throat.

Siena's breathless laughter coated his senses.

Addicting and sweet.

"Fuck me," she urged.

His hand slid along her throat, and pushed her head back again. He needed to see her eyes—wanted to look into them and see all the chaos he caused for her like this.

He loved that, too.

Love stared back.

His love lived inside this woman.

"Gonna kill me," he said.

John felt like a broken record with her sometimes.

It didn't make it any less true.

• • •

"You'll meet me at the warehouse, then?" John asked.

"I don't think you need me there, son," his father replied on the other end of the call.

"Maybe not, but I want you there. It helps, you know."

"What does?"

"When I have someone to keep me in line."

Lucian cleared his throat. "And that's me, is it?"

"Sometimes Andino. Leonard suggested I be more open to you, though."

"I do like Leonard."

John rolled his eyes upward. "Not news, Papa."

"I will be at the warehouse. Say in what, an hour?"

"Or two. I have to grab the fucker first."

"I thought you already did that."

"I got distracted."

John's gaze drifted to Siena's sleeping form, but he didn't mention to his father where he was. He didn't want anyone concerning themselves about his choices, or what he was doing on the personal side of his life. They kept telling him to have patience, but things were not always so simple for him.

Especially not Siena.

Siena was not simple at all.

"I will see you in a while, John," his father said.

"All right. Thanks."

Hanging up the phone, John gave Siena his attention again. He had been up for a good hour—compliments of his internal clock that didn't know how to let him sleep in. Not that he could afford to do that today, anyway. He'd taken a quick shower, pulled on his clothes from the day before, and swallowed down his meds before calling his father.

He only had a few more minutes before he needed to leave. Soon, Siena's enforcer would be probably getting up, and making his way over to check in on her. She let John know the guy's usual schedule for her in the mornings.

Running his fingers over Siena's naked shoulder, his gaze traveled to her nightstand. He'd left a burner phone for her there, and a hastily written note.

It wasn't much.

He would never leave her without an explanation, now.

He promised.

Keep the phone out of sight. I'll only call early in the morning. I had some business to do early, and didn't want to wake you up. I'll call tomorrow. Love you. —J

Duty called.

John gave Siena one more look, and then he was gone.

• • •

John backed his Mercedes through the opened bay doors of the warehouse. Darkness cloaked his vehicle, and as soon as the front of his car was entirely inside, the bay doors began to close. John only got out of his car once the doors had closed completely.

He found his father standing by the switch used to open and close the bay doors. Lucian said nothing as John moved to the back of the Mercedes, and popped open the trunk.

Still unconscious, the enforcer John had picked up shortly after he left Siena's place was bleeding like a gutted pig all over the damn trunk. That was going to need to be cleaned, for fuck's sake. There was nothing he hated more than bloodstains.

"Fucking mess," John muttered.

Uncaring that it would hurt the man, he reached into the trunk, and dragged the man out by his already broken arm. That had happened in the struggle of John wrapping a wire around the guy's throat, and dragging him across a concrete parking lot.

Shit, the guy should have just come with no fight.

That was always easier.

"And which one is this?" Lucian asked, coming closer.

"Kev's man, specifically," John answered.

He let the guy fall to the floor of the warehouse. The thump of the unconscious man was almost sickening, in a way.

"Brad, or some shit," John said. "He's the one Kev uses whenever he wants something done. I've watched him for a week, so I feel pretty good we'll get something useful from him."

"As long as you don't kill him first."

There was that, too, yeah.

John reared back, and kicked the unconscious enforcer in the side of his chest. Likely breaking a rib or two. Brad's hazy eyes flew wide, and his mouth opened with a shout. The guy coughed, and clutched at his chest as he rolled over to his side.

He didn't seem to know where he was, or what the fuck was happening.

This could be a little confusing.

"Where's the fucking hose?" John asked.

Lucian nodded to something over John's shoulder.

"Keep him awake," John said.

His father started nudging the groaning enforcer with the tip of his shoe in all the sensitive spots. Like his aching chest, and his broken arm. John found the hose, turned on the water, and headed back to Brad.

Lucian stepped back from the man at the same time John turned the hose on him. Ice-cold water blasted Brad right in the face, and then the rest of him, too. John didn't stop until the guy was fully awake, and soaked to the goddamn bone.

Sometimes, cold water could be as good as torture.

It all depended on the man.

"Stop, fuck, stop!"

John lowered the hose. "Who did Kev have make the hit on my sister's husband?"

Brad blinked up at John from his back. Water coated his eyelashes, and dripped from his cheeks. "You think I'll tell you that, Marcello?"

To his father, but never looking away from Brad, John said, "In the back of my car—grab the black bag, thanks."

"You got it, son."

"I think you're going to tell me quite a bit, actually," John told Brad. "I mean, by the time I'm done with you. And don't think that just because you give me information means I won't kill you in the end. No, that's not the case. I will kill you regardless. How fast I kill you depends on the kind of information you give me. Do you understand?"

Brad sneered.

John smiled.

Soon, Lucian had dropped the black bag at John's feet. Bending down, John upended the bag and let the contents spill out where Brad could get a good look at them.

Just to make the point of each thing clear, John went through all of them. "A couple of knives—I like to watch people bleed, you know. Small ice picks because when I drive them up under your fingernails, you'll choke on your own vomit. A stun-gun. We all know what that does, right? It'll be better, though, because you're soaked with water, now. Vice grips—they're great to pull out shit. Teeth, whatever. And a gun."

John smiled at the man again, knowing damn well he looked cold. "Take your pick."

Brad stumbled over his words.

John nodded. "Yeah, we're not playing games now. You need to start talking."

Like most fuckers, Brad was stubborn. John used the stun-gun first, and watched the foolish idiot jump halfway across the warehouse floor before the shocks finally stopped running through his system. He let the guy bleed a little bit when he drove a knife into his kneecap, and then sighed—annoyed—when Brad *cried* when the ice picks came out to play.

Bending down in front of the now bound, soaked, bleeding, and soon-to-die Calabrese enforcer, John tipped his head to the side.

Maybe his father was right.

Maybe he hadn't needed somebody to keep him in line after all.

"I just want information, Brad," John said, "and I have all day. We would really like to give my sister something to make her husband's funeral a little bit better. You could help us out here."

"Y-y-you fuck—"

John stabbed the stun-gun into Brad's neck for a couple of quick seconds. It was another minute before the guy stopped jerking all over the place.

"Next time," John told him, "I am going to shove this fucking thing down your throat, and stab your eye out with the goddamn ice pick. See, I would have taken information for my sister about William, and probably called it a day. You couldn't make shit easy on me, though, could you? Now I'm going to expect a hell of a lot more."

Brad swallowed hard.

John nodded. "Yeah, I told you I wasn't fucking playing around, asshole. Start talking."

The enforcer would still die, though.

It was just how shit worked.

• • •

John slipped into the third pew behind his sisters and mother. He didn't want to impose his presence on them right now, considering everything.

At the front of the church, William's black casket rested high enough for everyone to see it whether they were standing up, or sitting down. The silver accents and bars shined brightly under the flickering candles.

"When do you think you can come over again?" Siena asked.

That burner phone he left for her was coming in handy. Talking with her early in the morning gave John something to get through the day, really.

"Not sure," John replied honestly.

He knew that wasn't a good enough answer for her, but it would have to do. After all, they had delivered the dead enforcer's body to the doorstep of Kev Calabrese's new place of residence—his mother's brownstone. It had only been a few days since John extracted information from the guy, and then killed him, but he kept him on ice to keep the body from going into decomposition.

He hoped Kev liked their present.

"I'll try to figure out something soon," he said. "But I have to go—I need to get inside. This funeral is about to get started."

"Don't forget to tell Andino about Kev and Darren for me."

"I won't forget to tell Andino, love. Relax."

"Okay."

"*Ti amo*, Siena."

"I love you, too, John."

He hung up the call, slid the phone into his jacket pocket and headed into the church.

John slipped into the third pew behind his sisters and mother. He didn't want to impose his presence on them right now, considering everything.

At the front of the church, William's black casket rested high enough for everyone to see it whether they were standing up, or sitting down. The silver accents and bars shined brightly under the flickering candles.

At the same time he chose a seat, Andino came to sit beside him in the pew. Ahead of them, Lucian sat down next to Cella who was currently holding onto her eight month old child like Tiffany was the only life line she had left in life.

Maybe the baby was.

Who knew?

"Tell me what?" Andino asked.

"Siena—I guess the Calabrese brothers are planning to make work and life a special kind of hell for us. They figure if they can't get to us with violence and whatever else, then picking away at business will do the trick."

Andino scowled. "Fucking bastards."

"They're not even worth all of this, Andino."

Not the death of their family members.

Not his sister's pain.

None of it.

Andino felt differently, apparently. "Anything can be worth something, John. It's all about what you get in the end from it, really. Take that as you may."

Maybe that was part of the problem.

John saw one thing.

Andino saw another.

"I take it you met up with Siena somehow?" Andino asked. "I didn't get the chance to get over there last week during her yoga time."

John shrugged. "I had a way in. I took it."

"Don't blame you."

Ahead of them, Lucian murmured something to Cella which caused John's sister to break in to tears. More tears. The woman hadn't stopped crying.

John's guilt increased.

He knew what his father told her.

William's killer would be dead tonight.

They had a name.

They knew who did it.

She could thank John for that, but he would never expect it from his sister. He only hoped that someday, she did not feel like she did right now. He hoped that someday, she would be happy again.

His part in it made no difference.

He didn't want recognition.

"It's almost over," Andino said beside John. "We'll get them. We'll end them. Soon."

CHAPTER NINE

SIENA WAS beginning to hate the passage of time. Or rather, how time no longer passed by for her the way it used to. Before all of this had happened—before John came into her life, and was then taken from her—she never paid much attention to getting through her days, or how slowly they crawled by.

None of that ever seemed important before. She got through the days by focusing on her work, and getting lost in books. By using the black and white simplicity she applied to her love of numbers, and the little joys she got in her private moments alone.

Back then, she had yet to find something that was worth counting her seconds, minutes, hours, and days for.

It was no longer that easy.

Now, time felt like a snail sliding ridiculously slow across ice. No amount of work could keep her distracted or focused enough, and she worked all the damn time. *Still.* Her eyes continued to travel to wherever the clock was on the wall, and she often found herself counting down.

It had become a game of sorts.

Twenty days since I last saw John.

Twelve hours to John's next phone call.

Three days until yoga.

Whatever she had to tell herself to get through the fucking day, and into the next, that's exactly what Siena did.

Problem for her was, that method only went so far, and her distractions were not without some kind of consequence. Mostly, her work.

Siena blinked, and rubbed the heels of her palms against her eyes. The numbers on the screen might as well have just bled together for all she understood of the mess in front of her. She wasn't even sure where some of these goddamn numbers had come from, or how she got them to this point.

Her bottom line number in the Excel spreadsheet lit up bright red. A sure sign that the total had ended up in the negative, which meant nothing good because that wasn't where those numbers were supposed to be. Not even close. That told her she had done something wrong at some fucking point.

But where?

How?

Which account had the mistake?

Siena sighed, and pressed her fingertips into her temples to relieve some of the pressure starting to form there. A migraine from eye-strain and stress, likely. She was getting them far more often than she liked lately.

In her head, she started going back through numbers, accounts, and their individual books. She had worked on at least fifteen different accounts for Kev's restaurant today—a pretty average day, all things considered.

Still, she needed to find that error.

The books couldn't ever be filed in the red.

She was paying heavily for her distractions. More hours at a computer fixing books she should have already had done a week or more ago. A sore back, and stiff fingers from working so much because this shit had to be done, and she was the only one doing it for her brothers' businesses.

"You're still not done yet?"

Siena quickly glanced up from the numbers on the screen to find Kev standing in the doorway. He stared back at her, seemingly unbothered or unknowing of her troubles. She couldn't decide if that was a good thing, or not.

"No, I'm not done yet," she finally said.

Kev looked at the watch on his wrist. "It's almost five, Siena."

"I'm aware, Kev."

She had been watching the clock, after all.

"Jason had shit to do today, Siena. He's been waiting on your slow ass all day."

"Jason?"

Who the fuck was *Jason*?

"Your enforcer," Kev said as though he were talking to a small, dumb child.

"You know," Siena replied, "that's the first time someone has ever told me his name. And that includes him."

"Huh." Kev shrugged. "Guess it wasn't important for you to know."

Nothing ever was.

"I won't be much longer," Siena said, waving a hand and going back to the computer screen. "Tell him a half hour, at most."

Or she would make it that long.

One or the other.

"I told you—he's got shit to do," Kev said. "Just go. It's not like you can't pick up where you left off tomorrow, or something."

Except that's not how Siena had been taught to do things, and work. It was not the proper way to do things. What accounts she opened and started in a day, she had to finish inputting and calculating numbers.

That way, there was less chance of more mistakes should she come back to it, and forget her place. In her business of cooking and falsifying books, she could not afford very many goddamn mistakes before it became noticeable.

Numbers were unforgiving that way.

Kev didn't understand.

Arguing wouldn't help.

Siena decided to take this small blessing for what it was, anyway. There was no way her brother would take her request for a break seriously. He would just laugh, and refuse while telling her she didn't need a fucking break.

She could be having a stroke, and he would still want her to show up to work the next day. So was her goddamn life.

"Fine," Siena said heavily as she pushed up from the chair. Quickly, she closed the books out. She didn't even bother to save the work she had done for the day because it all needed to be redone, anyway. Then, she looked at Kev with raised hands. "I'm done. Happy?"

"I will be when you get out of my office. Jason is waiting in his car outside."

Good for him.

Kev plopped his ass down in the chair as soon as Siena moved out of the way. He had already put the phone from the desk to his ear by the time Siena stepped out of the office. She closed the door behind her, but it wasn't enough to hide Kev's conversation. Like their father's voice had once done her brother's also carried through walls.

Siena took the second or two she had to lean against the hallway wall, and press her fingers to her temples once more. Without the unforgiving brightness of the screen in her eyes, the pounding in her head subsided just enough to make the oncoming migraine a little more bearable.

At least, for now.

Behind her, she could hear Kev talking on the phone. She only knew he was talking to Darren—wherever he was today—because Kev used her other brother's name.

"When it comes to this, Darren, no news *is* bad news," Kev snapped.

Somebody needed to give her brothers' lessons on privacy. Neither of them understood how loud their voices could be.

It was sad, really.

"You're telling me that not one effort we've made to fuck with the Marcello family's business on the streets—or otherwise—has worked? Not one fucking thing?"

A beat of silence passed.

And then, "Then we're going to go back to my way—*yes*, exactly that, Darren."

Siena should move, as her enforcer was waiting for her, and Kev might come out of the office soon. Still, she stayed right where she was.

"Your way isn't working either," Kev snarled. "At least with my way, we were knocking them down. Even if it was one by fucking one. Let's try my way one more time—something a bit more violent. It's my choice, and I made it."

Shit.

That didn't sound good.

Kev's conversation continued on with Darren, but Siena only listened for long enough to learn that he wasn't giving anything about his plans away. Nothing that she could use to tell John, or Andino.

The vibration of the cell phone made Siena quickly step further away from the office door, and dig around inside her bag to answer the call. She put it to her ear, and asked quietly, "Hello?"

"Is Meghan there?"

Siena smirked a little. "Wrong number, sorry."

As she pulled the phone away a little, she heard the guy say, "Andino is in the back alley of the restaurant. Ten minutes, at most."

Click.

Siena dropped the phone into her bag, and looked between the bustling restaurant just down the hallway, and the back exit that was just a few feet away. It wasn't the back alley, but it would lead her to the back alley, plus give her a way back in.

Kev's conversation was still going full force behind her. It was a risk. But frankly, everything she did lately was risky.

Siena slipped out the exit door, and tried not to roll her ankles as she ran toward the back alley behind the restaurant. Sure enough, she found an unknown red car running in the back alley parked between two other businesses.

Andino didn't drive a red car, but he was behind the wheel of the vehicle. Siena slipped into the passenger seat without thinking about it.

"New car?" she asked.

Andino laughed. "Borrowed, actually. Your brothers' people know my shit."

"Oh."

"I have a favor to ask."

Siena looked over at the man. "Sure."

"It's not going to be easy."

She scoffed.

"Nothing in this life is ever easy, Andino."

"Fair enough," he murmured.

"By the way, Kev is pissed that nothing they're doing to the Marcellos is working at the moment, so he's decided to go back to his old ways."

Andino scowled. "Violent means."

"You could say that. He didn't specify what or who, though."

"Shit."

"Sorry."

Andino shrugged. "No worries. I'm hoping this plan I have for you will end a lot of it. Or shit, at the very least, make your other brother stop and reconsider some of his fucking options at the moment."

Siena's brow furrowed. "You're going to have to explain that to me."

"How much do you care for your brothers?"

All she could do was dead-stare Andino right in the face. She had no appropriate response because none would be good enough. Her care and concern for either one of her brothers was so low, it couldn't even be measured.

Hate was not a good enough word.

Truly.

"Let me guess," Andino drawled, "if you don't have anything good to say, then say nothing at all."

"Something like that," she replied.

"That makes this easier. How opposed are you to murder?"

A lump formed in her throat instantly.

His suggestion was blatant, and cold.

Still, Siena barely had to think about it at all. "It's all for him, right?"

For John.

For *them.*

For forever.

"I need Kev gone." Andino passed over a small clear bag with one tablet inside. "Arsenic pressed into a pill. It'll dissolve quickly in something like liquor, or anything with a good amount of acid."

"Like juice, or soda."

"Exactly."

Siena nodded. "That's a terrible way to die."

Andino laughed. "Fuck, you know what, if I wanted easy right now I'd have blown up his restaurant once I knew you were gone from it. Unfortunately, that draws a lot of attention, and I'm trying to follow some kind of rules at the moment."

Jesus.

That lump was still firm in her throat.

"Make sure there's a lot of people around, and not only you and someone else. You don't want suspicion being drawn to you on this, either," Andino said.

"Definitely not."

"You don't have to let me know when it's done, either. I'll get word."

Siena glanced down at the pill in the bag. "John won't like me doing this."

Hell, even *she* was struggling with the idea of actually being the cause of someone's death. She wasn't quite ready to use murder in context with everything, but she was not so naive that she didn't realize that's exactly what it meant.

John would understand why she dirtied her hands in this way eventually, sure, but that didn't mean he would like it.

Not at all.

"Well," Andino murmured, "we're just not going to tell him until after."

Yeah.

Shit.

"I should go before someone notices me gone."

Andino nodded. "Yeah, go."

• • •

Siena barely blinked, and two weeks passed her by just like that. As though she hadn't even been a part of it at all. It was strange how when something was weighing on a person's mind, everything else in their life became inconsequential. Nothing else mattered but that one thing they couldn't seem to shake.

Not long ago, she had been wishing for time to speed up, and make life a little more bearable. Oh, sure, she could absolutely see the irony in it. Now, here she was wondering where in the hell those two weeks had gone, and how she managed to spend them entirely lost to her own mind.

She felt like she was in a bubble, of sorts. All the time, and never ending. Floating high above everyone else, and looking down on them while they continued living their lives. The world kept moving, but she was frozen—suspended.

She could hear their conversations, and see their expressions and gestures. Yet, everything still felt a little cloudy and muffled to her. She was sure this was what people called an out-of-body experience.

Was it supposed to last this long?

Was it supposed to be this confusing?

Siena didn't know.

If anyone noticed her disengaged attitude, or distracted behaviors, no one mentioned anything to her about it. Not even John when he caught her zoning out during their early morning phone calls.

For that, she felt most guilty. She couldn't explain to him, though.

Andino was clear.

Siena just needed to get this done.

And by *this*, she meant killing her own brother.

Strolling through her mother's brownstone, Siena saw far more faces than she cared to count. Many, she recognized, but there were a few whom she couldn't place. Her brothers' men, their families, and friends.

All the people who should gather for a party when there was something worthy to celebrate. Today, they were celebrating Kev's birthday. Apparently, a new boss should always have his momentous events celebrated by his men.

Siena didn't know if that was actually true or not, and she really didn't care at the moment. Kev was simply celebrating something only to never see it through. He wouldn't see the end of his birthday—he wouldn't wake up the morning after being a day older than he was right now.

She had to make sure of it.

She was going to make sure of it.

The filled-to-the brim brownstone was exactly the kind of circumstance Siena needed to get this done. Andino's warning about making sure many people were around when she did the deed had not been simple. She always figured out ways in her mind about how the murder would be linked back to her.

Not tonight, though.

Balloons, streamers, and banners hung from the ceilings, and decorated the stairwell. A bit juvenile for a grown man, really, but their mother didn't know how to tone it down when it came to her sons.

A gold and black theme, it seemed. Even the cake had black frosting piped with gold trim. God knew Siena didn't want any of that overly sweet shit—she would probably throw it back up.

She already felt like puking. Her nerves worked overtime. She wasn't sure if it was because her anxiety was acting up, or due to the action she was about to take against her family.

Once again, betraying them. Once again, proving she was exactly what they all said.

The shame.

The disgraced one.

It was just too damn bad that none of those thoughts really stopped Siena's resolve to get this whole thing done and over with.

"Siena!"

Coraline's sharp bark made Siena hesitate as she tried to pass by a group of gathered men. Turning, she faced her scowling mother standing in the entryway between the hallway, and the living room.

"Yeah?"

"Your brother is going to blow out the candles on his cake, and cut it

104

for everyone to have a piece."

And that meant what exactly to Siena?

"So?" she asked.

Coraline cocked a brow. "Please have the catering people come in and bring the food into the dining room. They can set it out on the table, and everyone can pick what they want like a buffet."

Siena wondered if this was her chance …

She didn't have time to think on it.

"Sure, Ma."

"Well, hurry up!"

Jesus.

Siena made her way into the kitchen where a catering team had taken over the space. It looked as though they were mostly done with their preparations for the dinner, and wouldn't need much help moving things into the dining room.

Behind her, Siena heard her mother calling out, "Everyone to the dining room to wish Kev a happy birthday, grab some food, and have a piece of cake!"

People moved through the kitchen to the dining room. More simply used the hallway. Either way, Siena was acutely aware that people were leaving her alone, and she didn't have anyone looking over her shoulder at the moment.

Winning.

"Excuse me," Siena said to the lead caterer.

The woman wore the only white hat amongst the rest. She smiled at Siena, asking, "Yes, what can I do for you, Miss Calabrese?"

"We would like the food moved into the dining room as a spread— buffet-style, if you wouldn't mind."

"No problem at all."

One sharp whistle, and the catering crew was moving fast. Soon enough, they had almost everything moved from the kitchen in one go.

On the second round the servers made to the kitchen, Siena slipped out, and headed for the wet bar in the dining room. At her back, people sang Kev happy birthday. She kept her back turned to the people, and her brothers.

No one approached.

No one saw a thing.

She pulled the sleeves of her dress down over her fingers, and worked to open up liquor bottles, and set up the glass. The little pill she dropped into the screwdriver drink dissolved with three quick twirls of the spoon inside the glass.

Siena took a deep breath, and then another. It didn't help to settle her nerves, but for some reason, her racing heart had slowed down just enough to make her think she was in some kind of control of her emotions.

It was an illusion.

She would freak out later.

Break down later.

Not now, though.

As soon as the happy birthday song was over, Siena turned fast, and slid through the crowd of people already beginning to swarm the table and food. No one seemed to pay her any mind as she pushed through to the head of the table where Kev had decided was his permanent seat for the night.

Her brother had stood to accept a plate of food from their mother. He didn't see Siena set the glass down next to his napkin, still not letting her fingers touch anything lest she leave something unintended behind. She was grateful she had chosen the long sleeved dress that night instead of the other one she waffled on. Nobody saw her do a thing because like always, she blended in far too well. She was the forgotten one—the useless daughter who nobody thought to watch.

Here, Kev was a king.

Or, he thought so.

He expected people to wait on him—his men, sister, mother, and even his brother. It's what he had seen his father expect from everyone around them for his whole life, and Siena really didn't expect Kev to be any different in the grand scheme of things.

He was spoiled.

He was demanding.

He was excessive.

Siena was already at the other side of the dining room and picking up a paper plate to begin filling it with food by the time Kev sat back down in his chair. Not food she would eat, but something she could pick at until the action really got started.

Kev sat his plate of food down in front of him, and laughed at something Darren said beside him in the next chair. He picked up the screwdriver—his favorite drink, as everyone should know—like he expected it to be sitting right where it was … as he was the boss.

Everybody always catered to the boss.

Siena watched Kev down half the drink in one go. He ate a bit—finished the drink off right after. He didn't make it through a quarter of the way through his plate before he started foaming at the mouth.

Fuck.

Siena had been right.

It *was* a horrible way to die.

• • •

The hospital bustled with movement and people. In the corner, Siena found her mother sobbing as Darren tried to console Coraline.

It was pointless.

She couldn't be consoled. One of her prized things were gone.

Kev was dead.

"Are you listening to me, ma'am?"

Siena turned her attention back to the cop taking her statement. She had tossed the small bag the pill had been in on their drive to the hospital—the enforcer had been too busy barking to someone on the phone to notice her getting rid of evidence.

The cop had already swabbed her hands—and everyone else's, too. Not that any of them were very pleased about that. No one in their business particularly liked to be involved with cops in anyway, but it was difficult to refuse police when something like murder came into play.

Her fingers had never touched the pill, or the items used to mix the glass. She wasn't the least bit worried about being found out.

Everyone was either too confused, or too scared to realize she had been the one to set the glass in front of Kev just a few hours earlier.

"Ma'am?"

"I'm listening," Siena said.

"And then what happened after the song?" the cop asked.

"I got my plate ready like everyone else was doing."

"You didn't see anyone approaching your brother, or leaving something for him?"

"I saw him talking to my other brother. My mother brought him a plate."

"Think harder."

"There was no one," Siena said.

Her eyes were dry—no tears to be seen. She tried to conjure up some kind of emotional response to make this cop think she was in a state over Kev's death, but it was kind of pointless. She couldn't do it.

The man seemed to think it was something else entirely. He touched her shoulder with soft affection, and leaned in closer. "I know it's a shock you'll process all of this in time. I'm sorry for your loss."

"Thank you."

Maybe she should have felt like the biggest piece of shit for pulling this stunt—for doing this to her family.

Yet, she didn't.

All she could really think about was … getting out.

The cop turned to talk to his partner, and Siena's gaze drifted over the people in the waiting room. Her brother and mother were still fully distracted with each other, and the people surrounding them.

Siena's enforcer was another one distracted by barking into his phone. He'd been doing that all damn night.

She finally had a chance to get out. Five minutes to breathe alone. All she could think about was John.

No one noticed her standing there alone, dry-eyed.

No one noticed her leave, either.

• • •

Siena used the key John kept hidden in a safety box on the back deck of his Queens home to get inside his place. She hadn't called to let him know she was coming over only because she didn't dare use the phone given to her by her brothers.

She left the burner phone from John at her place, hidden in a spot where it wasn't likely to be discovered.

Quickly, she slipped through the dark, quiet house. Upstairs she went until she found John sleeping in his bed. His house was usually locked up tight—she had spent enough nights with him to know the slightest sound or creak would wake him up.

The fact he didn't move at all as she crossed the bedroom was a testament to how busy and stressed out he must have been. So much so, that sleep was probably his only escape from everything.

She didn't want to wake him.

She didn't want to sleep, either.

"John," Siena whispered.

His name barely left her lips before his eyes flew wide open. Dark hazel darted right, and found her standing next to his bed. He blinked once, and then twice, like he was trying to make sure it was actually her standing there.

John didn't saying anything.

No, he simply grabbed her and pulled her into the bed with him.

Siena's sudden laughter was muffled by the hard kiss John leveled to her mouth as his hands gripped fiercely to her sides. He rolled to his back and took her with him. Never once did they break their kiss.

She couldn't help herself but touch him. In nothing but boxer-briefs, she had all the access to his body that she wanted. Hard lines, and muscles that strained with every movement. The dark dusting of hair that led from his navel to the waistband of his boxer-briefs called her name.

John didn't say a word—only groaned—when Siena kissed down his throat, over his chest, and kept moving lower. He pushed his lower half against her body when she wrapped her fingers around the waistband of his boxer-briefs, and started to tug them down.

Already, he was hard.

Already, she wanted to taste him.

Soon, she would have to go again. Before the sun was up, likely. Before either of them could possibly talk properly, or get their fill of one another.

It sucked.

But that's just how it was.

For now ...

Siena's fingers wrapped tightly around the base of John's cock, and she took the head of him into her mouth. The unique taste of him and his precum burst along her taste buds. He flexed his hips upward making her take damn near all of him into her mouth at once.

Her eyes watered.

She loved it.

Siena stroked him at the same time she sucked him. She let her teeth work magic as they grazed the sensitive skin of his shaft, while her tongue flicked at the head of his dick every time she came back up to the top.

She could feel his heartbeat in his shaft.

Racing.

Thumping.

Out of control.

So close, so close ...

"Fuck, fuck, fuck," John groaned.

She looked up through her lashes, and he was already staring at her. Dark hazel met light blue, and Siena was lost for those few seconds.

Frozen.

Perfect.

So happy.

John brought her back from that bubble following her around with one loud, sharp shout of her name. He came hard, held her tight to his cock, and blew his load down her throat. She took every bit of him in, cleaned the rest of him up with her tongue, and then kissed her way back up his chest.

"Jesus fucking Christ," John muttered into his hand.

Siena kissed the back of it. "Hey."

He peeked out at her. "Hey. Nice way to wake up."

She grinned. "Couldn't help myself."

"Don't help yourself more often."

"Noted," she said with a laugh.

John cleared his throat, and love reflected back in his eyes as he stared at her "What in the hell are you doing here? Almost got yourself killed, Siena."

"You would not have done anything to me."

Silently, he reached his hand under his pillow, and when he slid it back out, a gun came with it. "We're a shoot first, ask later kind of family."

Yikes.

"Next time, I'll call."

"Please." He pulled her down for another quick kiss, then asked, "Seriously, though, what are you doing here? Don't they have you on lockdown, or something?"

"Usually. They're all kind of ... distracted tonight. Being at the hospital, and everything."

John raised a brow high. "Something happened?"

"Kev, yeah."

"Siena."

She looked away, but John's hand grabbed her chin, and turned her back to stare at him. He wouldn't let her go, either.

Andino did say *after*.

Siena couldn't lie to John.

"Kev's dead," she whispered.

John stiffened in the bed. "How? Shot, or something?"

She wasn't surprised that was the first thing he thought of. A lot of the warring between their families had been violent and bloody.

"No, he was poisoned at his birthday party tonight," she said quietly.

John blinked, and stilled. "Poisoned."

Siena shrugged. "Yeah."

"That's a very specific way to die. How do you know he was—" John's words cut off abruptly when Siena glanced away again. The truth was in her eyes. She wanted him to see it and figure it out much more than she wanted to explain it. "Siena."

She wouldn't look at him again.

He said her name again.

And again.

"Siena," John murmured, his hands grabbing tighter to her waist than before. "Don't tell me you were the one to do it."

"I did what I was told to do."

It was what she was best at, after all.

CHAPTER TEN

"YOU FUCKING asshole!"

Andino looked up from the papers on his desk, and narrowly missed John's oncoming fist by ducking. "Shit."

It didn't make a difference. John landed a punch to his cousin's jaw on the second swing, anyway.

The hit connected hard enough to send Andino's head flying to the side. John was already bracing for the impact that was sure to come back at him. Andino didn't disappoint. His cousin pushed out of the chair faster than he could blink, and came at him.

John was quick enough to duck the first swing Andino aimed for his head, but forgot that his cousin was a south paw, and sneaky as fuck. Ducking like he did only gave Andino the chance to land a hard punch against John's fucking kidney.

Jesus Christ.

That hurt.

Andino shoved John into the office door. John went right back for more. He shoved Andino hard, too, knocking his cousin into the chair, and desk. Not that it kept Andino down, or anything. He came right back for more, too.

So was their way.

Soon, the two cousins were pounding fists into one another on the floor of Andino's office, while the employees in the kitchen worked on like nothing was happening. Just another day working for Andino Marcello, apparently.

This wasn't the first time the two had gone to blows over something, and it likely wouldn't be the last. Sometimes, this was just how they dealt with any kind of shit between them, but this time, it was different for John.

He was pissed.

Really fucking pissed off.

Where in previous fights he would make sure to keep his punches clean, and not hit Andino somewhere it would do lasting damage—like his face—John just didn't care. He needed to get some of his goddamn anger out, and since Andino had been the cause of that anger in the first damn place, here they were.

It didn't take long before Andino figured out John was not going to calm, or back down. He tried holding John down, but that didn't do anything for either of them. Andino got his own hits thrown in, too, but John barely felt them at all.

Maybe after the third or so punch John landed to Andino's head did the trick—he didn't really know what it was—but his cousin figured out this was not like every other time they went to blows.

Either way, Andino pulled back, and rolled away from John. He laid to his back on the floor, and stared up at the ceiling. It took all the willpower John had not to roll over, and start fucking up the man again.

Outside the office, dishes clattered. Footsteps echoed just beyond their space as the employees continued to work.

It would be comical.

If it wasn't so fucking sad.

"So fucking lucky Snaps wasn't here today," Andino snarled under his breath.

John let out a hard exhale, and scrubbed his now-sore hands down his face. "Where is he?"

"Haven took him to the spa."

Side-eyeing his cousin, he said, "The fucking *spa*."

"He likes it, okay. They rub him down, bathe him, and give him treats. It's their thing—she takes him once a week."

"He goes to the spa once a week. Are you serious? He's a dog."

"A dog that would have ripped your face off for this bullshit."

Fair enough.

"Fuck," Andino muttered, touching the spot above his eyebrow with his fingertips. "I think you cracked something in my face."

"Not going to apologize for that."

"What the fuck is wrong with you?"

John's jaw clenched so hard, his goddamn molars ached. The anger that had damn near controlled him for the entire day before, and this morning, was still entirely present. Apparently, there was no getting rid of it.

He tried using one of Leonard's techniques, which meant John had to make a conscious choice to put his reactive nature aside when something got to him. Whatever it might be—anger, or something similarly overwhelming. He needed to try and give it some time to settle, and then handle it appropriately.

Clearly, that had not worked.

Here he was.

"They change your fucking meds, or something?" Andino asked.

That hit a nerve.

John's fist came out like lightening, and landed hard to Andino's kidney. His cousin's air came out in a sharp whoosh, and then a low *fuck* followed right behind. Sweet satisfaction curled through John.

"Don't take cheap shots at me about being bipolar, or my meds. You fucking asshole."

"All right, all right. I kind of deserved that one," Andino grumbled through pants of air. "Jesus Christ, that hurt."

"You deserved it a little more than kind of, prick," John replied. "You're putting her in a lot of fucking danger, Andino."

"What, who?"

Oh, so now his cousin wanted to play dumb?

John wasn't up for that.

"*Siena.*"

"Shit, John—"

Quick as a blink, John rolled over, got to his knees, and then stood from the floor. Andino stayed right where he was on his back, and looking up at John. In a way, it gave him the feeling that his cousin was the weaker between them for the moment.

In a sense.

It didn't matter who was the weaker one between them. Either way, John still had shit to say, and he needed it to be heard. He needed Andino to fucking *hear him*, and get it. Really fucking get it. He wasn't playing these stupid games anymore, and he didn't want Siena to be playing them, either.

"Siena showed up at my place the night before last," John said, "you know, after Kev Calabrese croaked at his birthday party. Somebody poisoned him, huh?"

Andino lifted a single brow. "Word made rounds, yeah. What about it?"

"That's how you want to play this?"

"John, come on, now."

"You had her do that job, Andi."

Andino sucked air through his teeth, but his cold gaze never wavered from John for a second. "It needed to be done, and I couldn't trust anyone else to do it. Who the hell else is that close to those brothers, John?"

"Any one of their fucking men, Andino!"

"Couldn't turn one. Or rather, I couldn't trust one to turn them. That's not my goal in this—that's not the job I need to be concerned about at the moment. I just need those goddamn brothers out of the fucking way. That's it."

John didn't have the first clue what his cousin was talking about. "You're trying to ruin that family, but you don't want the task of controlling them once you've done that?"

Andino rolled his eyes. "She got it done. What else is there to say?"

"Stop putting her in these fucking positions, that's what. At first it was just getting information from her which was dangerous enough considering how controlled she is by that family—now *this*?"

"Is it because you think Siena is too innocent to kill a man, or because you don't want her dirtying up those pretty hands of hers?"

John forced himself not to kick Andino as hard as he could in the guy's ribs. It took a hell of a lot more effort than he thought it would. "You're purposefully being an asshole right now, and I don't appreciate it."

"Because you're acting foolish, and letting your feelings cloud up what you should already know about a war like this. We do what we need to—use who we can use—and get it done. Finish it. We finish them. That's all that matters."

"Not to the sacrifice of *her!*"

"You assume she'll be a sacrifice because she cannot handle herself, or something like that. Maybe that's something you should handle with yourself, John, because Siena has her shit covered. She's gold. She knows exactly what she's doing."

He heard Andino.

He still didn't like it.

"Darren Calabrese is not a stupid fuck like you might think. Is he a little screwed up or distracted right now because Kev is dead? Sure, but that means *nothing*. If you don't think they weren't already suspicious that someone inside their circles were feeding us information, then you're delusional, Andino."

"I—"

"Darren, or somebody else who will let him know, is going to figure out what is going on. They will figure out that it is her. The more info from her you use, or the more you get her to do, the worse it will get for her. I won't have you putting her in that kind of danger, Andi. I just won't."

"Are you going to fucking let me talk, or what?"

John fixed his jacket, and gave his cousin one last look. "I said what I had to say, actually."

"Shame—you're missing out on the bigger picture entirely."

"Your picture isn't *my* picture, Andino."

After all, John's bigger picture showcased Siena. It seemed like Andino's only showcased ruining the Calabrese.

"Get the hell out," Andino mumbled.

Fine by John.

● ● ●

"John," Leonard barked.

114

John glanced away from the clock just long enough to give his therapist a look. "What?"

"You're all over the place."

"I noticed that, too."

John's father slipped through the living room of Leonard's home. Lucian now made it his job to occasionally show up at John's appointments. He tried to put his reasoning under the umbrella that Leonard was an old friend.

Frankly, John saw that guise for what it was.

"When was the last time you slept?" Leonard asked.

John sighed. "Last night."

"How long?"

Good catch, Doc.

"Enough," John replied.

"That's not a good enough answer for me," Leonard said. "Try again, and give me the truth."

"Four hours."

"One long stretch, or in total?"

"Total."

Leonard nodded, and stood from his chair. Strolling to the window, he looked out at the clear September sky. "Tell me about work, John."

John glanced at his father.

Lucian only shrugged as he sipped from a glass of bourbon.

"It's busy," John said.

"Dangerous, I think," Leonard countered. "I watch the news. I keep up with things. Seems the Marcello organization is in a major feud with the Calabrese faction at the moment. Three deaths this last week alone between the two."

"Two were theirs—Capos."

"A foot solider for us," Lucian put in. "Replaceable."

"Your woman—Siena."

John stiffened on the couch "What about her?"

"She comes from their side, doesn't she?"

"Yes."

"How often do you see her? Or even, when was the last time?"

John cleared his throat, and just as quickly as his father had slipped into the room, Lucian left it the same way he had come in. When privacy mattered in John's sessions, and his father was there, Lucian knew when it was time to step the hell away.

He appreciated it.

"The beginning of the month."

"Almost two weeks, then," Leonard supplied.

"Yeah."

"I suppose you're concerned about her."

"It's a lot more than just her, but yes, I focus on her a lot, too."

Leonard turned to face John with a pensive expression. "You're going too much, and not taking enough time for up here."

The therapist tapped his temple.

John got what the man was saying.

"I don't really have a choice at the moment, all things considered."

"You're going to put yourself back into a hypomanic phase, John."

"I have it under control."

Leonard stared hard at John.

It made him edgy.

"What?" John asked, irritated.

"Choose stability."

"I *am*."

"How structured have your days been since you left the facility, John?"

Well, that one, he had to stop and think about. It was not an easy answer because at the moment, his entire life just felt like one giant ball of chaos. One thing after another thing, after another thing. It never ended.

"I'm structured in the areas that need to be handled," John chose to say.

"Your bipolar. Managing it, you mean."

John nodded. "That's what's important, right?"

"Take that away, though, John. Remove your twice weekly appointments, your strict regimes for diet and exercise, and the other routines you have in place to manage your disorder. Is that the *only* thing keeping you on track right now?"

"Somedays, it's the only thing keeping me sane at the moment, yeah."

"You're playing a dangerous game with that."

"Not sure how to correct it right now, either."

Leonard tapped his watch with one finger, but never took his gaze away from John. "You allow me to do that for you. Sometimes, a break is good for you. I'm the one who—regardless of what is happening in your life—makes you take a moment to step back, objectify things around you, and relax."

"I don't find our sessions very relaxing."

Hard.

Sometimes irritating.

Often, invasive.

Leonard smirked. "Then explain to me why you've just spent the last fifteen minutes in a far calmer, less jittery place than you were when you walked in."

Shit.

"Well ..."

"It's fine to say that this is your safe place, John. We all have one, you know? Mine tends to be high in the sky, amongst the clouds."

"You're not my only safe place," John said. "I have others."

"Who?"

"My cousin, for one."

"Andino."

John's lip curled back at Andino's name. Clearly, he was still sore over their fight a few days before. Leonard didn't miss it.

"Is there trouble with your cousin?"

"I think he's causing problems to further his own agenda, and I'm not very fond of the way he's going about it."

"And so, you're too irritated with him to let your emotional guard down."

"You make me sound pathetic."

Leonard chuckled. "Far from it. I could not imagine what it must feel like to be you, John. To be constantly stuck in a high-intensity emotional headspace twenty-four-seven. To feel things much faster, and more extremely, than those around me. And yet, you do it every day, and handle yourself all the while. That's admirable, not pathetic."

Well, then.

"Mmm, your woman, too, I suppose," Leonard added after a moment.

John scrubbed a hand down his unshaven jaw—making a mental note to shave. "What about her?"

"She's a safe place for you, too."

"More so than anyone else."

Understatement.

"So you do have places you can go where you do not have to be on edge at every waking second," the man said.

"She's not around very much at the moment, so no, I'm stuck with—"

"Me," Leonard interrupted with a grin.

Again, the man tapped his watch. John didn't know what he was getting at.

"We'll add an extra hour onto the two sessions a week you already do, and add a third session on Wednesdays to break up your week."

John groaned under his breath. "I don't have time—"

"You will make time because you need to."

Fuck.

Leonard waved a finger at the doorway where Lucian had disappeared. "Go let your father know you'll both be here for a bit longer."

"Wait, you mean we start the extra hour today?" John asked.

"I did not stutter," Leonard murmured.

John found his father sitting on the front steps of Leonard's quiet Brooklyn home. Lucian alternated between sipping his bourbon, and smoking a cigarette. He offered the pack to his son, and John took one out.

Maybe a smoke would calm his nerves.

Who fucking knew?

John didn't smoke very often, now. Just whenever the urge struck, or he needed a bit of stress relief. That first drag off the cigarette burned his lungs like nothing else, but also felt like calm swimming through his veins.

"Are you done for the day?" Lucian asked.

"Not entirely. Another hour, or so."

"Okay."

John glanced over at his father, but found Lucian didn't seem the least bit bothered that he couldn't leave. In fact, Lucian seemed perfectly content to sit right where he was, and wait for his son.

"Thanks, Papa."

Lucian looked up from his seat. "For what, John?"

"This."

You.

Lucian seemed to understand, and only gave his son a nod in recognition. John was coming to learn that maybe he had more than a couple of safe places—in many ways, his father was becoming one, too.

"I didn't mean to overhear," Lucian said, "but I heard what you said regarding Andino."

John's irritation flashed through his gut.

Hot and poisoned.

Damn.

He wished he could let that go.

"He's putting Siena in danger again and again," John said. "And for what? Nothing."

"Not nothing, son, to—"

"Take over the Calabrese. He'll absorb the Calabrese Capos, streets, and their crews into the Marcellos, which will only make his organization bigger when he finally takes over Dante's position officially. So, that compared to Siena's life? *Nothing*, Papa. That's what."

Lucan looked over at John, and his familiar hazel gaze flashed with something John didn't recognize. "He's not explained this to you at all, has he?"

"Explained what?"

"You've got this all wrong, John."

"Again, wh—"

John's question was cut off by the sight of a black sedan with tinted windows slowing down in front of the drive leading up to Leonard's home. He saw the driver's side front and rear windows roll down a few inches, and gun metal glinted in the light.

"Shit," John hissed.

He grabbed his father, and took them both to the ground with enough force that he was worried he might have broken something.

Bullets rained down.

Relentless.

Violent.

Deafening.

John kept his father covered.

Fucking Calabrese.

More people were going to have to die for this.

Shame.

• • •

John scrubbed a hand down his face in frustration as more people flooded into the hospital room. Jordyn snapped at anyone who came too close to her husband while the nurse gave Lucian his first small dose of morphine.

Getting two ribs broken could be painful, after all.

"Give me the run down," Dante said, moving in beside his brother's bed.

Sweet Jesus.

If there was anyone's glare who could rival the Devil's, it was John's mother. Even his uncle couldn't help himself but take a quick step back when Jordyn leveled it on him. John held his chuckle back, but barely.

"Jordyn, it's—"

"Not fine, Lucian!"

John's father passed his two brothers a look, and gestured one finger toward the door. "And take my son with you when you go. Let Ma through when she gets here."

Italian men and their mothers …

It could not be a joke when it was the truth.

Dante waved a hand, and John followed behind him and his other uncle. Giovanni looked John up and down, and nodded to himself.

"What?" John asked once the door was closed behind them. "That look what the fuck was that for?"

Dante cocked a brow, but said nothing.

Gio shook his head, and glanced away. "Nothing. I was thinking, at least one of you made it out unscathed, I guess."

"I'm the one that broke his ribs," John pointed out. "I took him to the ground too—"

"You did fine," Dante interjected firm and fast. "You did *right.*"

John quieted at that, and nodded. "Where's Andino?"

"Trying to settle people into safe places tonight," Dante explained.

"He wanted to come, but I know the two of you are having some issues at the moment. Better for him to be elsewhere."

"He could have come."

Dante gave John a hard look. "Andino knows when to step back for someone else."

Fine.

John was not going to argue the point further. He didn't think it would get him anywhere. Looking back at his father's room, he saw one of his sisters slip inside.

Cella.

She still wouldn't look at him.

She never talked to him.

John shook it off, and went back to the conversation at hand. "The run down?"

"Yeah, give it to me."

"They caught us on the porch. Did a quick drive-by. Black sedan. Didn't even get the make or model as I wanted to get Dad down. By the time I looked up again, they were gone. I mean, we know *who* ordered it, right. There's no question there."

"Definitely no question," Dante agreed. "We still have to figure out what to do about these fucking foolish idiots."

"Maybe stop fucking around with them like Andino has been doing, and challenge them head-on. If it's a proper street war they want, then—"

"There is a method to Andino's madness," Giovanni said, stepping into the conversation only to defend his son. Or so it seemed. "Don't shit on his way of doing things just because you have a different opinion about how it could be done."

"Had I started something like this," John shot back, "I would have fucking finished it shortly after, too."

Dante cleared his throat, and moved subtly in between the nephew and uncle. "All right, that's enough. Take a fucking breath, and lower your damn voices. We're not here to give the hospital staff a show, huh?"

"Sorry," Gio muttered behind Dante.

John still gave his uncle a look that spoke volumes without him needing to say anything at all. "I stand by it, though."

"You can't be that fucking entitled, John." Giovanni shook his head, and smirked in that irritating way of his. "You think the rest of us are putting our asses on the line for this plan because Andino *thinks* it's a good idea? Are you really that selfish in your own head that you can't see he's—"

Dante turned around, and shoved Gio on his shoulder. Pointing a single finger to the hallway leading out of the hospital wing, he said, "Go wait for Papa and Ma, Gio."

"Dante—"

"*Go*, I said."

Andino might have been the boss in waiting.

Dante was still *the* boss.

Giovanni moved past Dante, but pointed a finger at John as he went by. "Clean up your fucking shit, John. You think going on like that is going to suit a man in your position once this is over? I don't think so."

John's brow furrowed. "What in the hell was that supposed to—"

"Excuse me?"

Dante spun around on his heel at the quiet voice. John found a young nurse standing there with a yellow bubble mailer in her hands. She offered it out, but neither of the men moved to take the item from her.

"What?" Dante barked.

The woman shrunk a bit.

"This was dropped off at the nurse's station in the next wing, and we were directed that it be delivered to a Johnathan Marcello. Apparently, his father is being treated in *this* wing. It must have been a mix up."

Dante passed John a look.

John reached for the mailer. It was only once the woman was gone that he turned to his uncle, concern writing heavily along his brow. "Open it, or no?"

"She was holding it pretty firmly, and she moved from one wing to another with it. I don't think there's anything explosive in it, otherwise it would have went boom already."

"Nice."

Dante shrugged. "Here."

John took the knife his uncle offered. "Thanks."

"Open it from the back end, just in case."

He did just that.

Papers and photographs spilled out.

John's throat closed up at the images staring back at him, and the information now freely available to anyone with the right contacts, and deep enough pockets.

Information about him.

His disorder. On record admissions to a mental facility. Somehow, a fucking patient record. Photographs of him on the grounds of the facility.

It was everything that stabbed John right to his core.

Everything he didn't want people to know.

His one weak spot.

Crazy.

The word was scrawled across several photos.

Disgrace.

Another word written in thick, red ink.

Why was he so calm all of the sudden?

It wasn't even the calm that scared him.

No, it was the darkness seeping into his mind at seeing his disorder exposed and mocked like this. It was knowing his family would be ridiculed for the things he had done, and how they protected and shielded him.

How much more could they take?

Was he really worth this kind of shit?

"Who else do you think got a package like this?" John asked.

"Let's hope not very many," Dante replied.

John doubted that would be the case.

CHAPTER ELEVEN

JASON BEAT THE sole of his shoe against the hallway floor with more force than was necessary to get his point across. Siena shot the enforcer a glare over her shoulder, but he only cocked an eyebrow back at her in silent response. He didn't move as she flipped through the keys on the ring to find the right one for her apartment door.

Asshole.

Apparently, she was taking too much time unlocking her door. The same way she took too much time to get into a car, or cross the goddamn street. Or getting to and from places. Even eating in front of a window took too much time.

Anything.

She just took too much time lately.

According to Jason, anyway.

Siena knew what the issue really was. Nobody in the Calabrese family felt safe ever since their attack on the Marcellos the week before. And rightfully so, likely. Siena only heard about the attack because the shooting was on the news, and the anchors had named names regarding the *victims* involved.

She wasn't exactly sure John would appreciate his father and him being called victims and then criminals in the same goddamn sentence. Just the victim portrayal would be enough to piss him off.

Nonetheless, no one in the Calabrese family felt very safe at the moment. They were back to violence and bloodshed by Darren's command, and yet, the Marcellos had yet to respond to this latest attack.

Everybody was on edge.

What would they do?

Who would it be?

How?

When?

Siena was often shuffled from place to place before she could even sit down and think about where she currently was. She might spend a half of a day in one place to work, and then be moved to another place before she could even finish.

She wasn't allowed to stay out very long in public, and heaven forbid she stop on the side of the street. Her enforcer was closer than ever, including driving her all over the place because she couldn't even use her car.

It was stifling.

Suffocating.

She was *dying*.

Finally, Siena got her door unlocked, and pushed it open. Turning as she entered the place, she gave Jason a wave and said, "See, there, all safe. Bye."

The guy opened his mouth.

Siena closed the door in his face.

It wasn't like the guy would run to Darren and tell on her for misbehaving, or anything. Darren was too caught up in his own bullshit to care very much about Siena at the moment. It was a blessing in disguise, really.

Opening up her door not long after she closed it, she peeked down the hallway to find that Jason was just closing his apartment door. The slam echoed.

Siena smiled.

Quietly, she shut her door again, and headed through her small apartment. Another benefit of Darren being caught up in Kev's murder, and trying to plan for the next attack from the Marcellos was that he had yet to move Siena from her place. Shit, maybe he even forgot that it had been him who was so outspoken about letting her move back.

Who knew?

Who cared?

Not her.

All that mattered was she was still in her place, and that gave her a little bit of freedom to move. At least, where John was concerned.

In her bedroom, she bent down and pulled out a shoebox from under the bed. Flipping off the top, she dug through some magazines to find the item hidden beneath. She dug out the burner cell phone John had provided, and turned the home screen on.

Instantly, her heart dropped.

There was no messages. No missed calls.

Nothing.

Today marked one entire week since John had contacted her. The last time had been the morning of the shooting—he mentioned he would be going to his therapist's, and if he could, would call her that night.

He hadn't called.

Not then.

Not since.

Siena was started to get worried. It wasn't like John to break his word, and after everything that was going on between their families and on the streets, she really needed him to check in with her.

She needed to know he was okay.

Something.

Anything.

Was there a reason he went off the radar?

Siena didn't know that, either. The last time she had spoken to Andino was weeks ago, as it seemed he no longer needed information from her, or rather, knew she would pass it through Johnathan, anyway. She didn't know if she could get any information from him about John, either.

She dialed John's number, and put the phone to her ear. It rang and rang, but no one picked up. She tried again, and then again. She sent a text message, and waited five minutes to see if she would get a response.

Nothing.

Her worry picked up a notch.

Her anxiety thrummed deep.

Siena glanced out her bedroom window to find the sun was still high, and bright. It wasn't even supper time, but Darren didn't want her out in public too much. Someone might come after her, apparently.

She didn't think anyone was coming for her.

Siena knew better ...

It was a huge risk.

She shouldn't leave when it wasn't even dark. Someone might see her, or follow her. It was a dumb move to make, and yet, her heart screamed louder than the warning bells ringing over and over again in her head.

Still, she sent one last text to John letting him know she was coming over, and to expect her. She kept an eye out when she left her apartment building and hailed a cab. She glanced up and watched the windows of Jason's apartment, but never saw a single curtain move as she left the place.

It all seemed good.

She thought she was in the clear.

She didn't see anybody ...

But that didn't mean nobody saw her.

• • •

"Your front door is unlocked."

John didn't look up from the things he had spread out on his bed. "You said you were coming over. I left it open for you when I got home."

"You couldn't call me back? Send a text?"

"No."

That was all he offered.

No.

Siena could see in the way John's gaze narrowed as he fingered the edge of a piece of paper that something was weighing on him. On his mind, likely. Maybe it was the slope of his shoulders, too, or how he wouldn't look at her.

She came a little closer.

"What's all this?"

It looked as though he had dumped out a bubble mailer if the empty package tossed to the pillow was any indication.

"My latest surprise," he said dryly.

"What?"

John looked up from the stuff on the bed.

Pain stared back at her.

"I keep getting these—this shit," he said, waving at the papers on the bed. "It's like they want to remind me how easy it is to dredge shit up from my past. It feels like they're telling me they can put my life and business on display. I don't know how they keep finding this shit, Siena."

She grabbed a document on the bed, and looked it over.

A police report, it seemed.

A sixteen year old Johnathan Marcello had stolen a neighbor's car, and crashed it on the interstate. He tested positive for two different kinds of drugs, and had a blood alcohol level slightly over the limit.

Holy shit.

Siena understood that this event that had been documented in John's life—when he was younger, of course—was shortly before the time his bipolar disorder had finally been properly diagnosed. It was likely one of the many manic episodes that had led up to the final diagnosis.

"This accident was brushed under the rug," John said, taking the paper from Siena. "Or it was supposed to be. My family paid people off—got serious about trying to figure out what in the hell was going on with me, then."

"What happened to the case and file?"

John shrugged. "Should have been destroyed. Some went on record— few hours of probation, some fines. I once spent sixty days in a juvenile detention center for other shit. Of course, none of them ever actually had my disorder on record. That was all before I got diagnosed, and then even after, we were careful about keeping it off record when shit went down."

He gestured behind him to other opened bubble mailers on the floor.

"What is this?"

"Me," John said. "Me and bipolar."

Siena blinked, and then looked at John. "Someone is sending you these?"

He nodded. "Every day, usually. I come home, and one is on my doorstep. I come out of a place, and one is stuffed under the wiper of my car. I'm not the only one to get a package, either. Some of my people—my family, too. Associates of mine."

"John—"

"It makes people look at me differently, and that irritates me like nothing fucking else. Like I might blow up, or freak out. They don't trust me, or something."

"Or is that just how it makes you feel to have other people know," she said.

Siena didn't even pose it as a question.

John didn't respond.

She figured it was probably a bit of both, really.

"They're fucking with me, and I don't like it."

"Darren's people?" she asked.

She didn't really need to ask.

She already *knew*.

John looked up from the stuff on his bed, and finally met her gaze. She didn't like what stared back, or how distant he seemed. She knew that John didn't rapid cycle from high to lows all the time, but things could tip him one way or the other.

High, or low.

Good, or not.

Manic, settled, or depressed.

She wondered how low he was right then.

How low did he feel?

How dark was he in his mind?

"None of this is important," she told him, grabbing one of the papers, and shaking it hard. "Not to you, or your family. You know it isn't important. None of this has ever made any difference to them, John."

She tossed the paper away, grabbed another, and then did the same thing. She continued until all the crap was gone from the bed.

John never moved, or said a word.

Siena felt marginally better, but she doubted John did. "I'm worried about you, John."

"I'm sorry I didn't call."

"You haven't called in a *week*."

"It's nonstop lately."

"What is?"

"This," he said, waving at the mailers, "and this."

He pointed to his head.

"So *call me*," she said.

127

"I'm trying to handle it, Siena."

"Alone?"

"There's enough going on without me—"

Siena heard enough. She moved around the corner of the bed, and stepped in front of John. She put her body between him and the bed to make him look away from the spot that had been filled with things he likely regretted, and events that made him ashamed.

She knew what he had been doing.

Going over everything.

Reliving mistakes.

Wishing for different things.

Eating guilt like a second meal.

Fuck all that noise.

Siena reached up and cupped John's face. His hazel eyes locked on hers, and for a second, that darkness dimming his gaze disappeared. He focused on her, and nothing else seemed to matter to him.

She wished she could be here more.

Give him more.

Do more.

"Stop giving my brother and his people what they want by getting messed up over all of this," she said quietly. "You know that's their goal—don't do it, John. Nothing else matters but right here, and right now. Everybody else around you is going to tell you the same thing. You have too many other things to worry about right now."

He couldn't be off his game.

Not now.

The risk was too high.

She wondered if anybody else had told him that.

Did anyone else even know his state of mind?

John's fingers circled around Siena's wrists, held tight, and then he kissed her. A soft, quick kiss that didn't stay long, and yet still lingered once his lips were gone from hers. He gave her a crooked smile, and she gave him one back.

"Thank you," he said in a rough murmur.

He never needed to thank her.

Not for loving him.

"Don't worry me again."

He nodded. "I was just going to jump in the shower, and got distracted. I was out for a jog before I came home."

"To another mailer?"

"Yeah."

Fuck Darren.

"Go have your shower," Siena said. "I'll still be here."

"Better be."

John let her go, and Siena tried not to show how the loss of him made her heart heavy all over again. She watched over her shoulder as he disappeared into the connecting bathroom. She took a seat on the edge of the bed as the shower turned on, and eyed the mailers on the floor.

Her anger grew.

She wanted to kill Darren, too.

How much longer was this going to last?

The silence echoed from the bathroom. Siena looked over her shoulder to see the curve of John's naked back, but he wasn't moving. The shower continued raining on, and while he was naked, he didn't make a move to get in the water.

She was inside the bathroom before she had even really thought about it. John stayed stone still as she slipped in behind him, and let her hands travel over his naked back. A soft, light touch that eased some of the tension in his muscles.

"It'll pass," he murmured.

His mood.

This nonsense.

Everything.

Siena nodded, and pressed a kiss to the spot between his shoulder blades. "It'll pass, John."

"You probably shouldn't have come over here today."

"Probably not. I needed to see you, though."

"Worrying you, huh?"

"Yeah."

"Sorry, *mia cara bella.*"

Siena smiled, and pressed her forehead to his warm back. His muscles jumped from her touch that time. "I always have you on the back of my mind, John."

"Always have my back, too, huh?"

"Forever."

"*Sempre.*"

And always.

John stepped into the walk-in shower, and Siena decided she didn't like him being that far away in those moments. She wanted to be close to him for as long as she could. Quickly, she shed her dress, and undergarments. Stepping into the shower, she found herself tugged into John, and then his arms wrapped around her.

Water pounded down.

Steam wrapped around them.

The world stopped.

That was just fine, too.

It took only an innocent kiss to her forehead that led to another kiss on her lips which started an entirely different fire. One that stroked her from the inside out, the same way his fingers felt stroking her pussy when they slipped between her thighs.

Before she even knew what had happened, Siena was backed against the shower wall, and lifted from the floor. Cold tiles met her back, but she barely felt it at all. She was too focused on the way John's mouth felt slipping down her throat. The way his tongue lapped at her skin, and his breath came out harder when his cock rubbed against her center.

One of his hands tangled into her hair, while his other kept her held up under the curve of her ass. His fingertips dug into her skin in the best way—a shock of pain that swam through her blood, but only made her want more.

"Love me, *love me.*"

It was as good as *please, please* to him.

She didn't need to say more, or ask for anything else. It was only a quick shift of his hips, and her hand sliding between their bodies to line his cock up with her center. She took in one good breath before his cock filled her full.

She needed that breath.

He took the rest while he fucked her.

John kissed her again, then. All tongue and teeth warring. A hard kiss that left her lips numb, and her tongue tingling. She found he kissed the same way he fucked.

Deep and fast.

Unforgiving, and passionate.

A sweet dance she had come to crave.

Constantly.

John buried his face into her neck, and his teeth left marks behind on her pulse point. Each thrust of his cock brought her a little bit closer to the edge. Every time he withdrew, his length dragged across every single one of her most sensitive spots. Her heels dug into his back while her words urged him on, whispered fast and low into his hair.

There, there ... almost there.

"Come on, give it to me, love," she heard him grunt against her neck.

His fingers dug deeper.

Her nails drew lines across his shoulders.

The orgasm came on swift, and left her a mess in his arms. John didn't seem to mind. It was only then that his pace slowed, and he went back to kissing her. Her mouth, cheeks, the tip of her nose, and down over her jaw. His thrusts came at a leisurely pace. He took his time getting himself to where he wanted, and Siena didn't mind at all.

She wanted to do this for the rest of her life with him.

Calm him.

Love him.

Have him.

Someday, someday … someday.

Her mind chanted it.

Someday soon.

He would be all hers, then.

John came with a shaky exhale, and his eyes locked on hers. His thumbs trembled when he stroked them over her jaw, and then her lips.

One softer kiss to her lips …

A quiet, "I love you, my girl."

And then the phone rang.

Reality was always waiting to call them home.

• • •

He would be so angry with you for this.

Siena's inner voice taunted her, but she pushed it aside to deal with her current task. There would come a day in their life when she would no longer have to do something like this. There would come a day when John would have her every single day—he could come to her, and never have to worry about needing someone else to have his back like she did.

That's what she kept telling herself, anyway.

It made this easier.

She had almost talked herself out of it, but ended up just doing it. Dialing a familiar number before she could think twice, she put the phone to her ear, and waited the ringing out.

One ring.

Two.

Three.

She thought it might go to voicemail.

Thankfully, it didn't.

"*Ciao.*"

The Italian greeting almost made her smile.

"Lucian?"

A beat of silence passed before John's father asked, "Siena?"

"One and only."

Her joke fell flat, but she figured that. Sometimes, shitty humor was the only way she knew how to deal with things that stressed her out.

She had way too much stress lately.

"New number?" Lucian asked.

She laughed. "A burner from John, actually."

"Ah, I see."

Siena wasn't exactly surprised that Lucian didn't quite know what to make of her call. Sure, she had been given his number from Andino in case she needed another way to get ahold of him while John was in the facility. Lucian had periodically got messages through to her about John while he was away, too.

Still, their conversations were short, and to the point. He wasn't, however, rude to her or anything. Always respectful, and kind, but never personal. Siena kind of got the feeling that was just how Lucian approached people, and how he handled them.

She didn't take it personally.

"What can I do for you?" Lucian asked.

"Check on John for me, that would be great."

She didn't mention that she was at John's place, or that he had taken off shortly after she arrived because someone called him away.

"Why do you need me to do that?"

"He hasn't called in a while."

Not a lie.

"Oh?" Lucian asked.

"Usually, he calls every day."

"He's been a little off lately," Lucian said.

Good.

Someone had noticed it. Someone was taking note. Someone could help.

Siena wasn't entirely comfortable with outing John's business to anyone, even if it was his father. That's why she chose to hold off on telling Lucian that she suspected John was in a rough place because she *saw* him in a rough place.

John wouldn't want her bringing that up, either. His lines in the sand about his disorder, and how he wanted to handle it with those close to him were clearly drawn. Siena was not about to cross one of those lines.

Still ...

She had to do something.

John needed *something*.

This was the best she could do—a call, a suggestion, and a simple request. No information, and no personal details that crossed a line. John would get someone to check in, and talk to him more than he had talked to her.

It was the best she could do.

It was all she could do right then.

Siena hated that.

"He's keeping up with everything, right?" she asked.

Her unspoken question hung heavily between them.

His meds?

His therapy?

Everything else?

Lucian seemed to understand what she didn't say. "He is."

"I hear a *but* in there."

"But," Lucian said, chuckling dryly, "he got some unsettling things thrown his way lately. I don't think he handled it well. That's to be expected."

Siena's gaze drifted to the packages in the corner. It looked like John had gotten more than *one* unsettling thing thrown his way, actually.

Did Lucian know about those?

She hated her brother for doing that to John. She had made a promise months ago that no one would ever use John's own mind against him again, and yet, here they were.

It was happening.

Again.

"Could you check in on him for me?" she asked. "Just don't mention I asked. I know everything is all over the place lately—I need to know he's okay, that's all."

John loved his family. Siena saw in his expressions when he spoke about them, and heard it in his voice when one of their names were brought up. John was careful in the way he talked about others, sure, but he couldn't hide anything from Siena.

He loved his family so much.

"I will," Lucian promised. "I was going that way tomorrow."

"Great. Thanks."

"Be safe, Siena. This war is almost over."

"I'm trying."

"That's all we can ask."

Lucian said a quick goodbye, and then hung up the phone.

Siena pulled a pad and pen from the nightstand next to John's side of the bed. She scribbled a quick note for John as she looked around his empty bedroom.

Call me. Love you. —S.

She had thought to stay and wait for him. Maybe he would get back before she had to leave again, but that didn't seem to be the case. She needed to get back home just in case someone dropped by, or shit, Darren decided to call her away from her place.

She couldn't afford to be caught stepping out of line right now. Who fucking knew what Darren would do?

Her heart felt heavy as she slipped out of the room, and headed down the stairs, and left his house. She still kept an eye out for someone she might recognize.

Nothing seemed out of place.

That didn't mean it was safe.

CHAPTER TWELVE

JOHN STEPPED out of his car, and tightened the neck of his leather jacket to keep the cool mid-September air away from his body. Only part of his mind was on the warehouse in front of him. The other part was back with Siena where he had left her at his place.

He figured by the time he got back, she wasn't even going to be there. She mentioned she would need to leave as to not be noticed missing.

It sucked.

It was their relationship in a nutshell.

Fuck.

She didn't know it, but she had helped him more than he could explain just by showing up to his place. Over the last little while, his mind had disintegrated into darker thoughts and places. It was a dangerous game for him to play because it meant nothing good was to come.

Depression was a bitch.

It could claw its way into John's mind and life before he even realized the whore was there. And once she was in, she didn't let go.

Siena's presence was enough to filter through all the noise swimming in his mind, and the darkness thickening his blood. There was something about that woman keeping him from getting too deep into a headspace that he wouldn't be able to get out of.

She fought for him.

She loved him.

She had his back.

What more could he want?

What more did he need?

Her.

He needed her.

Forever. To wake up to her every morning, and keep her close at night. He wanted her laughter filling up their house, and her warmth in his bed.

He didn't want an hour here and there when it could be fit in when someone wasn't looking. He didn't want to sneak in and out of her life. He didn't want it like this.

And yet, this was all he had.

John needed to take what he could get.

For now.

John tightened his jacket more, and jogged toward the warehouse. A white car drove by, but because of the speed and the clear windows, he didn't think much of it as he crossed the street. Inside the warehouse, he found one of the Marcello Capo's crews hard at work.

None of the fourteen guys noticed John step into the place. They were too busy taking apart what seemed to be a truck of electronics. Flat screen televisions, mostly, but some other high value shit, too. It would sell damn well on the streets—a sort of gray market for stolen goods, and a fast way to get rid of hot items.

The guys worked quickly to unload the truck, separate the goods, and destroy anything that might be trackable. They worked as a team, which was a sign of a good crew, and a nod to the Capo that ran them, too.

Speaking of the Capo …

John bypassed the working guys, and headed to the side of the warehouse. He moved up the metal spiral staircase, taking them two at a time. He didn't bother to knock on the office door upstairs—the only room up there—as the Capo who had called him earlier left it open.

"Marky," John greeted.

The man—who would usually be working behind his desk—was pacing from one side of his office, to the other side. He passed John a quick glance, and a nod but continued his pacing.

"You said something was up?"

Marky nodded. "I got a call—friend of a friend down in Brooklyn."

"All right. What about?"

"Supposedly, my associate overheard some talk. Apparently, the guys are in with the Calabrese people. Not deep involved, mind you."

"Not made, you mean."

"Yeah."

"Go on."

"He said they mentioned a new job. Burning some warehouses. One mentioned was one down this way. The only one down this way is mine, John."

Shit.

"Going back to that again?"

Marky shrugged. "It's concerning. Listen, we've gone through this nonsense with them—burning shit, and shooting up whatever they can. I can't afford to lose another business because of the goddamn Calabrese family."

"Don't blame you."

Their Capos were hemorrhaging money at the moment with all their losses. It didn't have to be the loss of life. The loss of a safe business, or place to do business, was just as bad in the grand scheme of things.

"I figured you're in close with Andino and Dante, and neither of them are very easy to reach at the moment."

"Truth. You know how the boss is, though. Dante has Giovanni for shit on the streets, and messages get relayed back depending on importance."

"Exactly, but this might not be considered important. It's only *talk*, John. My friend didn't even know the name of the guys, and shit, he was in the back of a strip club throwing dollar bills at a girl shaking her ass in front of him. It's not someone's solid word. I can't take that kind of shit to the boss, his underboss, or his consigliere. He doesn't like—"

"To have his time wasted, yeah. I got it."

John glanced around, and back at the opened door. He could still hear the men working away downstairs. Some of their murmurings and laughter climbed up high to reach them in the office.

"Do you think it's a smart idea to have your guys working in a warehouse at the moment, considering?" John asked.

"I don't have much of a choice, unless you could help me along there until this shit blows over."

"How so?"

"Like I said, you're in close with the boss, and Andino. I mean, sometimes it's Andino running the show, and sometimes it's Dante. Whoever makes the calls, I guess. Point is, if they want me to keep bringing in money and *safely*, I need a place to do that."

"I can try to work—"

John's words cut off at the scent of something reaching the doorway behind him. A strong smell that burned his nostrils with every sniff. An unmistakable smell. He sniffed again, and then took a step closer to the doorway.

What the fuck?

"John?"

"You don't have gas or anything in the warehouse, do you?"

"A tank in the back—the guys use it to fill up every once in a while. I keep it full for them to make sure they have gas if they're running low on cash, or whatever."

"A tank."

"Yeah, an above ground one."

Shit.

The smell was stronger, now. John left the office altogether, and leaned over the banister. He could see the guys of Marky's crew were hard at work, and seemingly oblivious to the fact something bad was going down.

"Bay doors at the back of the warehouse?" John asked over his shoulder.

"Yeah, why?"

"Get all these guys out," John said. "Now."

"What, wh—"

John shouted down to the guys working. "Get out of the warehouse! Go through the front, not the back! Get the fuck out now!"

Marky came out behind John just as the crackling started. The guys on the floor ran for the front, and John headed for the stairs. The smell of gas increased, and so did the smell of fire.

The tank in the back exploded just as John pushed Marky out the front door of the warehouse. The place was flattened by fire in less than five minutes.

It never stood a chance.

The fire department never even made it in time to try.

Beside him on the street, Marky watched as fire fighters shot their hoses at the smoldering pile of rubble. "That truck was a good hundred grand payout."

"Truck isn't worth the life of your crew."

"I won't have a crew if I can't keep them working, John," Marky muttered.

Shit.

Yeah.

"Let me call the boss," John said. "Enough is enough with this shit."

"About time someone else thinks so."

• • •

"Son."

John stiffened a bit at his father's voice traveling in from the front door. "In the kitchen."

Soon, Lucian's footsteps echoed closer until they stopped altogether. John continued on with his work.

"What are you doing here?"

"I wanted to stop by—check in. I can do that, can't I?"

"I suppose."

"Were you working last night?" Lucian asked.

John kept his back turned to his father as he finished dumping in bubble mailers and other shit into the garbage can. "Another attack."

Lucian sucked air though his teeth so hard, it whistled. "Shit."

"No one was hurt this time around."

"Small blessings."

If you wanted to call it that.

John turned to face his father, and found Lucian standing in the kitchen entryway. "I called Dante last night to let him know what happened before someone else did, and he directed me to Andino before I could even finish speaking."

"His right to do, I suppose."

"Andino told me not to counterattack."

Lucian didn't blink at that statement. "His right too, I guess."

And that was the whole fucking problem.

"Who is really the one running this family?"

"Pardon?" Lucian asked.

"Who is running the family? Andino, or Dante? Which one is it? Nobody seems to know right now, and that makes shit dangerous."

"Officially, it's Dante. Unofficially, it's Andino."

"Why doesn't everyone else understand that—*me*, for example?"

"They've made the choice to do it this way for their own reasons. I suppose to take other organizations by surprise when the time comes, but also, you know how this business and family goes, Johnathan."

Yeah.

"Don't question a boss."

"Exactly. There is method to their madness. You have to respect their right to make the final decision."

"The Calabrese tried to burn out one of our warehouses from the back last night. The Capo had a whole crew of guys working in there to get rid of a boosted truck full of electronics. The Capo never could have handled that situation by himself, and the crew probably would have been lost had I not smelled the fucking gasoline in time. The time for games is over—we need to start acting more than we have."

"We act when we need to," Lucian replied calmly. "Not every action a Marcello answers with is violent, or straightforward. That's where the Calabrese differ from us."

John was getting nowhere with this conversation, but he wasn't surprised. Everything his father was saying had been repeated to John for three decades—his entire life. He knew all of this was the truth, and yet, he was antsy and edgy.

Something needed to be done.

Soon.

"Shit, maybe ..."

"What?" Lucian asked quietly.

"Maybe a large part of my problem is that I'm just ... impatient," John muttered. "Tired of waiting for this to end. Tired of being fucked with all the time."

Lucian lifted a single brow. "Tired of being made to wait for her?"

That hit a nerve.

A good one—an honest one.

It still hit it.

John had never quite realized how well his father actually knew him, but the truth was, Lucian saw more things in John than he ever admitted out loud. Perhaps that was because his father loved him more than John understood, or even maybe Lucian just had a way about him that allowed him into other people's perspectives.

He really didn't know what it was.

"Siena is definitely a reason for my impatience," John admitted. "The longer I have to wait, the further away she seems."

"Good things come to those who learn how to first wait for them, John."

"Impart that wisdom on someone who gives a damn. At the moment, it isn't me."

Lucian chuckled. "So is the way of a Marcello man when it comes to his woman."

"Yeah, well ..."

The two remained quiet as John turned back to compact the evidence of his former misdeeds deeper into the garbage can. He didn't realize his father had come to stand beside him until Lucian's hand snaked into the trash bag, and pulled out one of the documents.

Lucian stayed deathly quiet as his gaze drifted over the crumpled documents, and took the words in. It was the record of an event he should recognize.

John, at newly turned seventeen, had taken off for a little over three days in a hypomanic episode, and damn near killed himself with liquor and pills while he chased a rush. It ended up being the first of many hospitalizations leading up to his first full blown manic episode, and final diagnosis.

It took all of John's willpower not to snatch the paper from his father, and shove it back where it belonged. In the goddamn garbage. He forced himself to remain still, and let his father take in the paper.

Lucian dropped it back down into the bag, and grabbed another. Then, another and another. He took his time reading each one until he seemed satisfied enough to know that everything in the bag was the same.

All about his son.

All about his disorder.

"What is all of this?" Lucian asked.

John stuffed his hands in his pockets. "Me."

Lucian gave him a look. "It is not *you*. It is moments in your life during darker times. Moments in which you were not entirely yourself. Moments when you still needed help you were not getting."

"Yeah, I know."

And he did know that now. But it took several fucking days looking at this shit for it to really sink in that all of this garbage meant nothing to John at the end of the day. These events in his life had passed long ago, and he no longer behaved this way.

"I thought there were only a few of these packages sent out to people you know," Lucian said quietly. "What did you do, go and collect every single one of them from everybody?"

John laughed.

Hard and bitter.

"No, these are all mine. All sent to me."

Lucian stilled, and his gaze darted to John. "Oh, I see."

"Another reason I am so impatient to get this over with when it comes to the Calabrese family," John muttered.

"You know," his father murmured, "growing up, everyone liked to tell me that my son was the wild one. He came from you, but he acts like a young Giovanni."

John chuckled, knowing some of the stunts his uncle had pulled growing up. Of course, Gio had not been bipolar, or anything of the sort, simply … a wild child, and far too free spirited for his own good, according to everyone.

"And then you got older," Lucian continued on, not letting John speak at all. "We learned you were not like Gio—you were you, and you had your own set of obstacles to overcome. Yet, you were so focused, John, even on your worst days, and in your darkest moments. You had a goal that never changed in your life, and I wasn't sure whether to be proud, or terrified because of it.

John knew exactly what his father meant. He was living that dream now. "Being a made man."

Lucian nodded. "I worried how *la famiglia* might treat you, considering everything. I worried that something would happen to forever brand you in Cosa Nostra. Once a man ruins himself in this life, he is done."

John cleared his throat. "I kind of did do that, though. The Andino episode years ago. Matteo a few months ago. No man in control of himself would—"

"Except none of those events have ever pushed you out of the family, or affected your ability to do exactly what you do best in this business. Men still want to work with you—you still make *money*. They still respect you, and hold a healthy amount of fear for you at the same time. You earned all of that and not in spite of your bipolar, but because of it, John."

Lucian clapped his son on the shoulder, adding, "Nothing the Calabrese fools might release about you or your history is a shock to anyone who knows you, or has watched you grow up, John. Old news, that's all. The men of our family may not speak about it at the dinner table, but they have seen enough and know enough, and yet, we are all still one."

True.

Sometimes, John needed things pointed out to him. It was easier for him to see the bigger picture when he had been focused on only one piece of it for too long.

"I misjudged our *la famiglia*," Lucian said. "And that was my fault. Don't make my mistakes, John. We may be bad men, but we are also good men, too."

"Yeah, I won't."

"Good," Lucian said, patting him on the shoulder once more. His father turned to head for the counter where the electric kettle sat waiting. "Coffee?"

"Sure. You know, that was my biggest fear growing up."

Lucian looked back at him. "What?"

"Being the shame or disgrace of this family. I figured, how far could I push, and how many people did I have to hurt before it was all over for me? I kept getting one more chance. No matter how far I alienated myself from everyone, I still had to be close enough to the edge of the family to see inside. I didn't feel right, otherwise."

"Of course you did. We just gave you time."

"You completely disregarded what I first said."

"No, I didn't," Lucian said, prepping a mug for instant coffee. "You're not a disgrace to this family. You could never be, John. That's it, that's all."

"I like how everything is black and white for you."

Lucian smirked over his shoulder. "Far from it—my life has been lived in shades of gray, son. Much like yours. Now, have a coffee. We have a meeting to get to."

"What meeting?"

"Andino called it. He's decided on a course of action."

"Finally."

Lucian gave him a look.

John shrugged. "I can't help how I feel. That's part of this whole being bipolar thing, all right. I feel what I feel, and I feel it much more than any of you ever do. I can't help it."

And right then, he was feeling really fucking irritated with his cousin.

"I know, but you can be quieter about it."

Fair enough.

• • •

John did not expect to see what he found waiting for him in his uncle's office. Instead of Dante sitting behind the desk—where the boss always sat when a meeting was held—it was only Andino.

His cousin waved a hand at the chair across from the desk, saying, "Sit, John."

John stayed standing. "Shouldn't Dante be here? His house, office, desk, and family."

Andino smirked a bit. "The pretenses about who is running this show is just about over. Are you going to sit, or not?"

"Made men should never appear level with their boss. Stand for respect, or sit when he's standing to allow his voice to carry. We all learned these things, Andi."

Andino nodded. "Except, you and I have always been on equal ground, cousin. Never one higher than the other."

"You are now."

"In appearance only." Andino pointed at the chair once more. "Sit."

John dropped his form into the chair, and only glanced back over his shoulder when the office door was closed behind him. "We're the only ones here for this, or what? Not a good sign for you, Andi."

Andino chuckled. "Keep poking my nerves, man."

"I kid."

"I know." Andino shrugged. "No one else is needed for this at the moment, John. You had some issues last night, huh?"

"Another burned warehouse."

Andino's expression turned pensive as he turned his head a bit to look out the window. "Shit, like we can fucking afford another loss like that."

"My thoughts, too."

Sighing, Andino looked back at John. "Unfortunately, I need you to stand down on all of this. Do not respond to that with another attack, just like we let the drive-by shooting on you and Lucian go unanswered, too."

Irritation simmered through John's blood.

"Seriously? What are you trying to—"

"The Calabrese need to believe we are subdued in every aspect, from business to family. By not answering them back, it will slow their violence. Give them the idea they have possibly strong-armed us into a corner. Regardless, it allows me to put feelers out, which I need at the moment. I have an end goal here, and I want to reach it soon."

Andino smiled coldly, "It's time to put the last part of this plan into motion, John. I can't afford for anything to ruin it. So, no attacks, no threats, no anything. I need quiet streets until I get the Calabrese into the position I want them in."

John tried to swallow down his rage, but it was damn hard.

If not downright impossible.

"And your goal is what?" he asked sharply. "To make the Marcellos look weak—incapable, easily manipulated, and broken by a few attacks? To let them think we've backed down, and that they've scared us?"

"Yes, that's exactly what I would like for them to assume."

Andino's admittance took John by surprise.

John straightened in his chair. "What kind of fucking boss does that make—"

"A very smart one," Andino replied. "A boss that they won't see coming, as they still don't know I am the boss. Think, John, they know I will be taking over, but not *when*. As of now, it is still assumed Dante is running the show. Perhaps Dante is too old—too tired—to keep up with this kind of nonsense. Consider *Dante* gives them a way out of this that would satisfy their need and want to have more control in New York."

Andino leaned forward, and steepled his fingers together. "Consider, cousin, that their greed and ignorance will put them in a position where they open up to us. Where we finally get our in to remove the issue entirely. Where they are the ones who are weak, manipulated, and *broken*."

John took in Andino's words.

He liked them.

And he didn't like them at the same time.

"I knew this was your plan all along," John murmured. "To take over that family, I mean."

"Wrong. Oh, I do want to reorganize and make it a faction of the Marcello family, yes," Andino said, giving John a look from the side, "but I have no intention of absorbing it into this family. It was never ours to begin with. It belonged to someone else."

Andino gave John another pointed look. "It has *always* belonged to someone else. Aren't you ready to take back what was rightfully yours, John?"

A heavy realization fell on John.

A weight on his shoulders.

A birthright denied.

A promise …

For a long while, John and Andino only stared at one another. John decided to be the first one to speak between them.

"That's why you had me sit—why we are equal," John said quietly.

Andino nodded. "We have always been equal, cousin, and we always will be."

"You didn't think to let me in on this bright idea of yours, or what?"

"I needed to position myself where I could not be challenged," his cousin admitted, "and while this plan of mine is for you, it is also for me. I married a woman not up to the standards Cosa Nostra demands—I have effectively guaranteed the line of Marcello bosses will end with any sons I have, if I do. But there's always you."

Andino smirked, tipping his head in John's direction, "There is always you in one of the Commission seats who will not deny my position, or my wife. There is Cross Donati as another boss—we know he'll marry one of our cousins—and because of that, will be unwilling to start a war for the sake of his own family. And there is Chicago—too far away, and too caught up in controlling their own city to worry about us. Vegas, too, but my uncle still runs that syndicate, so I felt comfortable enough to push that line there, too."

"But had the Calabrese been sitting in that seat ..."

John let his words trail off.

Andino cleared his throat, and sat back in the chair. "It would have been an opening for them. A weak spot in the Marcello chain to pick at until it broke. I love Haven—I wasn't giving her up for anything, or anybody. Not this life of ours, and not this family. You understand, don't you?"

John thought about Siena.

He thought about her.

About *them*.

"Yeah, I understand."

Andino smiled, although fainter than before. "Then let's finish this."

CHAPTER THIRTEEN

SIENA DIDN'T START in fear when someone crawled into bed with her before the sun had even properly come up in the sky. She didn't have to be scared when she knew who it was without even opening her eyes. His presence was like a tangible aura to her. Something that sunk deep into her senses, and made itself at home there.

She felt him.

Smelled him.

Loved him.

"Go back to sleep," she heard John murmur.

Siena reached for him the second John was close enough to grab, but he seemed to have other plans. His arms tangled around her—like strong, steel bars keeping her close to him, protected, and hidden from the world. He dragged her closer in the bed, tucked her head under his chin, and refused to let go.

Siena could have fallen back to sleep like that. It would have been easy given how comfortable and tired she was. Instead, she dared to tip her head back on the pillow, and look up at him. Dark hazel stared back—familiar eyes that hid so much from the world, but showcased nothing more than a beautiful soul to her.

She was happy to see he looked better than the last time they were together. Less darkness in his eyes, and fewer lines of worry and anxiety on his face. His voice hadn't held that same low, unsure quality as it had before, telling her that his mind was likely in a far better space than before.

It helped *her* anxiety that hadn't left since she took off from his place to know that he was doing better. She didn't need to know the reasons why, or what pushed him back in the other direction. Just knowing he was there was more than enough for her.

Ten days ago.

Yeah, Siena was keeping count, now. It was yet another way she had found to get through her days without John, and the time in between seeing him again. Marking off days in her mind was like a challenge of sorts—could they see each other sooner this time around than the last time?

Silly, sure.

It kept her going.

"When did you get here?" she asked.

Siena had the slightest feeling he had been there for longer than it took him to wake her up, and crawl into her bed.

"Long enough to make a coffee, and take my meds," he said. "It's four in the morning—go back to sleep, *amore*."

"Did you pick the lock again?"

Because he hadn't changed it like he said he would. This was the first time he had actually gotten back to her apartment since that first time after he got out of the facility. Things were always getting in the damn way.

So was their life.

"Yes," he said, "and I came in the back way with the extra building key you gave me. Now, stop talking, and go to sleep."

"But when I wake up, you're going to have to go."

"Sleep," he said again. "I'll be here."

Surrounded by John, his warmth, darkness, and soft sheets, Siena really didn't need to be told again. John's fingers stroked a gentle path up and down her naked spine, which was enough to make her close her eyes. The sensation sent her off to dreamland in seconds.

John's voice followed right behind. "I'll be here."

The next time Siena woke up, sunlight had filtered through the bedroom through the break in the curtains. Warm rays streaked lines over her naked back, and dust particles danced in the stream of light; her gaze followed the amusing sight.

"I need to dust," she said.

The form she was resting on started to chuckle. The sound rocked them both on the bed, and made her smile even wider.

"Did you pull me onto you, or did I climb on?" Siena asked.

"A little bit of both," John replied in a murmur.

"Huh."

"And you do need to dust."

Siena laughed, and tipped her head back to stare at John. He had sat higher on her bed to rest his back against the headboard. He looked entirely relaxed sitting there watching her—like this was the one place he was meant to be, and the only place he wanted to be.

Siena supposed it was.

Or she hoped it was.

And maybe, had the circumstances been different in their lives, they could have already been well into the start of their own life.

Together.

She pushed those sad thoughts away. It wasn't the time for them, and it wouldn't do her any good. Besides, she had John with her right now, and that was all that mattered to her. It was all she needed to make her whole day brighter.

"I've been busy," she admitted, "and for the record, I didn't even live here for *months*. Nobody lived here. I only got to come here once in a while if I needed to grab something specific, and I wasn't allowed to stay. Kev and Darren didn't want me getting any ideas about coming back to my apartment, you know."

John's gaze hardened momentarily—it always did that whenever she brought up how controlled her life was—but he still managed to offer her a smile. It didn't reach his eyes, but he tried. "I guess you can be excused, then."

"Geeze, thanks."

His hands squeezed her ass firmly. The action made Siena laugh.

She pushed up higher on her knees, and crawled up John's body where she stopped just a breath away from his lips. His gaze zoned in on her mouth, and his pupils dilated as he watched her lips curve into a grin. His tongue peeked out to wet the seam of his lips.

Then, the corner of his mouth quirked up in a half-assed smirk that instantly made her wet between her thighs. She found herself wondering what she might have to do to get him to put that tongue of his to work on her pussy.

Yeah, she went to that dirty place fast. All because of him, too. He didn't have to even try. He barely did a thing!

Goddamn.

This man was terribly sexy.

More than he could possibly know.

"Are you going to kiss me good morning, or what?" John asked.

Siena's gaze drifted to the clock on the nightstand. A time flashed back at her, and made her frown. Like she thought when he first woke her up, they wouldn't have very much time together. Life would come along to separate them all too soon.

"As long as that's all we do."

John's fingers dug into her backside even harder than before, and he grinded her lower half against his. He didn't even try to stifle the groan of her name. "That's unfair, and you give me more credit for my control than I actually have."

Siena laughed, and then pressed a fast kiss to John's lips. Her innocent gesture soon turned into something much hotter. Heated coals coaxed into a raging flame with every graze of their lips, and tease of his tongue. She loved the way he urged her to kiss him deeper with flicks of his tongue against hers, and then the way he bit her bottom lip just hard enough to take her breath away.

She found herself rolled over on the bed in a single breath, and John hovered above her. The hard lines of his body were like a canvas of art for her—unblemished and mostly unmarked. She could stare at him all day, and never be bored.

His fingers tangled with hers, and pressed them into the pillow above her head. He fit perfectly between her widened thighs, and she could feel his erection growing harder against her naked thigh with every shift of their bodies.

John dropped a kiss to her nose.

One to each eyelid.

A path across her jaw.

Dotted kisses to her cheeks.

It was so sweet, that all she could do was smile when he finally came back to her lips. For the moment, the two could pretend like a war wasn't raging outside their small bubble. That nothing was wrong in their life.

They could be *normal*.

"I missed you," he said quietly.

His words grazed her lips like his kiss had. A soft-spoken promise that only brushed along her surface, but somehow managed to reach deep into her heart, and grab tight. An assurance that would never let her go.

She couldn't let it go.

"I missed you, too," she said.

John grinned. "I figured I had the chance to come over, so I might as well take it."

"Not complaining."

"Didn't think you would."

All over again, she was struck by how at ease John seemed compared to the last time. "You look a lot better—headspace-wise, I mean."

"Do I?"

"Mmhmm."

John's lips curved a bit at the edges. "Choosing stability means being honest when I'm having trouble. Not to everyone, mind you. It's not about them—this is all about me, and my mental health."

"Absolutely."

"Leonard—the new therapist—dropped the mood stabilizer for a bit and changed it to an antidepressant until I level out again. Might take a couple weeks. Might be a month. All depends."

But …

John had gone and done that.

Asked for something different.

Acknowledged something was offset.

Knew he needed a change.

It was *huge*.

"It's not a big deal," he said at the sight of her growing grin.

"You know it kind of is, John."

"It's a good thing, yes."

"That, too." Siena looked over at the clock again. "I've got a little while before Jason will be knocking on my door again."

John's happiness was soon gone with those words. "Mmm."

"Kev's funeral," she explained.

"Ah. Shame."

"It is. I would rather stay in bed than go and put on yet another farce for him, even if the bastard is dead."

John stilled and quieted as his gaze traveled over Siena. She could hear his silent questions without actually needing him to ask them. She could feel the unspoken words burning between the two of them.

They hadn't talked about what she did.

Not *really*.

Seemed that silence was over.

"You don't regret it at all, do you?" John asked.

Siena didn't flinch. "Not when it's for you—for us."

"He was still your—"

"Nothing. He meant nothing."

John cleared his throat. "Jesus, woman, don't be so cold. I don't like you cold."

Siena smiled, unable to stop herself. "Never cold to you, John."

"Better not be."

He let go of her hands, and Siena used that freedom to cup his jaw, and pull him in for another lingering, burning kiss. That flame he created was now a devastating inferno, ravaging her insides in the best way.

"Do you ever think about the future?" she asked.

John—so close she could see the flakes of gold in his hazel eyes— smiled. "I do when I feel like punishing myself. Nothing is ever really guaranteed, you know."

She did know.

"Doesn't matter to me," Siena told him. "I still think about it. I need to. It helps."

"What do you think about, then?"

"Us."

John's smile deepened. "Be specific."

"Everything. A wedding. I'd go for ivory, likely. In a church, maybe, but I wouldn't be offended if it wasn't, too. I wouldn't want to walk alone, though."

"No?"

"You could walk with me. Be different."

John laughed. "I would absolutely walk with you, *donna*. You never have to be alone."

"And I think about what comes after all of that, too. Life, kids—"

Siena's words trailed off when she felt John stiffen above her. She met his gaze, but could plainly see the way he tried to hide his discomfort.

"What?" she asked.

"Kids is kind of touchy topic for me," he said, shrugging.

John dropped to the bed beside her. He used a hand to rest his head on as he stared at her, waiting for a reply. Siena didn't really know *how* to reply.

"Why?"

"It isn't obvious?" he asked.

"No."

John waved a hand toward his own body. "This, Siena."

"I'm lost."

"I didn't wake up one day *with* bipolar—I didn't catch it like a sickness, babe. I've had it in my genetics from the day I was born, and puberty was the switch turning it on for me. There's no cure for it, either. You learn to manage it, and to stay at relatively stable levels that still fluctuate no matter what you do. There's a genetic component. Something in my DNA that was there from someone else in my family. Passed on, you know?"

"John—"

"Having kids means continuing this on—or possibly. You don't know for sure, right? My parents had four kids, and I was the one that found the barrel of the gun in the game of genetic roulette, so to speak. I'm not sure I want to do this to one of my kids. I know what it felt like to be confused for more than half my life, and to constantly feel like I was drowning."

"But there's nothing wrong with you."

John gave her a look.

Siena only gave it right back.

"Siena," he said, a little too patronizing for her liking. "I didn't say something was *wrong*. There is something different, though."

"You don't want kids at all?"

"I didn't say that."

"You're not saying differently, either."

John frowned, and scrubbed a hand down his jaw. Rolling to his back, he stared at the ceiling. "I never gave it a lot of thought—settled myself on the idea it just wasn't going to be something I moved forward with."

"See, that kind of sounds like a strong *no*."

He looked over at her. The intensity of his gaze made her still in place.

Siena still managed to speak. "This is a hard line for me, John. I want children. I have *always* wanted children."

He nodded. "I never did."

Ouch.

"Until this, and you," he added in a murmur.

Relief so sweet it was almost poisonous swept through Siena's insides. "Oh?"

"Mmm." John sighed, and went back to staring at the ceiling. "Like everything in my life, I can't go into something like that without planning for it. It's a huge change, and—"

"I get it."

Quickly, Siena crossed the space between them, and crawled back on top of him. She straddled his waist, tangled their fingers together, and looked down at him.

"But there isn't, by the way," she said.

John cocked a brow. "What?"

"Something wrong with you. There *isn't*."

"It took me a long time to figure that out, though, Siena. I'm thirty-one now. I still wake up some mornings and think, *why can't my brain work like everybody else's?* I wonder why I have to struggle with emotions, and processing them, not to mention everything else that comes along with being bipolar. It took a long time to figure out nothing was wrong. It was hell."

"But you did. That's what matters most *today*."

John didn't deny it.

Siena felt like that was a battle won for him.

• • •

Siena's attention drifted between her brother saying one last goodbye to the closed casket keeping Kev's body hidden from view, and the sunlight streaming in through the colorful stained glass windows. She should have been more present, or at least, made the effort to seem like she gave some kind of damn.

She couldn't do it.

At least, she had managed to put on a proper black dress, sweep her hair into a simple chignon, and brush her face with a bit of makeup. It wasn't the effort she would usually put into getting ready for church or a funeral, but it was the best she could do for today. Anything more, and it might seem like she cared.

She didn't.

Darren nodded to one of his men when the guy came closer. It seemed like her brother had more of those—men to do his bidding—than she cared to count, now. Unlike Kev who only worked with a couple of people, and kept Darren the closest, her other brother was entirely different. He kept many men at his side, and handed out orders like a tyrant who was unwilling to be questioned or challenged.

The change had happened instantly.

Practically overnight.

Siena supposed she now understood what her father had meant when he once told her that while many bosses came into the position by chance, far more bosses in this life were simply made that way. Men born to be in a position of power because they had the temperament, control, and mindset to do the job.

Her brother was not the man born to do the job, but rather, one who had come into the seat by chance, and was making the best of what he had to work with. Sometimes, it was a fascinating show to watch, and other times, it was incredibly disconcerting to Siena.

Darren was a chameleon—able to change the exterior he offered to someone depending on the situation at hand. He might not be a boss on the inside, but he was fully capable of presenting the image of a boss on the outside when he needed to.

Unlike John.

A man who Siena thought would suit a position like a boss's seat far better than Darren. John, who commanded attention without needing to change his image to suit the needs of others in order to make his position and demands clear.

John was who John was.

Darren, on the other hand, wasn't quite sure who he was at the moment, but rather, only knew who he needed to be.

"Get up."

Siena glanced over at her mother's sharp order. "What?"

Coraline waved at the aisle. "Come on, we have to follow behind the casket. Stop acting like a daydreaming, foolish girl, Siena."

Jesus.

She pushed out of the pew to quickly follow behind the casket carrying her brother. Darren was one of the pallbearers, along with a few other men he had chosen to do the job with him. She kept her head down as she walked toward the entrance of the church, entirely uninterested in meeting the gazes of those who had come to say goodbye to Kev. The scent of the priest's incense clung heavily all around them.

Almost over.

She would soon be able to take off her mask again.

Be *free* again.

Siena's mother slid in beside her as they continued their trek behind the casket and procession. Coraline's mask of grief was all but gone in that moment, and instead, a cold, expressionless, and unfeeling one took its place.

For a second, it took Siena by surprise.

Her mother didn't give her the time to question it before she started talking. And when she did talk, it scared Siena to death.

153

"You should have been more careful with your business," her mother murmured. "And by business, I mean Johnathan Marcello."

Siena swallowed hard, and looked forward. She kept her gaze locked on the back of the shined, gleaming black casket with its gold-plated bars and details. "I have no idea what you're—"

"Don't play stupid with me," Coraline hissed low. All the while, her mother's face remained impassive. Her voice stayed too low for someone else to overhear, and her expression gave nothing away as to their conversation. Siena could not say her face looked the same. "I will not allow you to ruin what your brother is working so hard for simply because you cannot control your stupid little *heart*."

Her mother said the word with so much disgust, that Siena flinched.

"You think this little issue with the Marcello and Calabrese families is *new*?" Coraline scoffed low, and shook her head subtly. "No, Siena, it is far from new. Years—*decades*—in the making, really. It started with your grandfather, and then was passed onto your father. He passed it onto your brothers, and finally ... Jesus, *finally*, we have the chance to finish this. To either take a controlling portion, or ruin the Marcello family for good. Except here you are, getting in the goddamn way with that man."

Coraline sneered, but quickly replaced it with a sad smile when she waved to someone who reached out to touch her arm as she passed. Out of the corner of her mouth, her mother said, "Darren has the Marcellos where he needs them to be—soft, and pliable. Backed into a corner, so to speak. I love you, Siena, and that is the only reason I was willing to turn my cheek about what I knew you were doing, but if you don't stop, I won't be able to pretend anymore."

Siena's throat tightened more.

Her mother nodded. "And you do know what your brother would do to Johnathan should he find out you have been entertaining the man behind his back, don't you? I am sure you would hate for your crazy boyfriend—if you could even call him that—to die because of your stupidity."

"Ma—"

"Shut up," Coraline hissed.

The two walked out into the sunlight, and quieted for the moment. Siena took the second she had where her mother wasn't talking to suck in a deep gulp of air. It felt like the breath had been ripped right out of her lungs, and her chest was crushed.

How did her mother know she was still with John?

How had she known *anything*?

Siena was careful—she had to be. She made sure not to leave anything lying around where someone could find it. She was back at her own place which meant she didn't have to worry about someone listening through the walls, or just outside the door.

She didn't take risks.

She didn't dare.

Except …

She had.

Once, or twice.

Kev's casket was pushed into the back of the hearse by the pallbearers. The men all slapped the back of the casket with their palm—a final goodbye.

Siena's mother turned to her once more. "You are my daughter, Siena, and I do not want to see you become fodder to a man's games or plans. Play this right with me, and you could have far more than you ever dreamed of. Johnathan—is he *really* your highest bar to reach? He is what you really want? Why? You could have much more, darling."

She didn't reply.

Her mother apparently wasn't looking for one.

"The Marcellos have called a meeting with your brother. Darren expects it will either lead them into a peaceful resolution that puts the Calabrese higher, or it will dissolve into more violence that will lead them into a longer war. Either way, it will be happening soon. Should you do anything to cause your brother to call off that meeting—say, get caught with Johnathan—you will *not* like what I do."

It was always men who planned.

Men who played games.

Men who manipulated.

Siena learned in that moment that men often forgot women were the flies on the wall. Women were the ones who needed to be watched because they held more information than anyone possibly knew.

Women were the dangerous ones.

Women like her mother.

"How did you know?" Siena asked.

"About you and the Marcello man?"

Siena only nodded.

Coraline turned to face Siena with a cold smile. "I was coming to visit you a while back, but you rushed out of your place like a bat out of hell. Your enforcer didn't trail behind, so I thought I should. I saw where you went, and I saw you leave his place. I thought … maybe I should keep a closer eye on you. I am glad I did."

Fuck.

Nothing was ever safe.

Not in their life.

"You see," Coraline said, "your brothers are a lot like your father—or *was*, for Kev. They're stupid in the way they believe that their word is law, and because they have said it, us women will automatically follow it. I know better. Do you think I stumbled upon my marriage with your father because I loved him, and wanted to marry him?"

"I don't know why you married Daddy, no."

"Because I was told to, but not because I wanted to. I have learned over the years to make sure the men in my life take everything I give them at face value and never feel the need to dig deeper. I loved Matteo, I *did*—it took years, but I loved him. And I will not see everything he worked for ruined because one of his children cannot manage to step in line with the rest."

"I will stay in line, Ma."

Only long enough to watch the Marcellos ruin this family.

After that, it was fair game.

"You better, but should you think to do something to force my hand," her mother warned, "you will not like what I do. I will make my arranged marriage and carefully sheltered life look like a cake walk compared to your future after this, darling. I do not want to hurt you, but I absolutely will."

What could she possibly say to that? Nothing.

So she didn't.

Coraline moved down the stairs, calling over her shoulder, "Keep it in mind, Siena."

CHAPTER FOURTEEN

THE CONVERSATION filtered down the main hall of the large Amityville home as John strolled through the front door, and closed it behind him softly. He took quiet strides, following the conversation until muffled voices were much clearer.

"It'll take time," he heard his mother say.

"That's what everyone keeps telling me," Cella muttered heavily.

"It's okay to not be okay, Cella."

"Is it? I think it's easier to pretend, Ma."

"But you *shouldn't*."

"Yeah, I know."

John used two knuckles to knock on the wall as he stood in the entryway to his mother's living room. He didn't want to interrupt the conversation happening in the room between his sister, and his mother.

At the same time, he also didn't want to be caught eavesdropping on a conversation he knew really wasn't any of his business. Cella would not like to think that John was stepping in on her personal shit—mostly *because* it was John.

"Hey," John said when the two women looked his way.

"*Mio ragazzo.*" Jordyn smiled. "Come in, John.

John took a step in the room as Cella cleared her throat, and dropped one of the items of clothing she had been folding back into the basket on the couch. She wouldn't meet his gaze, but he didn't take it personally.

"Cella," John greeted.

"John."

Well, his name was better than nothing, he supposed. It was more than he had been getting where his sister was concerned.

Jordyn didn't look all too surprised to see John standing there, but then again, she had known he was coming over. After all, he had sought out his mother's help to try and make some kind of amends with Cella over what happened to her husband.

Jordyn had been all too willing to play the go-between in that regard.

She always disliked how John's sisters—mostly Liliana and Cella—were not willing to close some of the distance between them. John understood why, of course, given their history. It was not a good history shared between them. He was once known to burn bridges with harsh words.

Here he was trying to fix a bridge instead.

Funny how that worked.

Sure, William's death was not done by John's hand. It had not been him who pulled the trigger, and took the man away from his wife and child. Nonetheless, it had been—in a way—John's involvement and subsequent dealings with the Calabrese that started this feud between the two families.

So, maybe, it was his fault.

Shit.

He felt far too much guilt.

"John," his mother said, "I will go make you a coffee. Your father is upstairs having a nap, too. I'll let him know you're here."

Keeping a firm grip on the gift bag in his hand, John nodded to his mother and came closer to the couch. He didn't set the bag down, step in his sister's way, or even get in her personal space. John wasn't here to upset Cella in anyway, just ... try to apologize.

If he could.

If *she* would let him.

"Don't bother Dad," John told his mother. "Let him sleep. I bet his ribs are still sore."

"A little," Jordyn replied. "But he won't admit it."

John figured.

Lucian was too proud a man to tell someone he was in pain, or that someone had bested him in a way that kept him down for the count. That, and Marcello men just didn't talk about that kind of shit when it came to pain, or injuries. Weaknesses were not publically acknowledged as to not give someone a vulnerability to pick on.

So was their life.

So was their ways.

He gave Jordyn a quick kiss to her cheek, and let her pat the side of his face with her warm palm. He was trying to be more affectionate with his mother—affectionate gestures did not always come easy to John because a lot of the times, they just made him feel awkward and out of place.

This wasn't the same thing.

It was his mother.

He loved her.

He should show her.

"Thank you for trying," Jordyn murmured too low for Cella to hear. "Regardless of the rest, that *matters*, John."

He nodded once. "I know, Ma."

She patted his cheek once more, and then darted out of the living room. He knew she probably wouldn't come back, despite her declaring she was going to make him a coffee. He would likely have to go find her after this was all said and done.

"Do you have a minute?" John asked his sister.

Cella shrugged, and probably just to keep her hands busy, grabbed the item of clothing that she had previously discarded. A baby onesie. "I guess. What do you need?"

"Very little, actually."

"Not sure I'm the right one to help you then, John."

Probably not.

He was hoping to help her, maybe.

John eyed the baby onesie she folded with careful hands. "You're staying here, huh?"

Cella nodded. "It's easier. Ma helps me with Tiffany, and Daddy gives me someone to rage at when it's all …"

"A little too much," John finished for her.

"Basically."

"Dad's good like that."

"He is," Cella agreed. "And besides, it's hard being home. Seeing things, and being around things. I cleared a bit out because someone said that might help—it fucking didn't."

"People don't know anything about this kind of grief, Cella. Nobody really knows what it's like to lose someone—your spouse, I mean. They're well-intentioned, but a lot of the shit they say still sucks. I know you probably don't want to hurt anybody's feelings, but you can tell them to stop when you need them to fuck off. It's okay to do that."

Tears gathered in his sister's eyes, but she kept her passive expression turned down on her work. "So I am learning."

"And I'm sorry."

Cella's hands froze in her work. "Pardon?"

John shrugged when she shot him a look. "You blame me for things, and I get it. I didn't pull the trigger, but I'm a catalyst in a way to William dying."

"Are you?"

"The Calabrese, and Siena. I know my place—I know my choices. I know what they did. You weren't wrong when you said what you said, but you said it in the wrong way at the time. You were angry, though, so I get it."

"Do you love her?"

"Siena?"

Cella shrugged one shoulder. "Daddy says you're still seeing her sometimes."

"It's complicated given the situation, but yeah, I love her."

"She seems nice."

"She is wonderful." John scrubbed a hand down his jaw, and decided to just get this over with. Say the hard shit—stuff he hadn't ever said to his sister, but she still deserved to hear all the same. "I've taken a lot from you—and Liliana, too—over the years. Safety in your own home. Peace and quiet. Possessions. I've said a lot of shit, and done a lot of shit when we were growing up. It should have been a good time in your life, but I turned it into chaos. I recognize that, Cella. I know I can't change it, but I am sorry."

A single tear made a traitorous line down Cella's cheek. She didn't try to wipe it away, or even acknowledge that it had escaped.

"I do love you, John," Cella whispered. "I just have to do it from afar."

"Yeah, I know. We all have to do what we have to do for ourselves, so don't think I expect anything more from you than what you're willing to give."

"Thanks."

John placed the large gift bag on the coffee table, and took a step back. White tissue paper overflowed from the top. "Ma helped a little bit. I hope it helps you, and the baby, too."

Cella glanced at the bag, and then back to John. "Nothing really helps, John."

"Yeah, I got that. I'm sorry, Cella."

"I know. I wish it helped."

John headed out of the room when Cella went back to folding clothes, but didn't touch the gift bag. He didn't want to push or pressure his sister for anything. She was going through enough shit as it was.

He found his mother in the kitchen. She already had a cup of coffee waiting for him, and a seat open at the table.

"How did it go?" Jordyn asked as he sat down.

"Uh, well, she didn't tell me to fuck off."

"That's good."

John smirked. "She didn't say much else, either."

"Did she like—"

"She didn't open it with me there," he interjected.

Jordyn nodded, and took a quick sip from her coffee. "Oh, I see."

"It's got to be at her speed, Ma. On her time."

"You're right, John." His mother reached out and cupped his cheek. "You're good that way, my boy."

Something like that.

He stayed with his mother until he finished his coffee, but quickly got up to leave once it was done. He had business to do, and Andino to meet.

Things on the Calabrese side of business were starting to move forward. John was anxious as fuck to put it all to rest.

"I'll see you later, Ma," John said, dropping a kiss to the top of her head. "Tell my father I'll call him."

"Don't forget."

"I won't."

A quick *I love you* to his mother later, and John headed for the front entrance of the house. He had to pass by the living room on his way to the front door. The sight of his sister sitting on the couch stopped him for a minute.

She was holding his gift—hugging it, actually.

And crying.

John had managed to get one of William's T-shirts from Jordyn when Cella cleaned out some things. A soft, cotton T-shirt with one of the man's favorite band logos on the front. He'd sent it to someone his mother suggested, who made it into a throw pillow, of sorts. Something for Cella to keep, or hug. Something for her daughter to have when all that was left would be pictures, and dusty knickknacks.

John had nothing else to offer.

He didn't have the right words.

He *did* hope it helped.

Even if just a little.

• • •

"John."

Andino greeted John with a hand already outstretched to take his. The two shook before Andino sat down at the table. John fixed the lapels of his Armani blazer before he too sat down.

Waving two fingers at his empty placement, he said to the passing waiter, "Water, but put ice in it."

Andino smirked. "Always making it look like vodka, huh?"

John shrugged. "Do what I got to do, man. I'm not late, am I?"

"Right on time, actually."

Andino didn't explain more, instead standing from his seat. John looked over his shoulder to see a familiar man walk through the front door of the restaurant. At the sight of a familiar District Attorney, John stood from his seat to greet the man, too.

It paid to know people.

It *really* paid to use people.

"I thought it was strange that you didn't want to do this meeting in your own business," John said under his breath.

Andino nodded. "You know how these button-up-types are."

"Yeah. Can't be seen in the place of a mobster."

"I hate that fucking title."

They all did.

People used *mobster* or *gangster* like they were slurs. Especially people who fancied themselves firmly on the right side of the law. They didn't truly appreciate what it meant to be a *Mafioso*, or how the mafia had come to be the rock-solid foundation it was today.

Not that any of them cared to explain.

It was what it was.

"Arthur Lorde," Andino greeted, holding out a hand to shake.

The D.A. gave the place a look as he shook Andino's hand. "Shit, Andi, you couldn't make an effort to get us a better table? One that might not be so goddamn close to the windows."

"Relax," John said, "we don't use this place, either."

Arthur didn't look entirely convinced, but he nodded nonetheless. John didn't offer his hand to shake, but that was mostly because Andino had been the one to call this meeting. It was his job, and his show. John was just there to take attendance, and know what the hell was going on plan-wise.

Because he didn't know shit.

Not at the moment.

Andino gestured at the table. "Sit, Arthur, and we'll chat."

Arthur glanced at his watch as he sat down. "I don't have a lot of time here, Andi. I am running shorter and shorter on time lately."

"This won't take long."

Once all the men were sitting at the table, the waiter came back. He had John's water with ice ready, and a glass of what looked to be whiskey for Arthur.

"Still your preferred drink, right?" Andino asked.

Arthur nodded. "It is when we do business. What do you need, Andino?"

"Always to the point."

"I have to be with you and your father."

"I need quiet streets," Andino said. "Peaceful business. Less attention from the media, and officials. I would like for the detectives to quit calling my lawyers five times a day trying to get me in for different interviews. Do you get what I am getting at?"

"Don't you think you and your father have called in enough favors with me?"

Andino smirked. "I mean, you call them favors, but we call it repaying a debt. You know how this works Arthur."

The D.A.'s face reddened.

Andino nodded like he expected that. "Or blackmail. That works, too.

You see, we would really hate for information to get out on that dog fighting ring you had going on. Dad keeps impeccable records when it comes to his people, though, so something could still accidentally slip out should it need to."

Arthur cleared his throat. "There's no need to go down that road, now."

"So you keep saying."

"Andino—"

"And yet you give me trouble every time I need something from you," Andino interjected with a calm, cold tenor.

It was almost amusing to John how his cousin often reminded him of their uncle, Dante, at times like this. Giovanni—Andino's father—could, of course, be cold and harsh when needed, but this was something altogether different.

This was a strange kind of detachment that Giovanni—no matter the situation he was put in—just could not achieve. He was like John in the way that he reacted based on emotions, and it was often that same thing that worked to his benefit when it came to making a point, or getting what he wanted.

The cold detachment, though?

That was Dante Marcello all over.

"Maybe that's because you need things from me far too often," Arthur responded heatedly.

Andino kept his demeanor, unruffled and unbothered. "And I will continue to need things from you until you are useless to me. At the moment, you are not useless. Maybe you should count that amongst your good traits because once someone becomes useless to me, you would not be pleased to find out how I dispose of them."

John smiled to himself.

This was amusing.

He was glad he showed up.

"Jesus Christ." Arthur took a long sip of his whiskey, and then set the glass down a little harder than was necessary to the table. "You're fucking relentless, Andino."

"I have to be in my business."

Arthur pointed a finger at Andino, and shook it. "I almost prefer to walk into a meeting, and see your father sitting in a chair rather than you."

"As you should. Giovanni has a far greater tolerance for nonsense than I do."

"What do you need?"

"I told you—less attention, and peaceful streets."

"I don't understand what exactly that means."

"It means," John said, stepping into the conversation just because he could, "that things will be heating up soon between the Marcello and Calabrese families. As it is, we already have enough attention on us because of their little tricks. You like a quiet city—you prefer we Marcellos keep our business clean, and out of sight. We are trying to do that, but they are making it very difficult."

"I don't see how I can help you with that problem."

Andino chuckled. "I just need your word, Arthur. Nothing more."

"My word for what, exactly?"

"When the time comes, you will make every effort to help the Marcellos go back to their previous position in this city. Business that does not make headlines every other day, and so forth. We will make the streets quiet again."

Arthur sighed heavily, and cleared his throat. "Tell me, then, how I am supposed to help your family go back to the edges of society with the rest of the—"

"Careful," John murmured.

The man passed John a look.

John smiled coldly in response.

"You have the floor," Arthur said to Andino.

"I want a guarantee of freedom," Andino said. "For my men, and me. Whatever we do to quiet the city again, and make the streets safe, we will do it. And in return for giving you a peaceful city, and you know, not exposing your dog fighting history to anyone with a screen in front of them, you will make sure any and all attention or charges from officials can be either put away, or disabused in whatever fashion necessary. Not enough evidence. Destroy statements. Burn a goddamn police station to the ground. I really don't care—you will make it happen."

"You are asking for a lot," Arthur said.

Andino nodded. "And you have a lot of contacts in this city to make it work."

"What exactly are you planning to do that you need this kind of guarantee, Andino?"

Andino looked to John.

John responded for his cousin. "Watch the news. You'll see."

Andino flashed his teeth in a wicked smile. "It'll be a blast."

• • •

The lead up to anything should always come with a palpable feeling. Be it dread, excitement, or something altogether different. It should make a man's heart race, and his palms sweaty with the knowledge that everything he wanted or waited for was finally there.

It was finally happening.

It should thrum through his veins, and beat with his heart. He should be left awake in the night from the anticipation of *almost, almost.*

And yet, the one moment John had waited for had finally arrived, and there he was, entirely calm. Eerily so, even. He felt nothing but a confident assuredness that this was everything he had wanted to see come to fruition, and it was almost over.

Maybe that was it.

Maybe once this was finally done with, he could get that rush of excitement and relief that he had been missing for so long. Maybe once all of the things that had been standing in his way were finally gone for good, he could celebrate.

John would just have to wait and see.

An enforcer stepped up to his door as John pulled his car to a stop at the curb. The man opened the driver's door, and waited for John to exit the vehicle. He handed the keys over, but gave the enforcer a severe look.

"Only move it a block," John said. "No more."

"You sure?"

"Just keep it out of the immediate zone. I need to drive home, but I don't want to walk a damn mile to get my car after this is over."

"All right."

John turned to find his cousin was also getting out of his car. Two Marcello Capos had also been invited to the meeting of the bosses. Andino allowed Darren Calabrese to pick the venue of the meeting because really, it wouldn't make a difference.

It was all going to end the same way.

"No one else is coming?" John asked as Andino approached.

"We don't need anyone else."

John nodded. "Your call."

"Soon to be yours, too."

"Don't get ahead of yourself."

Andino clapped John hard on the shoulder, and turned them both to face a rundown restaurant that looked as though it had been out of business for a while. "John, I already told you. There's a boss's seat waiting for you, and that's right where you're headed. There's no argument. It's already been done."

Well ...

Almost.

"Hey," Andino snapped. "Be careful with that fucking thing, you foolish fucker."

The enforcer carrying a blue crystal vase full of colorful tiger lilies damn near missed a step at his boss's shout. The man straightened up, and held the vase a little more carefully, and took his steps a bit slower as he crossed the road.

Across the street, another enforcer stood waiting. He was the one who took the flowers from the first man, albeit with a hell of a lot more care. John watched the exchange with an amused fascination.

"Fucking idiots," Andino grumbled. "They're going to end this before I can even begin it."

"Give him some credit. I still can't believe you went with *flowers*."

Andino shrugged. "Haven thought it was a nice touch."

John smirked. "There's something cold about your wife."

"I know. It's what I love best about her. You ready?"

"Are they inside?"

"According to our men, yes," Andino said.

John nodded. "Then yes, I am ready."

The two cousins crossed the street without as much as a look around them. They didn't have a reason to be concerned until they got inside the restaurant, and even then, it was only because they needed to get out alive afterward. Neither of the two were very concerned about an ambush of sorts from the Calabrese for several reasons.

For one, the Calabrese *needed* this meeting to go well. Darren was out to get something from the Marcellos—be it more control, power, or influence in New York—but he needed an actual agreement to get it. And he needed to be alive, too. Earning himself a grave would do absolutely nothing for his end goal.

For two, killing John and Andino wouldn't achieve very much for Darren, anyway. In the grand scheme of the Marcello family, John was only a simple Capo. Two other Capos had come along, too, although they would remain outside in waiting vehicles until the others left. Killing a Capo would mean nothing except more bloodshed.

As for Andino?

He was just one of three high-ranking men in the Marcello family. Killing the underboss—as no one outside the family was aware that Andino had taken control of the Marcello organization—was not going to cause the family to crumble. There were still two other men with heavy influence and control.

Darren was greedy.

He made rash decisions.

He was violent.

Stupid, though?

No, he wasn't stupid.

The one enforcer stayed back a step, and kept hold of the flowers as Andino and John stepped up to the entrance of the rundown business. The other enforcer—the one Andino had snapped at—came to open the door of the place, and let John and Andino inside.

John let Andino go first, as a boss should, and then followed right behind. He was entirely unsurprised by the ripped up floors, overturned tables, and wires hanging from an exposed ceiling. Who knew who owned this place, but John was grateful for the venue. It didn't look like the place had been used in a while, or that anyone had worked in it for God knew how long.

It meant less clean up.

Less lives lost.

Small blessings.

Darren Calabrese stood in the middle of the floor flanked by three men. He kept his hands folded at his back as he stared expressionless at John and Andino. None of them moved until the other two Marcello enforcers had also entered the restaurant, and stood waiting behind their respective boss.

It was all about the respect in Cosa Nostra.

John doubted that would ever change.

"I'm happy to see you can follow direction," Andino said dryly. "Three men to you, and three to us."

"Inside," Darren agreed.

John smiled. "We're aware of your men outside, and how many there are. We had a three block radius scouted before we ever even came within five miles of this place today, Darren. We're not stupid."

Darren's cheek twitched, but otherwise, he gave nothing away. "I can assume the two of you brought a small army of your own, then."

"You can," Andino said.

"Where is Dante?" Darren let his arms fall open to his sides, as though he were asking for some kind of gift to be handed to him. "I thought I would be dealing with the boss today, and not his underboss, and a useless Capo, too. What good does that do me?"

John let the insult roll off his shoulders. It wasn't meant to do anything but be fucking offensive, anyway. "It wasn't very fucking long ago that you too were nothing more than a Capo, Darren. It would do you well to remember that."

Darren altogether ignored John, not that it was surprising. After all, the asshole had spent a whole week sending John package after package detailing how much of a shame he thought the Marcello man was.

"The boss?" Darren asked Andino again. "Where is he?"

"You *are* looking at the boss of the Marcello family," Andino said, smirking just enough to look self-serving *and* smug as fuck at the same time. It was a look to be respected and appreciated, really. "I can't help it if you're unable to keep up with the politics of families outside of yours, Darren."

The enforcers flanking Darren passed looks between one another. Darren, to his credit, barely blinked a lash at Andino's admission. It didn't matter—John knew the truth. The damage was done for Darren with his men in that moment. He had likely assured them that this would all go exactly according to his plans because he knew all there was to know about the Marcellos.

The truth was clear now.

He knew nothing.

It was simple, but effective.

A man needed all the faith and trust from his men that he could get in this business. It was the one thing that might save his life, or end it at one point or another. It was a good lesson to learn, and one of the first John had ever been taught when it came to being a made man navigating this very dangerous life.

"Then you misrepresented to me what this meeting would be," Darren said, taking a step forward. "This is a farce, and I can't say that I want to continue—"

"Are you interested in settling this feud once and for all, or continuing on with the bloodshed?" Andino interrupted with a cocked brow. "Because I know which category the Marcellos fall under, and as I told you when I asked for this meeting, we are willing to do whatever necessary to finish this *appropriately*."

Darren hesitated in his next step. "Anything? You're absolutely sure about that?"

"I said what I said."

"And we don't repeat ourselves," John added for his cousin.

Darren passed John a look that lingered for a beat too long before he said, "I want him to leave, then."

"John stays."

"You're making this very difficult for me to want to work with you, Andino."

At that, John scoffed.

All eyes turned in his direction.

"Work with us?" John asked.

"Him, not *you*. I have little interest in working with a dishonored made man, regardless of which asshole is his father, or which bitch pushed him out into the world."

John's lips curved into a wicked smile. "Too far, Darren. You went a little too far with that one."

"Deny any of it is true."

"I don't have to do anything for you, and frankly, if you thought *I* would ever work with you after the things you've done, you're the one who was mistaken."

Andino looked to John, and nodded.

John looked back to Darren. "You were right—this was a farce. A fake meeting. Nothing could ever come from it. Much like you being the boss in your organization. A little prince playing pretend in a king's throne, Darren. That's all you are."

He turned his back to Darren, adding, "And I will greatly enjoy taking that throne, and your crown from you."

"I'll kill you, Marcello!"

Darren's worlds stabbed uselessly into John's back.

They meant nothing.

One of the enforcer's followed John out, while Andino stayed a bit behind in the doorway with the other one.

"Shame," Andino said behind John, "as this could have gone down far differently. Or ... not. Here, a gift, Darren. We thought you might appreciate a kind gesture from us."

John didn't look back to see what happened, but he knew what the plan was. The flowers would be set directly in front of the door—carefully, of course, as to shake them or move them too much would set off the chemical mixture inside the vase. The door would be closed, and Darren would need to move the vase before he could exit the place.

A seemingly innocent vase.

Innocuous flowers.

All harmless, really.

Until they weren't ...

"Move your ass," Andino barked at the enforcer.

John finally looked over his shoulder.

Through the front window of the rundown restaurant's door, he saw Darren kick the vase of flowers. The explosion was beautiful.

Not as big as they had hoped, but enough to blow the windows out.

Enough to knock them to the ground.

John wasn't sure how long he stayed like that—prone on his back and staring up at a clear early October sky—but the sound of laughter brought him back down to reality.

It took him a minute to realize it was his own laughter.

He was the one laughing.

He finally felt that relief.

It was glorious.

CHAPTER FIFTEEN

"PASS ME THE bowl of flour, and I'll show you what to do if it seems like the dough gets a little too sticky," Siena said.

Greta pushed the bowl across to Siena, while Giulia hoisted herself up on the edge of the counter. The two girls watched silently as Siena added just a tablespoon of flour at a time to the bread dough before she rolled it and kneaded it again and again.

"You have to make sure it mixes all the way through—you don't want one part of the bread to have too much flour while the other parts don't have enough. Always make sure you knead it really well after you add any extra in."

"What would happen if the dough was too wet when it cooked?" Giulia asked.

"Depends, really. It might be too dense—it might not rise high enough. It could still be doughy in spots, and it'll have that dough-ish taste."

"You can't just … cook it for longer?" Greta asked. "Make up for the difference, or something?"

"No, it doesn't work that way, unfortunately. Bread has to be made just so—even the dough has to be the right consistency every time to make it perfect. If you add something, or take something away, you have to account for it somewhere else. If your kitchen is hotter than normal, you need to account for that, too."

"Ugh," Greta groaned.

Giulia echoed her sister's sentiment. "This seems like a lot of work for just *bread*."

"Sure, but if you master bread, then the rest is kind of easy at the end of the day. And we Italians do love us some bread."

"Truth," Greta said.

"It's really that particular, though?" Giulia asked. "I feel like I should have been taking notes from the start, or something."

Siena laughed a little, and gave her half-sister a smile. "The only thing more fickle than a man on this earth, is bread."

Greta and Giulia passed a grin between one another. Their girlish laughter filled up Siena's apartment. She took the moment to slow her kneading of the dough, and soak in their happiness. So much had been taken from these two young girls, and she wondered how much they would have to sacrifice before they could finally get their own happily ever after.

She was the one left caring for them a lot of the time. Sure, their useless aunt gave them a home to live in, and beds to sleep in. The woman fed them, and kept them clothed—*mostly*. That was the extent of their aunt's involvement in their lives.

She didn't care for them on a deeper level. They had no woman to go to when they needed a private chat. They had no voice to be their reason, or to give them direction when they needed that, too. They were, essentially, alone.

"Ma tried to teach me how to make bread once," Greta said.

Siena passed the older of the two girls a look. "How did that turn out?"

"I wasn't paying attention the way she wanted me to. She got mad. I got mad. We yelled a lot, and she kicked me out of the kitchen. I guess …"

"What?"

Giulia picked at her nails, avoiding everyone's gaze and looking all kinds of awkward for the moment. It wasn't very often the girls talked about their mother. They buried all their feelings, and memories of their mother somewhere deep, and kept them locked up tight where no one could reach. Siena didn't think that was very healthy to do, honestly. Someday, they were going to have to deal with the murder of their mother, and the things that preceded it.

Right now, though, they couldn't do any of that. It wasn't a topic that Kev or Darren had wanted them to chat about, really. It might upset Coraline, after all.

Not that Siena's mother made very much of an effort to be around the girls. Because she absolutely didn't if she could help it.

"I guess," Greta continued after a long stretch of silence, "I wish I had listened now. Been better that day—on a lot of other days, too."

Without even thinking about it, Siena pulled her hands away from the bread, and reached out to her half-sister. She touched the girl's cheek with a dough- and flour-covered hand to give Greta a gentle pat. It left fingerprints of flour behind, but Greta didn't seem to mind.

"Your ma loved you, Greta. Regardless if you were terrible, or wonderful. She's your ma, so you know what that means, right?"

"What?"

"That she loved you just as much on your best days as she did on your worst days. That's what good mothers do. And I know you have a whole bunch of good memories to think about, but sometimes the bad ones slip through, too, right?"

Greta shrugged. "It makes me feel guilty sometimes."

"Don't. Okay? Just don't. Focus on all the good because you are going to have more than enough bad moments in your life to focus on at a later date. Right now, just focus on all the good you remember."

Her sister nodded. "Okay."

"Back to bread?"

Both girls agreed.

Siena made quick work of breaking the dough into three chunks. She passed a piece to Greta and Giulia before pushing the bowl of flour over, too.

"Put a little on your hands, but not too much," she said. "Keeps it from sticking. We'll knead it a bit more, and then put them in bowls to rise for thirty minutes to an hour."

"Okay," the girls echoed.

Siena continued chatting with her half-sisters while they worked just to keep them occupied in a verbal way. At least then, she hoped their attention would not go back to darker places in their thoughts.

Or ... that was her hope.

In the background of their work, the television played through breaking news on the major news network Siena liked to keep on daily. The news was always depressing, but in some ways, it also reminded her that her life could be a hell of a lot worse in ways.

Unfortunately, she also kept it on for another reason. Her family—and John's, at times—seemed to be the focus of New York related news a lot lately. Organized crime was making a comeback; not that it ever went away, the idiots. The streets were bloodier than ever between the crime families, and rivaled the Chicago War from two decades earlier.

Attention was never good in their life.

It hindered business.

Siena slowed in her work as a shot of a street came into view on the television.

"Some sort of explosive device was detonated on ..."

Siena blinked at the reporter's words. Not because of what the woman said, but because of what she saw on the television. She recognized the street they were showing—a Brooklyn street full of small businesses. Mostly restaurants, but a few other vendors, too.

And then the shot changed to a building. Windows blown out, and a door ripped off the hinges. The front charred from fire, and smoke still billowing out from the broken, gaping holes of the business.

Explosive device.

"A restaurant that was undergoing renovations and owned by—"

"Darren," Siena said quietly.

Her sisters looked to her, and then back to the television screen. They, too, stopped in their work to take in what they were seeing on the news.

The reporter continued talking. "Sources tell us prior to the incident, they had witnessed several men entering the restaurant at different times. The police have, so far, suggested it looked to be a meeting of sorts between the Calabrese and Marcello crime families. As you know, Gordon and Marney, there has been quite a bit of news about those families lately."

The shot switched back to the anchors at the station. A man and a woman with their makeup pressed with powder, and their hair perfectly coifed back with not a strand out of place. Siena always thought they looked sort of like dolls in a way.

Fake, and unrealistic.

Unmoving, and unfeeling.

"We have reports of deaths on the scene, too, don't we?" the woman asked.

"At least two."

Siena held her breath.

She *wondered* ...

She *feared* ...

Her hands started shaking against the counter top.

Please give a name ... please, please, please give a name, but don't be his name. Don't be John's name. Give me a name.

"Others were apprehended at the scene," the reporter on location stated. "Of course, the police were unwilling to release the names, as they have not yet stated what or *who* was the cause of the explosion, but we did get word elsewhere of the names of suspects apprehended."

Siena gripped the edge of the countertop so tightly that her knuckles turned white from the pressure. She didn't dare look away from the screen for fear she might miss something important. Her stomach had all but climbed up into her throat, while her heart had altogether stopped beating for the moment.

"Several members of the Marcello family—Andino and Johnathan Marcello being the two most recognizable figures apprehended at the moment," the reporter continued.

Siena felt like her fucking knees gave out, though somehow, she managed to stay upright. Her stomach dropped back down into place while her heart began a slow beat once more.

Not dead, not dead ... not dead.

Just in custody.

A knock echoed on Siena's apartment door, but she was only half paying attention at that point. It took Greta poking her in the shoulder when the knock echoed a second time for Siena to snap out of her daze.

As she crossed the space to answer the door, she kept reminding herself that apprehended and in custody did not necessarily mean arrested. It simply meant they were with police, and likely being questioned.

Was it good?

Fuck no.

It was still *workable*.

This life taught her that.

Siena was still looking over her shoulder at the television when she opened the door to her apartment. She didn't even get the chance to turn around and greet whoever was at her door before a form flew at her.

"You little *bitch*!"

Siena first felt her mother's fingernails rake down her face before Coraline slapped her. The surprise attack—and the sting of the pain—was enough to set her off-balance. Her vision swam as she put her hands up in front of her face to defend whatever might be coming next, but it did no good.

Her mother hit her again.

And then again.

Unsteady from the surprise, Siena lost her footing as she quickly tried to back away from Coraline's attack. Her back hit the floor hard enough to take her breath right out of her lungs, but she didn't even have enough time to recover from that.

"How *dare* you?" Coraline screeched.

The sharp points of her mother's heels hit her body. Her sides, and her temple.

"Ma, stop!"

"You knew, didn't you? You knew what they were going to do! I warned you, Siena, I *warned you*!"

Another kick landed to the side of Siena's head.

She was not a weak girl—not an incapable woman. She could and would defend herself, but something made her turn away from her mother's attack, and simply *protect* herself instead of fighting back.

Maybe because it was her mother. She had once loved his woman. She thought Coraline loved her, too.

It was painful to be wrong.

So very painful.

"Stop!"

"Leave her alone!"

Greta and Giulia's voices filtered through the ringing in Siena's ears. That last kick to her head had done a number because her vision was fuzzy, and everything sounded like it was under water.

Siena blinked in just enough time to see one of her half-sisters fly at Coraline. She wasn't sure which one, but the other girl came right after her, too.

Coraline landed on her back as she was shoved away from Siena's prone form. It took another few seconds, and more shouting, before Siena finally gained enough of her bearings to try and move. She rolled over to her knees, and coughed painfully as she clutched her head.

"Little whores," Coraline spat, standing up slowly. "Just like your mother."

"Say that again, and I'll cut your fucking tongue out," Greta hissed.

Siena looked to the side to see Greta wielding a knife. One of the kitchen knives Siena had used earlier for their lunch.

"What are you going to do, little girl?" Coraline taunted. "Do you honestly think you could use that on me?"

"Try me," Greta urged right back.

This was getting worse by the second.

So bad.

"Ma, *leave*," Siena whispered.

Goddamn.

Her head pounded.

It hurt … bad.

"Leave," Siena said louder. "Now!"

Siena looked at the floor, and the lines of the hardwood seemed to swim. She only heard the slam of the apartment door before her sisters were at her side again.

"It's all right, it's fine," Siena tried to assure them.

Greta touched the side of Siena's face, and her fingertips came back red. "You're bleeding."

"It's fine."

"Giulia, get something frozen from the freezer for her head," Greta barked.

"Okay!"

"I'm *fine*," Siena said.

Then, she promptly vomited all over the floor.

Yeah, that wasn't good.

Greta made Siena look her in the eyes. "She kicked you really hard in the head. A lot. Maybe you should go to the—"

No.

She had to stay.

What if John came?

What if …

"It's fine," Siena repeated.

She was becoming a broken record.

Greta frowned. "I'm sorry you don't have a good ma, either."

Yeah.

Siena was sorry for that, too.

"There's a phone under my bed in a box," Siena said, struggling with every word. "A shoebox—it's black, like the phone. There's a contact. John. Just … call until he answers."

"John?"

"John," Siena echoed.

And then everything went black.

• • •

Siena was alternating between icing the lump on the side of her head, and pressing the frozen bag of mixed vegetables to her cheek where Coraline had scratched her viciously. The scratches felt like they were on fire whenever something cold wasn't being pressed against them to level out the heat.

At least, her vision had cleared and her head had stopped pounding. That only took a good six hours. She probably should have listened to Greta, and took the young girl's advice to go to the hospital.

Siena likely had a concussion, and needed to be looked at. Still, she stayed at her apartment. Neither Greta, nor Giulia left, either. In fact, they stayed right by Siena's side the entire time to make sure she was okay. They wouldn't let her sleep, or even close her eyes for more than a couple of seconds at a time.

They were sweet girls.

Good girls.

They did not deserve the hell that had been brought down on their lives by their half-brothers. Siena was never more aware of that fact than now.

"Greta?"

"Hmm?"

The girl looked over at Siena with worry creasing her brow. Siena instantly wanted to take that away. Greta was only seventeen. She didn't need to be worrying herself with the problems of the adults around her.

This life made girls grow up too early.

It always did.

"Ginevra is in Canada," Siena said quietly.

Greta stilled. "What?"

"On the day she was supposed to get married, a gift was sent to her private room when it was just me and her in there. That was intentional— planned ahead of time. The gift was a letter with instructions, new identification documents, and a way to get out of the country."

Tears filled Greta's eyes.

Giulia had fallen asleep on the chair across from where they sat on the couch.

"So, she's okay?" Greta asked.

"She is great," Siena said, "as far as I know now. I haven't gotten any information on her since she left. That was kind of the deal."

"Will she come back?"

"Maybe."

"When could she come back?" Greta pressed.

"When it's safe."

When all the men threatening her safety and life are gone from this city. Siena didn't say that out loud, though. She knew they were one step closer after today to finally getting Ginevra back to her younger sisters.

Kev was gone.

Darren ... might be, too.

Siena didn't really know at this point. She had been watching the news, and waiting for any snippet of information that might give the names of the two men deceased from the explosion at the restaurant. Nothing had come up yet.

Her mother had not come back for round two, thankfully, but that also meant she couldn't get any information out of Coraline, either. The enforcer who had dropped the girls off earlier that day had yet to come back and get them.

Siena figured that was because too much was going on outside of her apartment at the moment. A whole world of new trouble had just popped up for all the men of the Calabrese family, and it was all about damage control right now.

They needed to get this situation under control before they even considered dealing with something less important. They had better things to deal with than two *principessas* who needed nothing more than to be returned to their aunt's home.

Greta and Giulia likely didn't even mind.

Neither did Siena.

"Okay."

"I'm sorry I didn't tell you months ago," Siena said softly.

Greta shook her head fast, and wiped her eyes with the heels of her palms. "No, it's okay. I understand, really. Thank—"

The front door of Siena's apartment opened with such force that it smashed into the wall. The noise made Siena jump, Greta duck, and woke a very confused Giulia up from her sleep.

Jerking in surprise was not a good thing for Siena's current state. Pain swelled in the side of her head all over again, and made her double over on the couch. She pressed the frozen bag of mixed vegetables harder to her temple in a shitty attempt to relieve some of the sudden pressure. Her stomach threatened to revolt all over again.

"Oh, my God," she groaned.

"Siena? Shit … babe."

John's voice was the only thing that felt remotely *good* in that moment. Siena didn't even have time to lift her head up before he was in front of her. Kneeling down, his hands found her thighs, and his gaze locked on hers.

Warm hazel.

True love.

Calm and beautiful.

For a second, her vision focused, and Siena was good again. At least, for a moment.

"Don't move," she told him.

John's brow furrowed. "Why would I move?"

"Just … don't. If you move, I might get dizzy again, and I don't want to puke."

"What happened?"

His harsh demand made her flinch. He didn't miss it.

"Shit, sorry. Sorry, babe. I would have been here sooner after I got the messages on my phone, but I wasn't even given my phone until they released me once my attorney got there. Here, let me look at you."

Soft fingertips drifted over her face. The sensation was such a stark contrast to the pain and heat coursing through her head. He peeled her fingers away from her cheek, and then convinced her to drop the frozen bag, too.

Siena watched John's gaze drift over her face, and injuries. His fingers followed the same path—careful not to press too hard, or hurt her as he checked her out. As the silent seconds ticked on, she could plainly see his rage growing.

He hid it, sure.

She still saw it.

"What happened?" he asked one more time.

Calmer.

Quieter.

Still as stone.

"It's okay," she told him.

John made a grunt under his breath—dismissive, yet heated. "Nope. Try again."

"Her mom," Greta said. "She came over, yelled at Siena, and hurt her."

John's gaze darted to the girl beside Siena. "And who are you?"

"One of Matteo's other daughters," Siena muttered.

To his credit, John didn't blink a lash at that. Nor did he out the fact he had been the one to take Greta's beloved father away, either.

"Well … hello," John said. "You were the one that called me?"

Greta nodded.

"Thank you."

"Siena looks after us," Greta said as though that explained her loyalty.

"Who are *you*?" Giulia asked.

John glanced over his shoulder at the girl. "Johnathan."

"Johnathan *who*?"

"Marcello."

The two girls passed looks between one another like that explained *everything*. Their silent conversations could sometimes be annoying, but in that moment, Siena had other things to focus on.

John, mostly.

Always John.

His hands cupped her face, and he brought her in closer. He pressed a soft kiss to her lips, and a tear escaped the corner of Siena's eye. He made quick work of wiping it away, though.

"I saw the news," Siena whispered.

John nodded. "It went well."

"Could have told me."

"This wasn't really my show. More … Andino's."

Siena nodded once. "Oh, I see."

"Your head has one hell of a knot on it, and those scratches look really bad." John looked her injuries over *again*. "I don't like the looks of this—you should go get checked out."

"I'm fine."

"You're not fine."

"I *am*."

"Siena, I am taking you to—"

"I can't leave, John," she said. "I don't have an enforcer with me, and it'll only cause problems. I wanted you here because I was scared."

A small smile edged at the corner of John's lips. "You can do whatever the fuck you want to do. Don't you realize what happened today?"

"A lot happened."

And she was still trying to figure it all out. She supposed her scrambled head wasn't really helping her case at the moment.

"Darren is as good as dead, Siena," John murmured, holding her face so she couldn't look away from him. "The cops let it slip when they were hounding me—he's on life support until someone pulls the plug, and he's not coming out of it. This is almost over. We're so fucking close, love."

A small swell of relief threatened to drown Siena.

Reality was a quick bitch, too.

Darren wasn't *dead*.

Not entirely.

Not yet …

"Everything is going to change," John said. "Starting now. I promise."

• • •

Siena stared down at the prone form resting in the hospital bed. Monitors beeped, displaying heart rate, oxygen levels, and a non-existent brain function. Stiff, white blankets that had been warmed before being brought in were tucked firmly around Darren's form.

According to the nurse, the blankets were new. Over seventy percent of Darren's body had suffered severe burns in the blast, and being covered was typically considered a major no-no. However, the lack of brain function, and the stress his body was under meant Darren had not been placed on the burn victim ward.

There was no point.

John had been right.

Darren was not coming back from this.

A tube down his throat attached to a respirator kept him breathing. His heart only continued to beat because of the oxygen being pumped into his body. His brain was not working, and thus, not allowing his body to breathe on his own.

CT scans, MRIs, and reflective tests all showcased the same thing for Darren. He was, entirely, braindead. He was not going to wake up one day, and he was not going to get better as time passed on.

Ever.

The nurse and doctor moved quietly throughout the room. They worked in tandem which was interesting to watch. As soon as the doctor reached for something, the nurse came right behind him to finish what he left behind. Or better yet, should he need something, the nurse was already there to fulfill his unspoken request.

It was only once their attention turned back on Siena that she straightened a bit more, and waited for their next move.

"You can wait to sign the documents, if you so choose," the doctor reminded her.

"My lawyer was clear. We went through the proper channels. Darren has no wife, no children, and at the moment, no parent we can make contact with. I am—according to the law, and the judge that signed off on my lawyer's petition—Darren's only next of kin. And I made my decision."

She said all of this with a cold detachment that likely didn't escape the doctor or nurse's notice. At the moment, it was the best she could offer them. She *had* gone through a lawyer to get this finished—it only took about a week when her mother couldn't be contacted, and did not appeal the decision to make Siena her brother's next of kin capable of making life or death decisions for his person.

Who knew where Coraline was?

Siena had no idea.

"Could we get started?" Siena asked.

The doctor cleared his throat, and nodded once. "Yes, sure, of course. Once you sign the documents, and witness us turn off the machines, and remove the tube, you will not need to remain in the—"

"I will stay."

The man gave her a look. "Many don't prefer to stay and watch, and it can take a while."

Siena stared back, unaffected. "I will stay."

Until the bastard's heart stopped beating.

Until he couldn't hurt them again.

Until she was safe.

Her sisters.

John.

Siena would fucking *stay*.

"Okay," the doctor murmured. "Let's get started on these final forms."

The next several minutes were a blur. Siena checking boxes, and signing her signature on too many dotted lines to count. It was all the same thing over and over again, simply reworded a different way, and on a new page.

Did she understand …

Does she agree …

No liability …

"And here," the doctor said one final time.

Siena scribbled her name a little harder than before.

Done and done.

She stepped back, and found a chair in the corner of the room to make herself comfortable for the next little while. For all the machines and wires hooked up to Darren, it took only a couple of quick minutes to remove them from his body.

"Would you leave that one on?" Siena asked.

The doctor hesitated as his hand hovered over the monitor. "You want me to leave the heart rate monitor on?"

She needed to know.

She *had* to.

"Yes, if it's possible."

The nurse and doctor shared a look before the man nodded once at her. "Yes, I can leave it on. It might be upsetting, however, and—"

"I can assure you it won't be."

And it wasn't.

When his heart stopped ...
When it was still ...
When it was silent ...
Darren was dead.
Siena only felt relief.

• • •

Siena stepped out of the hospital room to find the enforcer that had been placed at the door before she went in had not moved an inch from his post. The man greeted her with a kind smile, and a nod.

"Siena," he said.

Respectful.

Caring.

Soft-spoken.

This enforcer—a man who introduced himself by name, with a smile, and a handshake the first time they met—was not like any other guard Siena had ever had. He did not treat her like a piece of property to *la famiglia* that he was simply protecting.

He was not a Calabrese enforcer.

He was a Marcello enforcer.

And he was hers, now.

John had said everything would change the day the bomb blew a week before, and he had not been lying.

Everything was different.

"Pink," she greeted.

Yep.

That was his nickname.

Pink.

Siena didn't know how he got it, and she didn't care to learn. It just made her smile every time she used it.

"You're the only one who can't say my name with a straight face," Pink said.

"Come on, it's *cute*."

"I've heard all the comments, Siena. They don't surprise me or bother me anymore. Come on, the boss is waiting for you."

"Where did John go?"

"To grab a coffee downstairs."

"Oh."

"He's waiting for you—figured he would get back up here by the time you were done," Pink explained.

Siena shrugged. "It's okay. I don't mind chasing after him."

She had all the time in the world to do that, now.

182

Pink guided Siena through the upper level of the hospital, and then down to the main floor where John had apparently gone. They did not find him at the coffee shop, but rather, outside surrounded by several men.

Most of which, Siena recognized.

They were her brothers' men.

Or … they used to be.

John, in his tweed coat and black Armani suit, with a hand flicking outward to showcase a diamond encrusted Rolex in a dismissive gesture, looked entirely at ease. Despite, apparently, the stiffened postures and angry expressions of the men around him.

"You seem to think you have control now," John said, "or even that *dead* men have control of this family now, and I am not very sorry to inform you that you are all mistaken. Your first—and *last*—mistake with me will be to ever underestimate or question my authority."

"We don't answer to you, Marcello, not now, and not—"

"You will address me as your boss, or as the Don, or you will address me from your broken knees with my gun in your mouth. *Try again.*"

Pink kept Siena back a few steps by holding onto her shoulder with one beefy hand. She saw a few gazes of the men drift in her direction, but they quickly went back to John.

"So, that's how it is, then?" another one asked. "The Marcellos are just going to come in to our organization, and clean fucking house like this?"

"I'm not cleaning anything," John said, "this is *my* house. It has always been mine. Someone else was looking after it for a time. Mind you, they did a shit job about it, but you've got a new boss to correct that issue now."

"This is not your *famiglia!*"

John pointed a single finger at the man, and then looked over at the guy who had driven him and Siena to the hospital earlier while Pink followed behind in Siena's car. "He will be the first to learn. Tonight, don't stall."

"Yes, boss."

The man in question made a move like he was going to come forward, and John didn't wait for him to make the choice. Instead, John was the one to go forward himself until he was standing toe-to-toe with the man.

"Do you have something to say?" John asked. "Now would be the time."

The man swallowed hard. "You're a fucking lunatic. Crazy—a *shame*. No Calabrese man will ever accept you as their boss. You don't have what it takes, and they'll ruin you, Johnathan. Mark my fucking words."

For a brief second, Siena's heart clenched for John. He had been right—everything was changing for them. Starting with the Calabrese family. He and his men had slid into the organization, and within a week's time, made it abundantly clear there was new leadership in charge.

That didn't mean it was easy.

Or that the men were agreeable.

She knew that everything that man had just thrown at John were some of his worst fears being laid out on the ground in front of him to see, and for everyone else to dissect. That he was not good enough—that he would never be.

But they didn't know him.

Not like she did.

Siena caught sight of John's slow, cold smile starting to grow. His next words came out calm, and sure. The most sure she had ever heard him speak.

"This is no longer a Calabrese family—there's a Marcello running this shit now. Keep calling me crazy, and your wife will get you back in pieces. I don't have what it takes? You think this position just *came to me*? You think this isn't mine to take?"

John took another step closer, crowding the man and smiling wickedly all the while. "Check my bloodlines, motherfucker. I was made by men—and raised by men—you can only dream to be. My bloodlines? They're written in fucking red. Grovatti blood. My life? It's written all over this city. Marcello legacy. You'll understand what all that means really soon. It's a promise. I don't break those."

Good God.

She loved this man.

CHAPTER SIXTEEN

"JAIL-GRAY LOOKS like shit on you," John noted.

Andino looked away from the clock on the wall to showcase one of his usual easygoing grins. "Right? But fuck, it was this, or the suit I was wearing last week when they threw me in here."

Yeah, fuck.

"What are you still doing in jail, huh? You should have been out by now, Andi. Arthur Lorde clearly isn't doing what he's supposed to be doing. You're still fucking in here. They've filed charges, man."

Andino shrugged. "But what do they have?"

"Andino—"

"No video surveillance. Darren Calabrese made sure he picked a spot where there were no cameras around to spot us going in and out. No witnesses to say I did anything except *be* there. No *live* victims—the other enforcer Darren brought along died yesterday. They couldn't even hold you and the other guys, John. They have nothing. Arthur is likely just biding his time."

John sometimes wished he could have the same bright optimism as the people around him, but his mind didn't work that way. He first went to the worst place imaginable, and then worked back from that to get to a relatively decent place.

"You're forgetting details," John pointed out.

"Do tell."

"The detectives are hounding everybody. My lawyer's phone won't stop ringing. They're threatening charges on us still, even though they released us. The only reason they're holding you is in hopes they'll get someone else to roll for your sake."

"Maybe someone will do just that," Andino said. "It would be a win-win all the way around the board. I'll get out of this shithole, and they'll get someone to eviscerate on the news, so they don't have to lose face."

"You're missing the point, Andino."

His cousin sighed, and his green gaze drifted to John's. "I'm not, man.

I get this is not going the way I planned. You're right, too. I should have been out of here by now, but at the moment, it is a waiting game. This whole life is one giant waiting game, anyway. I can wait for one more thing, surely."

John knew that feeling.

At first, a little boy waited to grow up, so he could be the same as the men around him. Then the grown-up boy waited to be made. Being a made man only took a man to waiting for several different things—money, honor, death, or jail time.

Funny how that worked.

"Haven is …"

Andino's gaze darted to John again. "What?"

"Your wife is very upset."

Putting it lightly.

Haven Marcello was in one hell of a fit. Damn, the woman wasn't even Italian, but she knew how to raise hell like any good old Italian woman at the end of the day. She was a nasty thing when she thought something or someone was fucking with her life, and her husband.

Not that John blamed her.

This shit was bad.

"You'll figure it out," Andino told John.

"Was that part of your plan, too?" he asked.

Andino smiled. "What, leaving you to hold the ball for me?"

"I suppose you could put it that way."

"Man, I have held the ball for you time and time again in our life. I didn't mind doing it, either. No, it wasn't part of the plan, but here we are. I have all the faith that you'll do whatever you need to do, so we can get back to controlling this fucking city like we were always meant to."

John nodded. "Ride or die, right?"

"Since the days we were fucking born, John."

Yep.

It wasn't long before the damn jail guard came around to knock his baton against the metal table to signal it was time to wrap up the visit. John didn't know if that was some kind of shit the jail had worked out with the detectives or not, but they didn't allow Andino's visitors to linger for too long.

Mostly because the bastards couldn't stay too close. Certainly not close enough to overhear their conversations—the man was allowed privacy, after all, even if said man was a fucking criminal in jail on suspicion of murdering a handful of people with a simple explosive device.

"Tell my wife—"

John looked at Andino, noting the way his words cut off. "What? I'll pass whatever along. I know taking your calls upsets her."

So was the way with women married to a man like them. Those ladies fought tooth and nail for their men's freedom, but at the end of the day, they were still women looking down a long, hard road that might just lead them straight to hell.

It was a big undertaking.

It wasn't for the faint of heart.

"I was going to say you could tell her to relax," Andino said, grinning a little, "but I don't think you could handle Haven in one of her moods. She's not like Siena, you know?"

"Definitely not as mild-mannered and sweet, no."

Andino smirked. "She can be. You just have to stroke her the right—"

"Thanks for that, but no thanks."

His cousin's laughter lit up the visitation area. "Tell her I love her, man."

"Will do, Andi."

It was the best a man in this life could offer to a woman he loved. His faith, and undying loyalty. He could hope for forever, but promising it was never really a guarantee he could keep. She could share his life, but John wasn't sure the life was ever really theirs to actually *have*.

"I'll be seeing you around," John said, fixing his Armani blazer as he stood.

No goodbyes.

Those were too final.

"Of course you fucking will."

John was collecting the items he had been asked to hand over coming into the jail when a familiar detective saddled in beside him. He only knew who the detective was because the guy was giving his best effort to put Andino behind bars for a twenty to life sentence. He was also the same asshole that had been the one to release John as he taunted him about his cousin.

He shoved his phone, wallet, and a roll of cash into his pants pocket, all the while, ignoring the detective. He wasn't speaking first. Made men didn't talk to cops of any sort if they could help it.

"No greeting for me today?" Detective Rosencauld asked with a shit-eating grin. "Not even a *go fuck yourself* for good measure, John?"

"What do you want?"

John checked the time on his watch, and then headed for the entrance of the jail. Rosencauld followed close behind at the same time, never missing a step with John. It was both amusing and annoying.

"Your visit with Andino didn't last long. Your cousin didn't have orders to give today, or what?"

"I don't take orders from Andino," John replied, opening the doors and heading out into the mid-October day.

Taking over his own organization as a boss meant John answered to only himself, which was something he hadn't realized he needed in the grand scheme of things. It was simply easier when he was the one calling the shots for his own people.

Not that the Calabrese fools made it easy.

"Is that because he's family, or …?"

"That's because none of your fucking business," John said.

Waiting at the side of the road was a black town car. One of John's enforcers—one of several men he had brought over from the Marcello side to help control the Calabrese organization—waited with the door already open to the car. Smoke puffed from the tailpipe, telling him the man had kept the engine running during his visit.

"Have a good day," John said to Rosencauld as he slipped into the back of the car. He went to close the door, but the detective grabbed it at the last second. John gave the man a single look—promised violence silently for stepping in his way. "Do you have something else you need?"

"Just one thing, John."

"Which is what, exactly?"

"No matter who steps in to try and shut this investigation down, I am not going away. Papers can go missing, and witnesses can recant, but I'm still going to be here at the end of the day. Don't forget it."

John only smiled. "Keep reaching. You might actually grab something. Heath."

At the call of his name, the enforcer stepped in to crowd the detective away from the car, and further from John. Heath was a bull of a man—as wide as he was tall, and all muscle, too. He slammed the passenger door shut, and stood in front of it until Rosencauld backed off entirely, and headed for the jail again.

"Fucking asshole," John muttered.

But his mind had found that goddamn detective to be something worth thinking about, apparently. His focus zoned in on the things the man had said, and everything he suggested. Even as Health climbed into the car, and chatted away while he drove, John was still laser focused on a few passing comments from Rosencauld.

No matter how many times John tried to shake the comments, or forget the man who really couldn't do anything to him or Andino as long as everything went right, the thoughts wouldn't leave.

It wasn't even so much the detective as just everything about this whole situation in general. Andino didn't know, but John *had* been working to get his cousin out. He didn't stop—from morning until night. He was sleeping maybe three hours a night, and running all goddamn day, too.

He didn't feel it, though.

Not exhaustion, anyway.

It was everything else that he felt too much of lately. It was everything else that kept his attention obsessive, and unwilling to let him go. He had been taken out of the deep swell of depression, and thrown into the hyper-focused, fixated state he was now.

That probably should have been a sign.

• • •

John's gaze zoned in on the clock as voices echoed around him. Leaning back in the kitchen chair, Siena moved around the arguing men like their raised voices and irritation didn't bother her in the least.

She dropped a kiss to the top of John's head as she passed his chair at the head of the table. It was the only thing to break his focus away from the clock, and the countdown he had begun silently in his head.

"Coffee?" she asked him.

John shook his head once. "No, thanks."

"Cake?"

He smiled, because *fuck*, here she was in his house, and making cake. It was everything he wanted and so much more, but at the same time, he wished that was all they were doing together at the moment.

Instead, they could not focus on the fact they were actually together. That she was with him—had been with him, and waking up in his bed every morning for over a week. No, they had to let other things take center stage in their life at the moment, and deal with it first.

They came second.

"Not right now," he said to her offer of cake.

Siena nodded, and patted his cheek before heading off to the island again. John's attention went back to the clock while the men around him raged on. His family—uncles, and his father.

"Has someone updated Haven today?" Giovanni asked.

John held up a single finger. "She yelled a lot."

Lucian frowned at his son. "I'm sure she's having a difficult time."

"Didn't say I blamed her."

"What about that goddamn deal Andino put in with the District Attorney?" Dante asked. "Arthur, or whatever the fuck his name is. Why hasn't something come of that yet? The boss of the Marcello family cannot remain in lockup for very long. It's *dangerous*."

Gazes drifted to John, but he was still staring at the clock. He felt them looking at him, though, and waiting for a response. He didn't have very goddamn much to give them right now. He knew as much as they did, honestly.

"We're quite aware of how fucking dangerous is it for him to be in there," Lucian snapped back.

John did look away from the clock at that statement. It was very unlike his father to be sharp in his words or tone, but especially to his brothers. Lucian Marcello had long since perfected the art of cold words, and a detached delivery. Even when it came to family. It was how he managed to distance himself from an argument with people he cared about.

"I'm just saying—"

"I know what you're not saying, too, Dante," Lucian muttered. "I don't think we have to worry about someone putting a hit on Andino while he's in lockup. That's not the kind of issue we have been having lately. John has a bribe in with two of the guards as well, so he's being fucking watched as much as we can watch him."

"Scum has a way of surfacing when they think they have a chance to be overlooked, Lucian," Dante replied.

Lucian opened his mouth to respond, but John stepped in to save his father the trouble. He knew his father was speaking for John, in a way. He rarely ever did that, but John's distraction at this meeting was not going unnoticed, either. He couldn't exactly help it at the moment.

Talking would do nothing.

Talking *had* done nothing.

John needed to do something.

"I will figure it out," John said simply.

Dante looked at John, and so did Giovanni. John's father, on the other hand, only leaned back in his chair like he knew the discussion was just about over with entirely. Lucian was smart that way—he could recognize when John had found his limit of politeness for the day. John had found his limit.

"And just how—"

"I will let you know," John said, standing from his chair. "I shouldn't have to make this clear, but this was a plan Andino put into motion. It was his choice to make, and he knew the risks. It was a plan he brought me in on for obvious reasons."

John's gaze drifted to where Siena was wiping down the island counter. She kept her gaze on her work, but he had no doubt she was listening to him. The woman was smart like that, and he appreciated it.

"So that means it's our issue to clean at the end of the day," John continued, giving Dante and Giovanni a look. "Let us do that without stepping in where you're only stepping on my fucking toes."

"John—"

He held a single hand up, and then just walked away from the table and conversation altogether. He left his father, and his uncles behind.

John had said his peace.

He gave his order.

He meant it.

"Where is he going?" Giovanni demanded.

"We're not done talking, John," Dante called.

"Actually," Lucian said, "he is done, and he can be done whenever he wants to be, brothers. Benefit of being the boss—a benefit you used all the damn time, Dante. A boss is a boss is a boss, even if he is the boss of another family. He said what he said. It's done. Let it be done."

• • •

"John?"

"Hmm?"

"What are you doing?"

"Looking for the fucking cake, Siena."

"What?" she asked.

Her sleepy confusion might have been cute any other time if John wasn't so goddamn fixated on finding the cake she had mentioned the night before. He felt her come closer as he peered into the fridge again, and moved things around.

There wasn't even that much in there. It wasn't like the fucking cake had got out, and walked away or some nonsense.

"Did you put it in the cupboard or something?" he asked.

Because it wasn't on the counter in a dish, either.

Standing, he shut the fridge door, and turned to face Siena. She had leaned one hip against the kitchen island like it was going to keep her standing. Her droopy eyelids spoke to how tired she was.

"You want *cake*?" she asked.

John shrugged. "Yeah, the chocolate cake. You had it out yesterday when everybody was here. Where is it?"

He had pretty much gone through his office, and then the living room on a cleaning spree. Everything was meticulously shiny again. There was no dust to be found, but he only felt marginally better, really.

"You want the cake," Siena said again.

John just stared at her. "That's what I said."

"Holy shit, John, it's …" Siena looked at the clock on the wall, blinked twice, and then looked at the watch on her wrist. "It's three in the morning."

"Is it?"

What did that matter?

"I still want the cake," he told her.

Siena shook her head, and rubbed her hand against her eyes. Finally looking a little bit more awake than before, she took another look at him, too. "When did you go to bed, John?"

Well …

"I didn't."

"Why does the living room smell like bleach?"

"I cleaned."

Siena smacked her tongue against the roof of her mouth, and nodded. "You didn't sleep last night, either. I saw the shelves on the way down the stairs, too. You moved everything around again."

"I didn't like the way it was."

"Yeah, I bet." Siena tightened the belt on her thigh-high, white silk robe, accentuating her tiny waist a bit more. "You just, what, suddenly wanted cake?"

"Listen, I'll just go drive around until I find fucking cake, Siena."

"It wasn't a big cake, John. They finished it off. I'll make you one tomorrow."

No, he kind of wanted one now. And when he fixated on something—like cake at the moment—he was willing to do just about whatever he had to in order to get it. It was not as simple as a promise of *eventually* getting what he wanted.

"That's not going to work," John said.

Her blue eyes showed no surprise, and little concern at that point. "Do I have to take your keys from you?"

"Why would you—"

Siena started ticking things off her fingers in that calm, sweet way of hers that always lulled John into a sense of comfort. "You're not sleeping. You're fixating on different things. Your energy is through the roof. If and when you sleep, it's maybe an hour at a time. You're watching clocks like time is the only thing tangible to understand at the moment. You're distracted at every turn unless it's something you're obsessing over. You're not quite nasty—*yet*—but your moods are flipping up and down depending on who's around at any given time."

John cleared his throat, not bothering to deny anything Siena just said. None of it was a lie, and he knew it. "It'll settle."

"Likely not at the moment," Siena countered. "Leonard has had you off your stabilizers for the antidepressants for what, a couple of weeks or more?"

"Something like that."

"I think you need to get him to switch them back over now, John."

John's ability to rationalize emotions and his situation at any given time was often hindered by his current phase of bipolar. The more hypomanic he became, the less concerned he was over his behavior and actions. He gave it all very little thought because that was just how his disorder worked. Right and wrong became whatever he could get away with a lot of the time.

All over again, he was reminded of how difficult it was to live his life, be a made man in the utmost control of himself, and manage his disorder.

"It's all right," Siena said like she could read his mind. Her hand came up to stroke his jaw, and she pulled him close until the two of them were just a breath apart. Damn, he loved his woman. "We can call Leonard in the morning, and get the meds switched back around."

"Always have my back, huh?"

Siena flashed him a smile. "You know it."

"People *know* now—about me, I mean," he said.

"Yeah, I know."

"But they can't know this shit, too. They can't know these things, too."

"They won't."

Her words felt like a promise.

She didn't break promises, he knew.

"It'll always be just you and me for this," Siena told him. "We'll handle it. It's your life—your business. Those doors are shut, John."

"Where did you come from, *bella donna*? You seem a little too good to be true when it comes to us."

Siena laughed. "I came from Brooklyn. And you know damn well I was made for you, John."

He gave her a quick kiss and said, "Damn right."

"Are you still thinking about the cake?"

John grimaced because, yeah, he kind of was. He really wanted some of that, and it wasn't just going to go away because he knew he was being irrational. "I can't—"

"Help it, yeah. I know. How about I distract you instead?"

Her tone dripped with sex.

It couldn't be missed.

John grinned. "I'll give you a head start."

Siena cocked a brow. "A head start?"

"Mmm, make it to the bed, and I'll bend you over. Let me catch you, and you'll suck me off and get fucked right then and there."

Her eyes widened, and glinted with lust. "That sounds like a win-win for me."

"Me, too. You get three seconds. *Go.*"

John's attention switched from chocolate cake to sex just like that. All it took was Siena darting away from him with a sexy, teasing wink thrown back over her shoulder. Her robe flicked outward as she spun around the island, and gave him the briefest peek at the swell of her bare ass.

Damn.

"You're not wearing panties?" he called after her.

"Nope."

Sweet and sexy all at once.

John groaned. "That's unfair. Had I known that, I wouldn't have given you a head start, Siena."

"Too late!"

Her voice echoed to him from outside the kitchen.

"Fucking tease."

Then, Siena's head popped back in the entryway of the kitchen. "Better make it worth my while, John."

Just as fast, she was gone again.

"Yep, time's up, babe."

Only her laughter answered him back.

John discarded clothing as he headed after Siena. He didn't really have that much on, anyway. A cotton shirt, and sleep pants. Like her, he hadn't pulled anything on underneath his nighttime clothes. His shirt hit the kitchen floor, and by the time he got to the staircase and could see Siena just reaching the top, he had shoved his sleep pants down, too.

Siena left her robe hanging off the bannister. He caught sight of her bare tits as she turned at the top of the stairs, and then quickly disappeared. But not before she graced him with a sensual smile that promised all kinds of sin.

Jesus.

"You're going to kill me, *donna*."

"I love you too much for that."

John rounded the top of the stairs only to be tackled from the side by Siena. Her unexpected attack came out of nowhere. He expected her to be down the hall in the bedroom, but apparently, that was not her plan.

He lost his footing, but somehow managed to keep ahold of both of them as they tumbled to the floor. His dark laughter lit up the hallway, but it quickly turned into a low groan when Siena's lips found his throat.

Her kisses trailed lower over his chest, and down to his stomach. Her fingernails dragged soft lines down his skin, making his nerves come alive, and his skin heat under her touch.

She barely had to do anything at all to drive him crazy. A simple touch. A quick kiss. A lingering look. One of her softly whispered words.

Sex was one thing.

Sex with Siena was something else entirely for John.

"Jesus Christ," he grunted when her hand snaked around his cock. A firm grip answered his harsh words, and then she stroked him as she leaned back up over his body at the same time. Her lips hovered over his, and her blue eyes locked with his gaze. "I think you like this, babe."

"Hmm, what?"

"Getting the upper hand on me."

"It doesn't happen very often."

"Do me a favor, huh?"

"What's that?" Siena asked.

"Get your mouth on my dick before I fucking explode."

Siena flashed him a smile, and without another word, she moved lower again. His fingers tangled into her hair as her mouth hovered over the head of his dick. Her tongue snaked out to strike against the tip, and taste him.

"Fucking tease," he told her again.

"*Barely*."

That was all she said before John lost his ability to breathe or speak. She took his cock in from the tip all the way to the base. He felt her throat muscles contract from how deep he was in her mouth, and then her lips closed around him.

Silken lips.

A rough tongue.

Hot wetness.

Christ.

"Love your fucking mouth," he mumbled.

John swore he saw Siena try to grin around his cock. He lost sight of her eyes as she dipped her head back down and swallowed his cock again. He loved the feeling of her mouth tight around his dick, and the way her tongue stroked his shaft as she pulled him out of her mouth once more.

Still, he needed to see her.

"Look at me, Siena."

Instantly, her eyes were back on him.

Blazing blue.

Raging lust.

Brimming love.

John tugged on Siena's hair with one hand, and grabbed her arm with his other. Yanking her up, he pulled her into his kiss with bruising force. She straddled his waist, and let her fingernails rake over his pecs hard enough to leave stinging red streaks behind. Her wet cunt grinded against his erection in the best fucking way possible.

"Get on me, girl," he growled against her lips. "Stop this fucking teasing, Siena."

She didn't need to be told again. Her hips shifted just the right way, and he positioned his cock where he wanted to be the very most. She fell down on his length with a sigh that melted into a satisfied moan.

"You like that?" he asked. "The way I fill you up, babe?"

"So much, John."

She rocked her hips, and fit her body even tighter against his. Every little flex of her inner muscles hugged him tight. He could feel her honey coating his shaft—he bet he could get her even wetter before they were done, though.

"You gonna ride me?" he asked.

"Yeah."

"You gonna fuck me, my pretty girl?"

"All night, if you want me to."

John grinned. "You better."

Her pace was frantic when she started riding him—a fast, hard rhythm that drove him insane. She tossed her head back, and her hair fell in a wavy, wild curtain over her tits. His hands cupped her breasts, and his thumbs tweaked at her hardened nipples.

"Come for me, Siena, and let me taste that cunt of yours."

"*Fuck.*"

He loved that.

Loved how she swore when she fucked him, and how good she sounded doing it. Not to mention, the way she *looked.*

Good God.

Siena's eyes flew wide, and found his. Her body tensed, and the broken cry that resounded matched the way her cunt squeezed him tight. He pulled her off his cock, and grabbed onto her ass to pull her higher.

Siena's hands slammed into the floor right above John's head as he yanked her down onto his mouth. He was right—she was fucking soaked.

Tart, hot, and slick.

Her arousal flooded his tongue as she finished her orgasm. He wanted to feel her coming again, though. Feel her shaking, and get her skin heating up under his touch all over again. His tongue struck out against her clit over and over.

Relentless. Fast. Unforgiving.

Siena trembled and shook as he ate her pussy until she came a second time.

"Again," he heard her whisper above him.

John kissed the hood of her clit, and looked up to find her watching him. "Whatever you want, babe."

• • •

John ticked his finger over his shoulder, and Pink followed behind at his boss's unspoken request. The enforcer was good like that. All the while, John continued chatting on the phone with the fucker giving him the most trouble at the moment.

"You mean to tell me there's nothing you can do at this point?" John asked.

"My hands are tied," Arthur Lorde said. "Unless you come up with something tangible enough to put reasonable doubt on the table, Andino is stuck where he is."

"The fact nothing ties him to the bomb—"

"It is now wide knowledge he is running the Marcello organization, Johnathan. He was there, in a business with men he was known to be having issues with, and they died. It is not a stretch for them to put two and two together to get four."

"Except you're talking a lot of circumstantial shit right now."

"They're putting things together."

"You agreed to help clear—"

"He did not say he was going to bomb a fucking restaurant in the middle of broad daylight in Brooklyn!"

The fucking bastard on the other end of the phone was lucky that John had been taking his mood stabilizers for a few days. Had they had this conversation a while ago when John's rationale was all but gone, he would have made a quick trip across town to break the motherfucker's teeth out of his head.

"Something tangible, you said?" John asked.

"Enough to cast a bigger shadow for reasonable doubt, at the very least. I need something *more*. Give me that, and this will go away."

"It'll be in your hands by tonight."

John hung up the phone without as much as a goodbye, or a fuck you.

Pink had stepped in front of his boss, and grabbed the door handle of a rundown warehouse in the heart of lower Brooklyn. He pulled it open, and let John walk into the dank-smelling, dark space.

John pointed to the side. "Go turn on the light, and then get your camera ready. Put the bag of shit aside, too."

"Got it, boss."

The second John spoke, the mumblings started from within the darkness. A sorrowful, terrified yammering that instantly made John's irritation spike a little bit higher. He shoved it down, and rubbed his hands together as he took a couple of steps into the darkness.

"No, no, please ... no," it continued on.

John sighed. "Hurry, Pink. It's been a while since he's seen any kind of light."

"Gotta find the fucking switch, boss—oh, there it is."

Instantly, the warehouse was lit up by huge overhead lights that were almost as bright as the goddamn sun. It even made John squint a bit, and he knew what was coming. In the middle of the warehouse, sitting in a pool of his own piss, excrement, vomit, and water that had been thrown on him occasionally was the Capo from the hospital.

The same man who had dared to speak out against John when he could have just as easily stepped back into his place. He was sure the Capo thought John just planned to kill him, but nothing was ever that simple.

At the bright lights overhead—the first time the man had seen any kind of light since that day a week ago—the Capo withered away from the brightness. He still wore his soiled clothing he had been brought in with, although, now also with the added accessories of chains that kept him locked in a spread eagle position on the warehouse floor.

In that pile.

Shit. Piss. Vomit. Water.

It was undignified, really.

Well, he *had* called John a disgrace. John just figured the Capo would appreciate a better understanding of what it felt like to have his dignity taken away altogether. The man had not been touched. Not beaten, or otherwise.

Not yet.

"Jesus, just *kill me*," he mumbled from the floor.

"Stop being dramatic, Roy," John murmured. "It's just a little light."

That probably felt like needles stabbing into the man's eyes.

"Why won't you just kill me?"

"This is better—more amusing," John supplied. "I was curious how much I could take away from you before you finally broke. I refused you light, food, and other than the warehouse, you have no real shelter. I took away your voice, as you can no longer communicate with anyone who will listen, or anyone who cares to. I removed your dignity the first time you pissed yourself, and I took your honor when you begged to be killed. Welcome to the land of the disgraced, Roy. We're a very pleasant bunch. I assure you."

"You're ... you are ..."

"Come on, find a noun or even an adjective to use. Pick one."

The man stammered on more.

John only nodded to himself.

Almost over.

Stepping back a few paces, John bent down to dig through the bag Pink had set aside. He pulled out a few items—a knife, ice pick, and two small handguns. John much preferred something a little heavier when it came to guns. An Eagle was perfect, but these would do the trick.

Keeping the items hidden at his back, John moved closer to Roy again. "I will let you clean up, and give you clothes. You will sit in a chair, and say exactly what you are told to say. And should you disobey, or fight, I will start with the ice pick. It will remove your ability to walk when I break it through your kneecaps before I start removing the tips of your fingers with a knife. Do you understand?"

Wild, terrified eyes stared back at John from the floor.

He only smiled.

"Wh-what?" Roy stammered.

"You will do as you are told, or for the unforeseeable future, this will be your life now. Darkness, humiliation, and pain. I won't kill you, no, but I will have someone come in everyday to remind you of why you should have simply listened to me in the first place. I will feed you just enough to keep you alive, and then make you wish you would die every single day for the rest of your life. You can choose allowing your wife to get your remains back a battered, unrecognizable mess, or something far easier to understand."

Roy gaped.

"Do you understand?" John asked, bringing the ice pick out to swing it back and forth. "Well?"

Weak men were predictable.

Roy was a weak man.

"Y-yes, I understand."

Just a little longer, Andi.

CHAPTER SEVENTEEN

"DO YOU WANT the good news first, or the good news last?" John asked.

Siena grinned. "Well, where does the bad news fit in?"

"That's the thing—there is no bad news."

Her laughter drew the attention of the other guests eating with them at the restaurant table, but John paid his family no mind.

"Just tell me," Siena said.

"Ginevra is coming back to the city this weekend—Greta and Giulia will be the first to greet her."

For a split second, Siena thought her heart had stopped. But no, the beats just took a chance to recharge before picking up an even faster pace.

"Really?"

The girls would be *ecstatic*.

They had been asking … and asking more.

Siena didn't know what to tell them.

"Really," John said.

Not even thinking about it, she leaned over to give him a quick kiss. She planned to pull away just as fast—no need to give everybody else a show, but John held her there for an extra beat in time.

"Since you're sharing news, what do you have on Andino?"

Siena frowned when John's attention drifted away from her momentarily to deal with the men who had filed into the restaurant moments before. His uncles, and his father, each took a seat at the table.

"Good morning to all of you, too," Siena said.

John shot her a sly smile. The rest of them had the decency to at least look a little bit sheepish.

"Our apologies," Lucian said, shrugging. "John is not very good at keeping people updated, and so, we have to chase him around to find out things we need to know. Isn't that right, John?"

John gave his father a look. "I update you all when there are things to report."

"Are there things to report?" Dante asked.

The quietest of the three men—Giovanni, Andino's father—rested back in the chair with a passive expression. It was almost like he didn't want to give off the aura of hope, lest karma come around and see it, only to knock him back down again. Still, the conversation held his attention, and he didn't look away once.

"Good news," John assured.

"How good?" Dante pressed.

"You really didn't think I would get this handled for Andino, did you?"

The three men quieted as they passed looks between one another. Siena cleared her throat, feeling just enough awkwardness to want to move to another table, maybe. John hadn't asked her to do that, though, so she stayed.

Finally, Giovanni spoke first. "We absolutely thought you could—"

"And would," Dante added.

"—get this done for Andino," Giovanni finished. "What we were concerned about was the fact you chose to keep us out of the loop, and went forward with your plans alone. That's not how this family works. We have always been a unit working together."

"Except that's not how *I* have to work," John replied.

Lucian grinned at his son. "And they know that now, too, John. Really. Changes like that take some adjustment, though. I think all things considered, they did pretty well stepping back as much as they could, and giving you faith."

John's jaw ticked—to Siena, a sure sign that his emotional currents were flip flopping back and forth. He was good at hiding when his high to low swings came on strong from others, but he still felt them. She couldn't imagine how hard that must be for him on a daily basis. The kind of struggle unique to him in his circle as no one else could possibly understand what it was like for him.

But his family was learning.

It seemed like they were getting it.

Finally.

Progress was progress. Whether John wanted to admit it or not, that progress would mean the world to him at the end of the day. He often alienated himself from his family, and his history with them kept him at arm's length a lot of the time.

Siena wanted to change that for him. He so loved his family, and they loved him. Look at all they had done for him.

"I think you will find," Dante said, leaning back in the chair, "that this business will be far more accommodating to you, John, once these changes become permanent."

"Which changes are those?" John asked.

Because there were a lot, Siena knew.

John had a good point.

"You controlling your own faction, and answering to yourself," Dante continued. "Andino—someone you trust and are close with—running his own faction, and answering to himself. I think, in ways, you will also ... help Andino in a way."

Giovanni looked to Dante. "How do you figure?"

Lucian laughed. "I think I might know."

"Go for it, then," Dante urged with a flick of his hand.

"John is the only person Andino wouldn't go to war with. Consider how Andino is, Gio ... you know it, and we all know it. His concern and care for others is fickle. He's just as quick to remove his loyalty from someone, as he is to promise it if it suits him. He is a *good* boss, but he is also a volatile one, too. You've seen his games—he manipulates, and he does whatever he needs to in order to get what he wants."

"Except with me," John murmured.

The men's gazes drifted to John again.

"Except with you," Lucian agreed. "With Dante's daughter marrying into the Donati family at the end of next month, you taking over the Calabrese faction, and Andino heading the Marcellos ... we are unlikely to ever see another war between the three Cosa Nostra families controlling this city. That's unheard of."

Giovanni chuckled. "Everything our father always wanted, in a way."

"It only took three generations to get there," Dante added with a smirk.

"You know, I haven't *officially* taken over the Calabrese family," John said.

Siena decided maybe then she should get up, and go to the bathroom. Or something to get away from the conversation. It wasn't as though any of the men made her feel unwelcomed, but her upbringing had taught her that this was not the sort of thing women were allowed to be a part of.

"I'm just going to go—"

"You can stay where you are," John said, giving her a look.

"It's business, and you know women don't entertain business, John."

"They do in this family," Dante said, "or they have started taking an interest over the years. You're fine to sit."

"See," John pointed out.

Fine.

"It's a matter of semantics," Lucian said, "as they know who their new boss is, and what's expected of them."

"Sure, but I still have to make a show of it, too. Drive the point home."

"We could help with that," Giovanni offered, grinning, "if you would like us to."

"How so?" John asked.

Before any of them could answer John's question, the restaurant door blew open, and with it, bringing cold late-October wind. Siena didn't recognize the disheveled looking man wearing a trench coat, and glaring, but the other men at the table seemed to. Their postures stiffened as the man came closer to their spot.

"Detective," John greeted.

"I don't know what you fucking did, but this isn't over," the man hissed.

"Now, Rosencauld—"

"Who did you pay, huh?" the detective spat out. "Who did you blackmail, or threaten? How did you do it?"

John only smiled up at the man from the side, and never once showed concern or irritation at the intrusion. "I didn't need to do anything. The evidence was on our side."

"Evidence like this?"

The man threw a tablet down on the table, and a video was already playing. On the screen, Siena saw a man she recognized—a Capo from the Calabrese family, although she had never had a real conversation with the man. The same Capo who had spoken against John outside of the hospital the day she pulled the plug on Darren's life support.

He stumbled through his words on the video, tears filled his frightened eyes, though he sat straight and proud on a chair. Darkness rested behind him, and nothing else.

He admitted to the bombing, and to setting it up. He admitted to killing *both* Siena's brothers, and to encouraging the feud between the families to worsen the peace in the city. He admitted where evidence could be found to connect him to everything he confessed. And then he killed himself with the gun sitting in his lap by swallowing a bullet.

Rosencauld pointed a shaking finger at John. "This isn't over."

John laughed. "Oh, it's been over for a while, detective. Have a good day."

The lesson was clear.

Don't fuck with the Marcellos.

"Andino will be out soon," John said after the man left. "*Very* soon."

• • •

Siena carefully maneuvered between the men sitting around the table. It was not her first time being in this spectacularly large home—the Marcello mansion—but she bet it was probably the first time for a lot of the Calabrese made men.

The fact they couldn't stop staring, wide-eyed and enraptured by the blatant show of wealth in status covering every inch, gave credence to their amazement. A few of the men had nodded to her in polite greeting as they were directed inside the home for the meeting, but more than a few wouldn't even look her in the eye.

It was going to take time.

They *would* give respect.

That was just how Cosa Nostra, and made men worked. They did not have to like the situation they currently found themselves in, or even agree with the new boss in charge. They did, however, have to offer respect at every turn.

It was that, or their life.

For most, it was an easy choice.

"Thank you," the last Capo at the table said when Siena set his glass of vodka down beside him.

"You're welcome."

She gave him a smile, but little else. She didn't linger to chat, either, instead heading for the front of the dining room where John had asked her to sit once she was done. She hadn't needed to be present for the meeting—probably shouldn't have been, anyway—but he asked for her to be there.

Siena didn't know how to refuse John.

Not really.

Still, she wasn't there to entertain the Calabrese men, or make nice with any of them, either. She was simply there for John, and so he could make his point clear with these people about where they now stood, where he positioned himself against them, and even Siena's place in the family.

As *his*.

All semantics.

Theatrics of the mafia.

It was what it was.

Sitting on a chair that was not pulled into the table, but set far enough back to make it clear Siena was not joining the men, she only took her attention away from their conversations when John came into the room. Despite the room being full of people waiting on him, he only looked at her.

Coming to stand at her side, his fingers drifted through her loose waves, and he quickly dropped a kiss to the top of her head. At home, in private, John dressed for comfort, or whatever he was doing that day.

Tonight, though, he wore one of his black Armani suits—black shirt, black vest, and black tie underneath. Black on black on black. It was quite a striking sight, and she thought he looked *most* handsome like this.

Sexy, too.

But she would save that for later.

"You good?" he asked her.

Siena nodded. "Of course."

"Good."

One more stroke of his fingers along the line of her jaw, and he turned to greet the men in the room. A wave of his hand to them, and their voices hushed.

John took the chair at the head of the table, and sat down. Glanced passes between one another, and Siena saw the arch of John's brow when he cocked it in challenge.

"You stand when a boss sits unless he has directed you otherwise," John murmured, "so move your asses."

It took a beat.

And then another second.

Chairs scraped as the men slowly rose to their feet. A couple of them grumbled under their breath, but didn't dare voice their complaints much louder than that. Once everyone was standing, John leaned back in the chair, and surveyed the men with his thumb and forefinger resting against his jaw.

"I thought you all might want to see what success in the criminal underworld really looks like," John said, waving his other hand at the opulence of the dining room.

The chandelier was bigger than a small car.

The table?

Flaked with gold.

"You could all learn a thing or two by accepting your fate of a new boss, and a new path for this family, but I assume there are some of you who plan to make this hard for me. Nonetheless, I brought you all here so you could have your *vote*. As we all do—we put in nominations for positions, and vote on them. This is no different. So, we will vote on the boss."

The men's gazes darted fast to John, and then between one another.

"Vote," one of the men echoed.

"That is what I said," John replied calmly.

"Yet, you present yourself as the boss, so where is the vote really?"

John smiled coldly. "I am giving you the illusion of a choice, and then I'm going to make my point very clear."

He lifted his fingers high, and snapped them twice. Siena stayed put on the chair with her hands folded in her lap, and quiet as could be. She knew what was coming, and it didn't shock her like it did the rest of the men to watch a good twenty more men file into the dining room.

Marcello men.

Enforcers.

Capos.

Trusted people.

Each had a gun in hand, though they kept the weapons lowered, and pointed to the ground at their front. Each man came to stand behind every standing Calabrese man, though they didn't speak, and in fact, didn't even look the other men in the eyes.

"I really don't mind wiping a family out and starting over," John said, shrugging. "It actually seems like the easier thing to do, but this takes work, too. Building a family, and working the streets takes time. I figure it will be far more beneficial for all of us to simply ... accept what's going to happen, and move on to better success."

"You can't be fucking serious," one of the men said.

John's gaze drifted to the Marcello man standing behind the Capo who spoke up. His head subtly moved to the side, and the man lifted the gun, and put it to the back of the man's head.

"You will, from this day forward, refer to me in only the best of ways, and with the utmost respect. You will stand when I enter a room as you should do for your boss, and you will behave as proper made men should in a family. Should I find out you even breathed a slur against me—call me crazy, inept, or anything—you will quickly find your way into a grave."

John smile, and leaned forward as he pointed a finger at the men. "You are *all* replaceable. Never think different. I do not care how long you have been a made man, or what got you to this point. You will respect me, or I will be forced to teach you how to respect me. I would much rather leave it to you to figure out."

Then, John looked over at Siena, and gave her a brief smile. "And my girl—Siena. You will see her quite frequently. With me, or at my home. She is an important presence in my life, and she is to be treated as such. She is to be treated with the same care and respect you would give to your mother, sister, or even your wife. As you want other made men to treat the women in your life, I expect the same. She is not your pet, or your servant. She does not answer to you, and what she does choose to do for you, you are to thank her each and every time you are graced with her presence.

"I intend for her to be my wife, and I expect you to treat her accordingly," John said with a wave of his hand.

Siena's throat tightened at those words. Of course, she wanted to marry John. She wanted to be with him forever—but he not used that word with her. He had not yet asked her, but still, happiness slipped through her veins like a drug.

"Do not make me regret choosing this way with you," John said. "Do not make me think the easier route would have simply been cleaning house one by one. That option, by the way, is still very much alive."

Instantly, every man but one sat when John stood from his chair. Siena could not hide her smile, but her concerned gaze drifted to the one man who had stayed standing.

"Do you have something to say?" John asked the man.

"I will not—"

John swept his hand in a sharp motion, and the sound that followed was both deafening, and morbid. The Marcello man standing behind the Calabrese Capo had raised his weapon faster than Siena could catch the move.

Now, the Capo was dead. His body slumped over the beautiful, large cherry oak dining table. His blood from the back of his blown out head mixed in with the ruddy brown of the shined table top.

John sighed, and then waved at the rest of the men. "Shall we start, then?"

Sometimes, a forceful show was the way to go.

Siena couldn't be prouder.

• • •

Siena made a run for the front door, and grabbed the bowl of mini chocolate bars on the way. "I got it this time, John!"

"I like to see them, too."

He slid in behind her with a grin just as she opened the door to showcase three little boys and one little girl in various ninja costumes. They were by far some of the cutest that had come through for Halloween.

Bending down, Siena held the bowl out for the kids to pick their favorite treats from the mix. "Go ahead, boys … and girl."

The little girl with the pink and black ninja costume preened at Siena. "I's can be a ninja, too!"

"You can be whatever you want to be," Siena told her.

John chuckled in the doorway, and helped her to say goodbye to the kids. Once they had darted back down the steps to where their parents were waiting, she and John headed back inside the house.

"Okay, those were my favorites of the night," she declared, setting the bowl aside.

John's laughter followed her into the kitchen. "You've said that for every kid that knocks on the door tonight."

"I can't help it. Look at them."

"So hey, my sister is coming down from California for a week or two," John said.

Siena turned to find he was leaning against the island. "The youngest one?"

"Lucia, yeah. She hasn't met you yet, and I was hoping we might be able to do something with her, or … try. Then she can get to know you, or something."

"Why try?"

John shrugged. "She's still pissed at me for shit that happened a while back. Maybe rightfully so, but it is what it is. I can't change the past, you know?"

Siena smiled softly. "I'm sure she'll forgive you—whatever it was."

"Yeah, maybe. Anyway, you wouldn't mind, would you?"

"Of course, not."

One of her favorite pop songs started to play from the living room, and Siena couldn't help but dance a little to the beat. She went back to working on the food for dinner that she had discarded when the kids knocked.

She could feel John's eyes on her as she moved, and it kind of felt like butterflies beating inside her stomach.

It was strange in some ways how much had changed in such a short amount of time. Her sheltered, carefully controlled life was gone, and she was *happy*.

Sure, things were still a little shaky in a lot of ways. John taking over the family. Her mother was still missing.

Siena was still happy.

She only had one person to thank for that, too.

"Siena."

She spun on her heels to face John at his call of her name, but she had to look down. He was down on one knee, and had one hand outstretched toward her. He opened up his palm, and sitting inside was the prettiest princess cut diamond resting on a thin, interwoven gold bands.

Her heart thundered.

Her muscles froze.

Her breath caught.

John smiled. "I'm sorry it took so long for me to do this, babe."

Siena shook her head. "Never apologize for you, John."

"I love you, Siena. You know that, don't you?"

God, he had to ask?

"I love you more than life itself, John."

"I know—look at all you've done for me. My father used to tell me that everyone has one person who is their person. One single soul meant for theirs. I didn't really believe that until I met you."

She quickly wiped the one tear that escaped from her eye. "You're my one person, John."

"And you're mine, *mia amore*."

"Hurry up and ask."

John laughed. "Siena, will you be my wife?"

"*Yes.*"

He was up off the floor before she had even finished speaking. His lips found hers as he pulled her impossibly close to his body. Love thrummed through her soul. Happiness buzzed through her mind.

Unfortunately, Siena knew …

Reality was never far behind in her life. She never seemed to hold onto happiness for very long before something came to take it away.

She hoped that wasn't the case this time.

God.

She hoped …

CHAPTER EIGHTEEN

JOHN LEANED BACK against the bar, and grinned wide at the sight of the man coming through the front doors of the Brooklyn pub. Andino brushed invisible dirt from his black tweed jacket as the door swung closed behind the three men who followed him in.

Andino's gaze swept the floor—a predatory gaze, in ways—as he looked for the fucker who had demanded a meeting with him for no other reason than because *they said so*. A meeting that needed to happen this very day. On Andino's release from jail. There couldn't be another time.

John hadn't given any other information about the meeting, either. Not that it was him who called it, or why he thought he had any kind of clout to call in a meeting with a Cosa Nostra Don. Knowing his cousin like he did, John figured Andino would show up just to make a point to whatever dumb fuck called him in that he answered to absolutely no one.

Seemed he had guessed right, after all. His cousin didn't look very pleased.

John smiled wider.

Finally, Andino's gaze found John leaning against the bar, and for a split second, his posture softened. His cousin took him in standing there once more, and raised an eyebrow from across the floor.

It was as though Andino was silently asking, *Really, John?*

"Hey, we have to get our kicks from somewhere, man."

Andino let out a laugh, and crossed the floor. His hand came out fast, and struck against John's already outstretched palm to clap, and then shake. Despite not being a physically affectionate kind of guy, John still pulled Andino in for a one-armed hug before he let him go again.

John took his place leaning against the bar once more as he flicked his hand at the two enforcers of his lingering close by. "Go have a drink, *cafones*. Relax a minute. We'll be staying a while before we move onto the next thing."

"You got it, boss."

Off the men went without a look back.

Andino, too, gave the two men who had followed him inside the bar a quick wave and a, "Scatter."

They *scattered*.

"You look good," John said, smirking. "I guess jail did something decent for you after all, huh?"

Andino flipped him the middle finger before taking one of the many stools at the bar. He gestured at the bartender with two fingers, and said, "Whiskey, neat."

Then, his attention was back on John.

"I can't believe you hauled my ass down to this dirty fucking pub for a drink *hours* after I get released."

John shrugged, and tipped his glass of water up for a drink. "Hey, I let you have some time with your wife. Mostly because she threatened everyone who even suggested they wanted to be at the house when you got home, but that's a story for another day. Bet you used and enjoyed every fucking minute with her, too."

Andino didn't deny it. "Yeah, and then I get a call about some arrogant, stupid fuck demanding a meeting with me like he's got some kind of right to."

John chuckled. "I knew you would come here just to beat someone's skull in."

"That's exactly what I was going to do, yeah."

Figures.

"Also," Andino said as he grabbed the glass of amber liquid from the bartender.

"What?"

"Thanks, John."

John nodded. "About time I save your ass for once, I guess."

Andino laughed hard. "Let's not make it a habit."

"You are the one with the level head."

"You've got your good qualities, too," Andino replied in kind.

Turning their backs to the bar, both men overlooked the quiet pub in comfortable silence. John enjoyed this—kind of needed it, really. It had been too long since he just sat down with Andino and did *nothing*.

"You must be busy as hell lately," Andino noted, shooting John a look.

"Christ, you don't even want to *know*."

"Try me."

"The Calabrese organization is a mess. Mind you, it's a mess I can handle, and one I am handling just fine. It's still a goddamn mess at the end of the day. I suspected a lot of the men would be difficult, and they are at times, but they're coming around too."

"How many did you have to kill to get them that way?"

John cleared his throat. "Half a dozen, or so."

"Better than I thought."

"Funny," John drawled. "It's not even the men, really. It's more than that. Their business is shit, Andi. They've depended on their affiliations with other families, and small time gangs to keep their crews moving product, and making money. I don't know if some of the younger made men even know how to go out on the streets, and hustle up a dollar. It's fucking outrageous. Imagine being the boss who drove your organization to that kind of breaking point. They're a goddamn shame."

Andino smirked.

John didn't miss it. "What?"

"Wasn't it you and Siena they called the disgrace of your families? Seems they had something to be hiding in their own closets. Makes sense why the brothers were so adamant about trying to get in more on our business. A slice they could take and claim for themselves, I suppose."

He scowled. "Yeah, well, now I'm left with what's left of what they were trying to hide."

Andino nodded. "Yeah, but you were always one of the best Capos the Marcello *famiglia* ever had, man. Those men have the best to learn from, John. You're going to do fucking fine, and be raking in all the money."

He couldn't help but smile at that. "Better be. I don't need to be wasting my time—I'm trying to live my life, for Christ's sake, not spend the rest of it working the streets as a Don."

"You'll get it straightened out. I have no doubt. I see you're all fucking dressed up, too."

His cousin reached up, and flicked one of the silver buttons on John's blazer.

"Armani," Andino said, cracking another smug smile. "The boss only wears the best."

"I've been wearing Armani since I was sixteen," John said, shaking his head. "The thought of wearing different brands when I know this one fits me well, and doesn't bother me, makes me want to stick an ice pick in my temple."

Andino's brow lifted high. "That's a little ... over the top."

John shrugged again. "Being bipolar sometimes is."

And he had his habits for a reason. Things he ate, and the stuff he did. The clothes he preferred to wear, and even the brand of shoes he had bought for years. He was always going to be a little particular, picky, moody, and obsessive.

It was just who John was.

"So what are you doing today?" Andino asked after another minute of silence.

"Taking a break from work to pester your dumb ass."

Andino shook his head, and grinned. "*After*, I mean."

"Taking my fiancée to meet Lucia."

"Bit that bullet, did you?"

"I waited long enough," John murmured. "I was not waiting one second longer."

"Not really by choice that you had to wait, man."

"Yeah, I know."

"How do you think little Lucy is going to be with Siena?"

John scoffed. "Siena, she'll love. It's me she hates, Andi."

"Not forever."

"Right now is hard enough."

Andino tipped his glass high. "Truth. Consider, though, that she feels so strongly in a negative way about you at the moment because she felt just as strongly about you in a positive way. That means good things—the bridge is not yet burned."

"Actually, that just makes me feel like even more of a piece of shit. She trusted me, and I took something away from her that she cared about."

"Give it time. Better days are ahead, John. Far better days are ahead."

Sure.

But for how long?

• • •

John stayed a few paces behind Siena and Lucia as the two navigated The Annex. Usually, he liked the market because it was yet another place where he could be surrounded by people, but he didn't need to engage them at the same time. He was all for anything that put him in a crowd, but didn't make him the center of attention at the same time.

He was only good with that when *he* wanted it.

Today, though, John was starting to feel like a third wheel as he watched Siena and Lucia chat, and laugh together. He was not privy to their conversation as he didn't want to intrude, mostly. Lucia had barely given him a hello when he picked her up earlier, but she took to Siena damn near instantly.

Small blessings.

He was counting those up.

"John, you're out of that jam you like, right?" Siena asked over her shoulder.

Lucia's gaze drifted to her brother when Siena mentioned his name, but just as fast, hazel fire turned to dark ice in a blink. She looked ahead once more, and didn't grace him with anymore of her attention.

John sighed.

Siena didn't miss the exchange, and frowned. Had his youngest sister not been standing right there, he would have reassured Siena everything was fine. He couldn't do that, so instead, his love was left to try and fix things.

John had come to learn that about Siena.

She was a *fixer*.

"We can grab some of the jam on the way out," he told her. "Don't worry about it, *bella*."

He meant for her not to worry about more than just the jam, and hoped his unspoken message got the point across. He seriously doubted that it did, though. Siena just didn't work that way when it came to John.

Always looking out for him.

Always having his back.

"No, I can make a trip around. I need to grab something else that way, too. You and Lucia keep going. She wants to grab—what is that, again?"

Lucia didn't look at John as she said, "Some bagged tea."

"Yeah, so take her," Siena said, dropping his sister's arm and giving him a pointed look. "And I will meet you at the entrance on the way out of the market."

John tried not to scowl as Siena dropped a quick kiss to his lips and murmured, "Stop pouting, John."

He was *not* fucking pouting.

"I will meet you at the entrance," John grumbled.

"Good."

Her hand patted his cheek affectionately, and then she was gone. Quickly disappearing into the crowd of people. Just as fast, one of the two enforcers that were following along, but also keeping their distance, split away from his partner without needing to be told. He followed behind Siena without her ever realizing he was even there.

That left John.

And Lucia.

Alone.

Together.

Fuck.

"Well, come on, then," Lucia said with a cool tone and a dismissive wave. "It's cold, and I don't want to freeze out here for too long."

John chuckled dryly, but followed along behind his sister. "You didn't mind five minutes ago when Siena was here."

He saw Lucia's shoulders stiffen from behind.

"Yeah, well …"

Time to bite another bullet.

"What do you need me to say, Lucia?" John asked quietly, speaking to the back of her head because she still wouldn't even look at him. "Tell me what to say so that we can move on, and I will do that. Sorry isn't going to be good enough—I get that. So what will do it for you?"

For the briefest second, his sister's posture softened. She stopped walking, but the people continued to blow by them in the market. No one around them seemed to feel the tension biting pain passing between the two siblings.

Slowly, Lucia turned around to face him. The coldness in her gaze had finally left, but he wasn't all too sure that he liked what replaced it, either. A line of watery tears that were damn near ready to fall, but somehow, she held the floodgates back.

"You're right," Lucia said quietly, "sorry *won't* be good enough, John."

"But I am sorry."

She nodded. "*Now.*"

"The day it happened. The day I found you. The day Renzo was taken away. That very second, Lucia, I was *sorry*. That was not what was supposed to happen."

Her jaw hardened, and goddamn, she looked so much like their father in that moment, it was unreal. Only their dad could hold back his emotions with a hardened jaw, and clipped words.

Lucia didn't do that, though. "Did you know he hated me?"

"Who?"

"Renzo," Lucia said. "At first, he thought I was just some little rich bitch with an air-filled head, and a pretty face. I didn't know what it was like to be poor, or to struggle. I didn't know the streets, or how hard they are on people like him. I didn't know what it was like to come where he comes from, or how to survive without a trust fund."

"Lucia—"

"He was right, too. And maybe I should have thanked him for making that obvious to me, you know? He woke me up. It took thirty days to change my life, and *seconds* to make it worse all over again."

John scrubbed a hand down his jaw, and glanced away. Silently, he dug in the inner pocket of his jacket, and pulled out a piece of information he had been keeping hidden for a while. He always planned to give it to Lucia, sure, but at the right time.

Now seemed like that time.

"Here," John said.

Lucia eyed the folded up piece of paper. "What is it?"

"A better apology."

His sister plucked the paper from his hand, but never took her gaze off him all the while. It was almost like she thought he was going to jump out and snatch the paper back, or some kind of nonsense.

Lucia unfolded the four squares of the paper, and silently read over the information. He saw the way her gaze flicked back and forth—how her fingers tightened to crumple the edges of the paper, and the way her eyes filled up with tears all over again.

"You don't have to say anything," John told her. "Not thank you, or fuck you, or anything, Lucia."

"Does Dad know you got this for me?" she asked.

John shook his head. "Nope. It's also not about Dad. It's about us. Sometimes, I think Dad just worries too much about us. He wants us to be safe, and happy, and fulfilled. In the process, his protective nature sometimes smothers us, too. And that's just Dad—he is who he is, and we have to love him regardless, Lucia."

"I do love Daddy, but—"

"You're angry with him, too."

A single tear dropped down Lucia's cheek, but she didn't move to wipe it away. "So fucking mad, John."

"It's cliché, kiddo, but what's meant to be, will be, and fuck the rest." John pointed at the paper, and said, "There's your lifeline, Lucia. You want to talk to Renzo—you want to *know*? He's right there. I'm sorry it's not more."

Lucia clenched the paper harder, and looked up at her brother. "This is perfect, John."

He smiled. "That's all I wanted to—"

His words cut off when a scream filled The Annex. A terrified scream that was accompanied by several other shrill shrieks. People began to scatter like horrified rats shoved in a very small space. One shoved John, which caused him to ram into Lucia. He grabbed hold of his sister with a fucking death grip to keep her from being shoved to the ground.

"What is happening?" Lucia asked.

John had no idea.

Another shrill scream echoed.

Someone shouted, "*She's got a gun!*"

John's blood ran cold. He didn't have any reason to think this was an attack on him, or Siena, but for some reason, he just … knew.

It had to be.

His luck had run out.

"Don't fucking move," he told his sister when he shoved her behind a vendor tent.

"John!"

"Don't move!"

John didn't look back as he darted in the direction that everybody was now running from. The same direction that Siena had went in earlier to get his fucking jam.

Jesus Christ.

For *jam*.

He would be lucky if he could ever put the shit in his mouth again after today. At the moment, it only made him want to vomit at just the thought alone.

John rammed through the oncoming people—he barely heard their shouts of terror, and he faintly registered the fear on their faces. He was laser focused on one thing, and one thing only. He didn't care about anybody else at the moment.

Siena. Siena. Siena.

His heart thundered her name. The organ practically jumped into his throat, and beat even harder there, too.

"You *ruined* us, you little bitch! Everything our family worked for, you ruined it! You disgraced our name, and our legacy and for what? So you could spread your legs for some Marcello—"

"Ma, put the gun down. Please, put the gun down. You're scaring people."

John pushed through the last few people, and came to an abrupt stop only fifteen feet away from the entrance of The Annex. Siena stood in a cleared circle with her mother only a couple of steps away.

Coraline Calabrese.

That fucking bitch.

John hadn't been able to get a lead on the woman once she disappeared after Darren's death, but he hadn't been too worried. He thought—stupidly, clearly—that the woman was just that ... a *woman*. Not one with any power, or capability to hurt them. She could go away and lick her wounds about her shattered family in private, and maybe come back to beg her daughter for forgiveness in the future.

He had been wrong.

So wrong.

They were going to pay for it.

Siena held up her hands, and in one, held the jar of jam John liked. A bright red, sweet mix of raspberries and strawberries. Her position almost looked resigned—she spoke so calmly, and without fear.

John reached for a non-existent gun at his back at the same time Coraline pulled back the hammer on the revolver. He didn't have a gun on him; it wasn't safe given his position, now. He had too much attention from cops and detectives, and his probation said he couldn't have any firearms on his person, legal or otherwise.

That's why he kept the enforcer's close.

Where the fuck were they?

Coraline's gun lit like a sparkler on the Fourth of July when she pulled the trigger. Another gunshot rang out right after.

John was already darting into the circle. His arms were already opened to grab Siena ... or in this case, to catch her.

He fell with her.

On damp pavement.

On cold ground.

Unfeeling.

So numb.

The jar of jam shattered—spilling sweet red all over the ground. It mixed in with the blood pumping from the love of his life in his hands, and the woman resting face-first on the ground with a blown out skull.

Siena stared up at him from his lap as red bloomed over her chest. It soaked through her white, off-the-shoulder dress in the most morbid way. "*John.*"

Panic and rage and fear and pain washed through John's senses all at the same time. He had never been very good at handling this kind of thing.

He raged.

Roared at the man who had shot Coraline.

Shouted at Siena, too.

"John," she breathed.

Dots of blood peppered her lips. Losing pink, and gaining the wrong shade of red, he thought.

"Look at me," he heard himself say. "Keep looking at me, my girl."

She did.

And then she didn't.

The noise in John's mind and emotions became impossibly louder. It became far more painful. It couldn't be contained.

He raged on.

• • •

"They were only trying to *defuse* the situation, John," someone said.

"Which is exactly what enforcers are taught to do," someone else added.

"You don't want them going out with guns blazing all the damn time—that's not how we fucking work, and you know it."

"They did their job, son," was the next sentence flung his way. "Coraline is dead—he took the shot the second he knew he had no choice."

Over his shoulder, John hurled with venom, "A fucking second too late!"

Silence answered him back.

His emotions were up.

Then they went *way* down.

Like a fucking swinging pendulum. One he couldn't possibly control no matter how much he tried to hide his issues.

He knew it was because today had just been too much—too much stimulation, and too much happening. His meds were not meant to combat these kinds of mood swings caused by traumatic events.

He tried to force himself to be quiet so his outbursts lessened.

John went back to staring at the clock.

Three hours in surgery …

Three more hours to go.

Or, that's what the nurse said when she came with an update.

Siena's heart had been nicked by the bullet. It ricocheted off a rib, punctured her lung, and grazed her heart. She'd been drowning and choking in her own blood while she laid in his lap, and that *killed* him.

He was never going to forget that.

Nothing was going to take that image away.

"And you want me to fucking let them go without punishment?"

His snarl echoed back in a silent waiting room.

He had tried to be quiet again.

He failed.

"John?"

He blinked as he stared at the clock. Every ten seconds, on the dot, he blinked again. Like a fucking robot. He heard them talking—his family, and his men. He heard their words and their justifications.

Part of him knew they were right.

Part of him didn't give a fuck.

That part was the one with bloodstained skin, and hatred in his heart. That part was the one who wanted to punish every stupid fuck that had failed to protect Siena today. That part was dead and dying and full of a rage so hot, it could only be the color black.

Like his mind.

Tar black.

"John?"

He looked to the side as someone tugged on his jacket, and found Lucia staring up at him. Her red-rimmed hazel eyes were a stark contrast to his dry, blazing gaze.

"Is she okay?" Lucia asked.

John shrugged, but even the action felt like it took too much effort. "I don't know."

"John, we need to talk about the enforcers—"

He found the men staring at him over his shoulder again—his father, uncles, Andino, and his own men.

They wanted to *talk*.

He wanted to *kill*.

John looked back at the clock. "I don't need to do anything at the moment."

Besides, his choice for those enforcers had already been made.

She lived—they lived.

It was that simple.

It was in God's hands now.
John's hands were tied.

CHAPTER NINETEEN

SIENA CRACKED aching eyelids open to see white stucco tile staring back at her from the ceiling. A strong antiseptic smell burned her lungs with every breath. The low, rhythmic beeps made her head pound. Something hurt like fucking hell in her chest.

She coughed.

Oh, God.

Yeah, shit, that hurt way worse.

Still, she refused to close her eyes and go back to sleep, no matter how much she wanted to do just that. She could tell she was in the hospital, but it was only after a few seconds of being lucid that she remembered why she had found herself there.

Her mother shot her.

Her own mother.

Siena blinked again.

"Look into this light for me, sweetheart, and follow it," she heard a man say.

That statement was quickly followed by a snarled grumble in the corner of the room—an angry, heated hiss of words that both worried her, and comforted her. Siena's bed was propped up higher, and her gaze found the person in question.

John.

His hard-set jaw, and blazing eyes would have nailed the doctor to the wall had the man been looking at John. He clearly didn't like the man using pet names on Siena, and while it was cute, she didn't even think she had the energy to smile at the moment.

"Follow the light, not the angry Marcello in the corner," the doctor said, grinning just a little.

Apparently, she could smile.

It didn't take that much effort after all.

"Sorry," she rasped.

"Johnathan," the doctor said, "I think the patient could use a bit of water. Three quarters of ice, one quarter of water, please."

"The nurse—"

"They are all busy at the moment. Siena will be fine for the entire forty seconds it will wake you to walk across the hall to the machine, and fill her a cup of water."

John looked like he struggled the most just to get up out of that chair. His blazing gaze flitted between the doctor, and Siena momentarily before settling on her. The anger there quickly bled away when she offered him a dry-lipped smile.

Or the best she could give.

"Please?" she asked him.

John nodded, but he didn't tear his gaze away from her until he was out of the room entirely.

"He's very protective of you," the doctor noted, still moving his light.

Siena followed it with her gaze as she had been instructed to do. "He can't really help it."

"He scares my nurses sometimes."

"Yeah, he can't really help that, either."

The doctor chuckled low, and clicked the button on the end of his mini-flashlight. The bright light turned off, and then he shoved it into his breast pocket.

"All in all, you're doing remarkably well. We expected you to wake up within a few hours of your surgery," he explained, "but maybe your body felt you needed the extra rest, as it's been twenty-four hours since you came out of the OR."

Siena almost felt like a sludge hammer had come and beat her right in the chest. "A whole day?"

"Your surgery took about five hours. There was a lung to repair, and a small piece of heart. Once in there, I found fragments from the bullet had embedded into different places. I didn't want to leave those in, so what should have been three hours turned into five. I suspected six—sometimes we all win."

Siena coughed, and pain followed all over again. Blinding, aching pain deep in her chest cavity that then spread throughout her entire nervous system. As though it was her body's way of trying to numb the pain a bit by spreading it out.

Still, it fucking hurt.

She pulled back the hospital gown to see the bandages wrapped around her chest. She suspected there was going to be a mighty scar left behind, but it was only details in the background of far bigger thoughts.

She had survived.

She was alive.

"How long is it going to feel like this?" she asked.

"Hmm, like what, sweetheart?"

"If he doesn't like it, then you probably shouldn't call me that."

The doctor grinned, saying, "You're probably right."

"It feels like I am breathing in acid."

"Ah. Well, until the wound in the lung heals, I imagine. You're breathing without a respirator, and came out of surgery like that, so it won't be long. You are young, and healthy. All good things. I suspect you will be discharged in a couple of weeks, and by then, you probably won't need the bandages. Your nurses will be in twice a day to check the surgery incision, and change the bandages when needed."

The doctor shrugged, adding, "You were incredibly lucky. Had the bullet been even a couple of millimeters to the left, your heart would have been useless. You'll need to take it easy for a month or so. No strenuous activity—nothing more than walking from one room to the next."

That sounded fun.

"I will make sure she rests," John said from the doorway.

John gave Siena a sexy wink, and crossed the room with a cup of ice water in his hand. The doctor gave her one last order to get some sleep, and keep the excitement to a minimum for the first couple of days, and then he left.

The sliding ICU doors closed shut behind him. It was only her and John left, then. The curtains covering the glass windows blocked out the outside world. John used a dial behind her head to turn down the lights in the room.

Another button quieted the machines.

Silently, John climbed into the bed with Siena. She hadn't even gotten the chance to ask him to do that—he already knew what she wanted.

The second he was there with her, and she was wrapped in his embrace, nothing else mattered. She cried because she was sad, and she was happy, and she was terrified. She was all of those things at once, and it was overwhelming.

John rocked her while his lips pressed against her forehead with a soft kiss—comfort, affection, and assurance all rolled into one. Next to the heartbeats between them, she couldn't hear anything else.

She didn't want to.

John tipped her head back, and used the pads of his thumbs to wipe away the tears from her cheeks. He quickly pressed one kiss, and then another just as fast to her smiling lips. All the worry he had shown earlier was gone for the moment. Sure, there was still a bit of concern flashing in his eyes, but nothing like before.

"I'm sorry," she said.

John's brow furrowed. "For what, *amore?*"

"Between us, I'm always the calm, levelheaded one. I know this probably upsets you. I'm sorry."

"*You* don't upset me. Ever."

His statement was so small, and yet firm and sure at the same time. As though it wasn't at all up for argument, and he didn't want to entertain it further. She chose to let it go because it didn't really matter.

John kissed her again—lingering longer the second time, and letting his tongue tease at the seam of her lips. It was not nearly as innocent or sweet as his first kisses. Siena's heart picked up the pace.

"You're not supposed to *excite* me," she whispered.

John laughed darkly. "My bad."

Then, she had another thought. "Is my mom—"

"Dead."

Flat. Dry. Cold.

His tone was all of that, and more.

Siena sucked in a shaky breath. "Yeah, okay."

"Sorry," he murmured. "I know that probably hurts."

"A little."

She was still her mom.

Coraline had given her life.

She simply hadn't cared about it.

"But probably not for the reasons you think," Siena added.

"I think—"

John's words cut off when a knock against glass echoed. Siena could see through the one sliding glass door with no curtain that people were waiting. A new family for her. People who loved her because John loved her.

His family.

"So much for no excitement," John muttered, climbing off the bed.

"They'll be good, and quiet."

"They're Marcellos. They don't know how to be good *or* quiet."

He was right.

But she had needed all their noise and love.

Just like she needed him.

• • •

Six weeks later …

The front door to the Queens home Siena now shared with John slammed shut, and she cursed under her breath. She didn't even have the time to hide the laundry basket she was hauling up the stairs before her lover came around the corner.

John's gaze drifted to the basket in Siena's hands, and then to where she stood halfway up the stairs. His eyes narrowed, and he gave her *that* look. The one a parent might give their child when they caught them doing something naughty.

"Oh, my God," she grumbled, "it is *just* clothes, John."

"You're not supposed to be doing anything but resting, Siena."

He came closer, and she shook her head.

Nope.

She was not doing this with him anymore. She was fine, and he was just going to have to let his overprotective nature down a little bit.

Holy fuck, she was lucky she could wipe her own ass the way he went on sometimes. The most she had gotten to do since leaving the hospital was attend Catherine Marcello's wedding to Cross Donati.

And even then, John barely left her side, or let her do anything more than walk a few steps before he told her to sit down. She knew he was concerned—he didn't want her to push too far, and hurt herself.

Siena was *fine*.

John was going to have to deal with it.

"Siena, put that damn basket down and go read one of your books, or something," John said, his foot landing to the bottom stairs.

She knew he was pissed.

How?

He hadn't taken his shoes off at the front door. There was nothing he hated more than dirt being tracked through the house because people didn't take off their shoes. The fact he was the one tracking dirt meant his focus was somewhere else entirely.

All on her, apparently.

"No," Siena said, turning her back to him.

"*Siena.*"

Her name practically yanked from his lips in a growl. A warning, if she ever heard one. John was not playing around, but neither was she.

Siena picked up her pace, and climbed the last few stairs without even losing a breath. She hoped that would be a clue to John—because her last three appointments had apparently not done that for him.

John was right behind her all the way. She made it to their bedroom, and dropped the basket on the floor beside the bed when he rushed into the room, too.

"What in the hell is wrong with you?" he asked.

"You."

John snapped back like she had struck out at him.

So, maybe she could have presented that statement a little bit easier than she had. Still, it needed to be said, and John needed to *hear* it for once.

"You hover, and you nitpick at every little thing I do," she told him. "You even get frustrated when I want to have a shower instead of a bath because I might be on my feet for too long. I couldn't even dance at your cousin's wedding—I wanted to dance with *you*. In case you forgot, I also have a job. Or I did, before you know, my brothers were killed. But now *I* own those businesses—they're mine, and I have to take care of them. I need to get out, and do shit, John. Work. Walk. See the goddamn sun."

He stared at her, unmoved and quiet.

Siena continued on, saying, "It's a laundry basket with a half of a load full of clothes. It weights six pounds at most. I can carry it from the downstairs, to the upstairs, and put it away without a problem. I am *fine*."

"Fine," John murmured.

"That's what I said."

"And I am your problem."

Siena pressed her lips together before saying, "I didn't mean it like that, and you know it, John. I just meant ... I know what happened was traumatic for you, and it scared you. You're not going to say that, though, because it's you. But I *know*. I do."

John glanced away, and scrubbed a hand down his face. "I don't want you to push yourself too hard, that's all."

"It's been six weeks. I am cleared. I can resume normal activity. You know this."

"But what if—"

"No."

"Siena, you have to—"

"No."

"You can't—"

"Nope."

John let out a frustrated grunt, saying, "Let me finish a sentence, *donna*."

"Unless that sentence is something about getting me on my knees, I really don't want to hear it. Because you know what, that's another thing. You won't even fuck me for fear I might get out of breath. That's kind of the point of *sex*, John."

"I know what sex does!"

"That is not the thing I want to hear," Siena said in a singsong fashion.

John gave her a look.

Another unspoken warning.

Siena wasn't having it.

"Killing me here," John muttered under his breath.

Siena grinned wickedly. "What if I helped you along, then? Do you think that would snap you out of this nonsense?"

"It's not nonsense. It's—"

John's words cut off when Siena pulled the straps of the dress she was wearing down over her shoulders. Without the straps to hold the flimsy fabric up, it simply fell down her body, and landed in a heap at her feet.

She wore nothing underneath.

No bra.

No panties.

This was planned.

She had a goal.

She was going to get it.

John made a noise under his breath, and then said, "What are you doing?"

Siena gave him a wink over her shoulder as she moved toward the bed. "What do you think?"

"You seriously want to fuck right now? We're having a discussion."

"No, you're having a discussion with yourself. I told you what I told you, John."

She bent over the bed to reach for one of the pillows, and pulled it toward her chest. Her scar had healed, but it could still be a little tender. Having something soft to rest on would help that little issue.

"Jesus *Christ*," John said low and husky.

Siena looked back at him.

She knew exactly what he was seeing—her bent over, and her bare ass high in the air. Given her legs were a little spread, he could probably see a peek of her pussy, too.

John's gaze lingered on her backside.

Siena smiled.

Good.

"Killing me here," he rumbled, moving closer with every word. "I know what you're doing, Siena."

Dark.

Rich.

Sinful.

His tone promised sex.

Siena's body hummed in anticipation. "Do you?"

She jumped—heating shooting through her body—when John's warm, rough palm slid from her ass to the top of her spine. His other hand landed a soft slap to her backside. Not enough to hurt, but just enough to *sting*.

It made her sigh.

"I am fine," she said, looking back at him.

John's hazel gaze found hers. "So you say."

"I am."

"Mmm."

He just needed a little more pressure applied, apparently.

Siena could do that.

She pushed her ass back into his groin before he could think to stop her. At the same time, she slid her hand between her thighs, and let the tips of her fingers run through her sex. Dampness met her fingertips, and she used that wetness to help her fingers slide in fast circles around her clit.

Jesus.

Already, her body was revving to go. Already, she was wet between her thighs. It had been too long for this, and she was not waiting one more fucking second.

"Siena," John murmured.

She kept playing, knowing damn well he could hear the sound of her fingers sliding through her arousal. "You should help me out here."

How was she already breathless?

How?

"Well," John drawled in that rumbly way of his, "I think you should get yourself off first, and then we'll talk about what comes after that."

Siena's eyes widened, and she found him grinning behind her. He lifted a single brow as if to ask her to challenge him while he shrugged off his suit jacket, and began unbuttoning his dress shirt.

Her fingers stopped working between her thighs. He didn't miss it.

"Don't stop now, Siena, you started this little game."

"But ... but I want *you* to—"

"I know what you want, and you can wait."

Fuck.

She as not a dumb woman.

She could see how this turned around on her.

His palm came down on her ass harder than the first time. The harsh, yet still lovely, sting sent her flying up to her tiptoes with a gasp.

"Play," John ordered. "And don't be fucking cute about it, either, or you'll wait longer, babe."

"Fuck you," she whispered through a laugh.

John flashed her a grin with teeth. "And we will be talking about the other shit you brought up after."

"Whatever," she said, working her fingers faster against her clit with every passing second. "I got what I wanted."

"Or you will soon," he countered.

"You know it, John."

"Widen those beautiful legs of yours. Show me that pussy—I want to see your fingers nice and wet. It's all mine, so let me see it."

Damn.

His filthy words flamed her desire higher.

Siena did what she was told, and made sure to let him see two of her fingers press deep into her sex before she dragged them back up to her clit. "You like that?"

"Just worry about you, babe."

Because yes, he did like it.

Siena heard the fabric of his shirt ruffle as he yanked it off, and then tossed it aside. She looked back at him again at the rustle of a buckle just in time to see him shove his pants down over his hips, and free his already hard cock from the confines of his boxer-briefs.

Not once did John's eyes drift away from where her fingers worked between her thighs. She saw lust glint there—a pure, carnal love at what he was seeing. That only made her hotter, and already, she felt like she was going to combust.

Her nerves sang.

Her skin hummed.

Her clit ached.

"Almost?" he asked.

"God, *yeah.*"

"God does not live in this bedroom, babe. It is just you, and me."

The spiral of her orgasm came on fast. A shot of cold down her spine, and a wave of heat in her gut. Pleasure started from somewhere in her center, and radiated outward until it reached the tips of her fingers and toes.

"Holy shit," Siena breathed into the pillow.

Intense, but not quite enough.

Wonderful, but it could have been more.

Good, but the relief didn't linger.

She couldn't make herself come like John could. It was sometimes strange to her how this man knew her body even better than she did.

John proved it in those seconds by letting one of his fists tangle in her hair, and sliding his hard length into her clenching sex before she had even finished panting her way through the orgasm. She felt him flex, and he was seated in deep.

Stretching her open.

Filling her full.

"Christ, I love the way you soak me," he said behind her.

His body fit perfectly against hers. So deep, her muscles hummed from clenching around him so tight. She vibrated all over.

She could feel that promise of another release—a better, stronger one—just beyond her grasp. She wouldn't be able to reach it herself.

No, he would have to take her there.

"Ask me for it," John murmured against the back of her neck.

His other hand slid around her throat. Long fingers wrapped along the delicate column, and held tight. She still had her breath, sure, but it caught in her throat a little with every exhale and swallow. His fingertips danced along her pulse point.

"Ask me for it, Siena."

"Please fuck me."

"Hmm? I didn't hear you, babe."

His lips grazed her neck, and then her ear. His words slipped over her skin with damningly sinful intent.

A wicked promise.

"Please fuck me, John," she said a little louder.

Not much, though.

She was airless.

Her mind muddy.

Her body needy.

"Please, *please* fuck me."

He either got the response he wanted, or he felt bad for teasing her like he had. She didn't even get the chance to take another breath, or prepare for him to take her again. He simply pulled back, and flexed forward all in the same second.

A hard thrust that sent her back up to her toes, and pushed her further into the pillow. She was right—the softness of the pillow cushioned her chest enough to keep the tenderness at bay.

She didn't even think about it at all as he pounded into her from behind. She couldn't think about anything except for his cock driving into her over and over again, and the way he held onto her hair and throat at the same time.

His pace was brutal.

Unforgiving.

So relentless.

John didn't slow at all when Siena's cries became a little higher, and her breaths came out shorter. He fucked her through the second orgasm, and then kept on going until she was shouting her way through a third.

Nobody owned her like he did.

Nobody loved her like he did.

Nobody could ever possibly be him to her.

"One more," she heard him say, his words mumbled into her hair. "Give me one more, babe."

"I can't—I *can't*."

She didn't think she could come again.

John had a different opinion. "You sure fucking can."

It took longer for the fourth orgasm to come. It took her fingers toying between her thighs, while he fucked her hard enough to make her bones ache in the best way. It took two of his fingers stuffed into her ass while he yanked her hair back, and whispered the dirtiest things in her ear.

God.

She loved all of it.

She didn't hurt a bit.

She really was just fine.

"Fuck, *yeah*."

She heard John's grunt through her mindless, pleased haze a second before his warm cum painted her back. His hand pressed hard against her shoulders, and she could feel the tremor working its way through his body just from the pressure alone as he tried to keep himself upright.

Siena laughed.

John chuckled, too.

"I still said what I said," she said, tasting sex and love on her tongue. "And I meant it—I am fine, John."

"Don't push me, Siena."

"Who else will?"

CHAPTER TWENTY

Two months later ...

JOHN LAUGHED AS the men crowded him into a hotel room. His father followed in behind his uncles, cousin, and grandfather with baby Tiffany on his hip.

"Come on," John said, "I am sure I can fucking dress myself, now."

"We have to make sure you don't run," Giovanni joked.

"And we have to have at least one drink before you head down," Andino added.

He gave his cousin a look. "I'm not drinking."

Dante gave John a light slap to his cheek as he passed. "One drink will not hurt you—we'll make it a beer."

Fine.

A beer he could do.

"Here," Andino said, throwing the garment bag at John.

"Christ, that's a four-thousand dollar Armani suit. Be easy, Andi."

Andino pointed a finger at his cousin. "Get your ass dressed."

Lucian gestured at the attached bathroom. "Get ready in there. We'll be waiting when you're done."

The rest of them were already done up, and waiting on him. Frankly, they had kept him running and on his feet from the moment he woke up to a splash of cold water being dumped on his face that morning.

Fucking Andino.

"I hope you all did this to Andi on his wedding day, too," John threw over his shoulder.

"Nope," someone called back.

"Assholes."

He shut their laughter out by closing the bathroom door. Finally, he had some kind of silence for the first time all day.

John stood there and soaked it in.

Soon, nothing would be quiet.

A room full of guests.

A dinner.

A party after.

It was a lot of stimulation, and probably the only thing about this whole day that had really concerned John. Still, anticipation curled heavily in his gut, mixing with the lingering longing that hadn't left him since he knew he loved Siena.

He was getting married to the love of his life today.

Nothing else mattered.

• • •

"All right, I'm fucking dressed," John said as he left the bathroom.

Surprisingly, only his father and Andino were left in the room. Well, and little baby Tiffany sleeping over her grandfather's shoulder.

"Where did everybody go?" John asked.

"To get the drinks," Andino said, flashing him a grin. Coming close to John, his cousin pulled him in for a one-armed hug. "You look good, man."

"I better."

Andino laughed. "Don't pump that ego up too big, huh?"

"Too late."

"It's a Marcello thing."

That was the excuse they all used.

Nothing ever changed.

"I have to go grab something from Haven, but I'll be back," Andino told him.

John nodded. "Sure, man."

Once Andino was gone from the room, John took a seat beside his father. Lucian gave him a small smile all the while patting his granddaughter's bottom in a rhythmic fashion to keep her asleep.

Things with Cella weren't necessarily better, but they weren't horrible, either. At least, his sister could stand to be in the same room with him, and didn't make it her second job to glare at him. She was still grieving, though, and so John opted to keep his distance.

Time would heal wounds.

After all, time had healed *his* wounds.

Well, time and Siena.

"You know I'm proud of you, don't you?" Lucian asked quietly.

John nodded. "I know, Dad."

He reached over and stroked the sleeping baby's cheek.

"She's precious," Lucian said. "I thought very little would compare to when my children were born, but let me say, grandchildren are something else entirely. I look forward to having more, and *soon*."

His father gave him a pointed look.

John rolled his eyes. "Not even trying to be sly."

"I have moved beyond that stage in my life. It doesn't get me what I want."

"Children are not on the table for a while."

Lucian frowned. "Why not?"

John shrugged, but didn't offer any information as to how much the thought of children terrified him to his core. He still struggled with the idea of passing on a life that sometimes felt like a punishment, rather than simply a difference.

"Ah," Lucian said like he could read John's mind.

John cocked an eyebrow. "What?"

"You still think about that genetics test we did years ago, don't you?"

"And the information you found about Lina."

Lina being his father's biological mother.

Lucian cleared his throat. "And yet, despite the fact she was bipolar, all I remember about my mother is how beautiful, loving, and wonderful she was, John."

"Perhaps your perspective is colored by the fact she died when you were like seven, or something."

"Perhaps, but I don't think it matters, either." Lucian smiled faintly again. "You should never—*ever*—be afraid to have a child just like you, son. You were an amazing boy who grew into an incredible man. You were perfect—more like me than your mother, but with just enough of Jordyn to color you up. You made your mother and I better people, John. You made us better parents. We learned to stop and take account of ourselves, and of others. We learned not to be ignorant in our thoughts and feelings about things people suffer with, and often suffer in silence."

Lucian shrugged, adding, "You were, and still are, one of our greatest gifts. And if anything I have ever done makes you afraid to be a father, then I am sorry."

"You are the best father."

"Who still makes mistakes sometimes," Lucian said.

"That's what humans do."

It had just taken him a long time to realize that.

"Please don't be afraid to have a child like you, John. Don't ever be afraid to become a better man because of it, either."

• • •

John stood at the end of the makeshift aisle. Silk and tulle and bushels of white and pink flowers covered the place in light colors, and floral scents. Guests had already filled the fifty or so white chairs set up—their ceremony was small, but their party would be massive.

Siena liked the harp, so a woman dressed in purple played one in the corner. An ordained minister waited behind John and Andino, ready to begin whenever those doors at the back opened.

They could have had this ceremony in a church, as would have been better for *la famiglia*, but John refused to wait. He would not spend time on useless couple's counseling when he already knew what he wanted for the rest of his life.

He didn't need a priest to confirm it.

Siena was his.

And he was hers.

Andino's hand clapped John on the shoulder. "You ready?"

John nodded.

Sweet Jesus.

He had been ready for his whole life. It just took three decades to finally meet her. Because that's what Siena was to him—his life.

"Yeah," John said.

Andino nodded to someone in the back, and the waiting man stepped up to the doors. He swung them open, and took a step back to get out of the way.

There, waiting, was Siena.

In her A-line, ivory lace wedding dress that swept the floor, and trailed behind her with a four foot train. Her veil kept her face hidden, but not quite enough. He could still see the way her painted red lips curved with love when his gaze landed on hers.

She was beautiful.

So perfect.

He was going to spend the rest of his life loving this woman, and making sure she knew it every second of every single fucking day of their lives.

She had been his catalyst.

She had been his saving grace.

She was his everything.

Loving her forever was the least he could do.

"Your turn," Andino said.

Yeah, it was his turn.

He promised, after all.

She wouldn't walk alone.

John made his way down the aisle in a quick stroll. Siena stayed still at the very end, waiting for him.

He probably should have waited until the end of the ceremony to do what he did.

It was the custom.

Tradition.

John didn't care about any of those things. The second he met her at the end, he bunched her veil up, flipped it back, and kissed her hard.

Laughter lit up the room.

Siena's smile curved against his.

"I love you," he told her.

"I love you, John."

"Are you ready?"

Siena nodded. "I have been ready."

They turned to face the now-standing guests.

A future was waiting.

Finally.

EPILOGUE

Three years later …

IF THERE WAS one thing—above all things—about her marriage and John that Siena thought was most important to remember, it was that surprises were not welcomed. Especially if said surprise meant a huge change in their lives, or something that could cause a massive emotional upheaval.

For other people, a change could be a good thing. A little stress, and a bit nerve-wracking, sure. They would, however, roll with the punches and accept the change.

For John, though, a change that could and would impact his entire life often led him to overthinking, panicking, and more. It almost guaranteed a hypomanic episode would be on the horizon, and once that was controlled, a short bout of depression to battle.

Siena never blamed him for these things.

She never wished for anything different.

Oh, she loved John.

Every part of him was hers to love.

So as she sat on the edge of the tub in their master bathroom, and stared at the little strip of plastic in her hand … she couldn't help but think of what this would mean, and what would come of it.

The pregnancy test flashed with the word *pregnant*.

Over and over.

It had been flashing that for thirty minutes now. Her heart was so full—happiness, trepidation, and joy. A love so fierce, she could hardly breathe. Already, she loved this baby. A child she didn't know, and would not see or hold for months. A child whose gender was still unknown, and whose name was yet to be picked.

And yet …

God, she loved this baby.

Still, the hesitance she felt was also very real.

Long ago, she and John had decided that children would be a very carefully planned event for them. When both of them were ready, and when everything was handled, then they would move forward *together* on having children.

This had not been planned at all.

Certainly not carefully.

A bout of a terrible chest cold that left Siena with a nasty infection, and led into pneumonia that she couldn't shake caused her to miss an appointment for her shot. She had been stuck in bed, and then in the hospital for two weeks when the pneumonia got really bad.

John had barely left her side, of course.

Once she was better, her doctor recommended she wait until her cycle started at least once—as she hadn't had a period in years since starting the shot—before they started the birth control again. They had been advised to use condoms as a backup method.

Yeah, well …

Her cycle never started. She and John didn't know what a fucking condom was considering they hadn't used them since the start of their relationship years ago.

They both knew better.

She knew better.

This was bound to happen.

Siena had promptly vomited every bit of the eggs and bacon mess John had left for her in the oven before he left for his morning jog. She had been keeping a pregnancy test hidden in her purse … just in case.

A part of her already knew.

Siena tapped the test against her palm again.

Pregnant, it flashed.

She was still trying to figure out a way to tell John and not surprise him, so to speak. She knew it was going to be practically fucking impossible. There could be no cute reveal that she secretly recorded, and then posted for the world to see. There could be no baby shoes in a gift box for him to open and be surprised.

None of that could happen.

She had to take away that element of shock so that this did not feel as though something John was not ready for in the first place.

Easier said than done.

Children had been his one sore topic for years. Not because he didn't want to be a father, but because she knew he worried that he was going to pass on the same genetics that had been given to him. Whatever it was in his DNA that left him with a disorder that clouded and colored his life, thoughts, and emotional processing a little bit differently than everyone else.

It didn't matter.

Children had always been non-negotiable for her. And she knew without a doubt that John would be the best father.

There was nothing wrong with him. There had never been anything wrong with him. Just like their children—nothing would ever be wrong with them, either. Regardless, they would be perfectly *them*. Little babies made by people who loved each other, and would love them.

They *would* have kids.

It was simply when.

Siena figured that time was now.

• • •

"John?"

"Hmm?"

He leaned over the top of her, and kissed the top of her head. In the vanity, her smile grew the longer his kiss lingered against the top of her head.

John's fingers tangled into the waves of her hair, and held firm. "Love you."

Siena reached up and patted his cheek—three day scruff tickled her fingertips. "I love you."

"What did you want, babe?"

"I was thinking ..."

"Keep going."

He straightened a bit, and she kept an eye on him in the vanity mirror. In sleep pants that hung low on his waist, and his chest bare, it was a little distracting.

Siena forced herself to pay attention to the topic at hand. "I was thinking about the bedroom across the hall."

"The empty one."

"We kept it empty for a reason."

John's fingertips drifted over her bare shoulder. "For the *someday* nursery, you said."

"Yeah, for that."

"What, did you want to turn it into a private office or something?"

She usually worked out of the house, and if she did work inside, she used his office. John never minded, or if he did, he never said anything about it.

"Or something," she replied.

John met her gaze in the mirror, and amusement stared back. "Okay, what, then?"

"What do you think about pastel green?"

"For a color?"

"Like paint," she said. "It's neutral."

"So is beige."

"But beige doesn't really fit for a nursery, John."

Momentarily, she saw him stiffen. Just as quick, though, he relaxed.

"No, I guess it doesn't."

"I would really like to start getting the nursery set up, John."

"Would you?"

Siena shrugged, and all her worries drifted away the second John bent down to kiss the top of her head again.

"All right," he murmured. "I think we can do that."

"Because we'll need one."

John's eyebrow arched a bit as he tipped his head up, and found her gaze in the mirror once more. "Will we?"

"What names do you like?"

His next swallow echoed.

The silence stretched on.

Siena waited John out.

"Luciano for a boy."

"For your dad," she said.

John nodded once. "And for my grandfather, yeah. Johnathan for a middle name."

"What about for a girl?"

"I don't know."

Siena grinned. "You better figure it out, don't you think? We'll need to know."

John sucked in a quiet breath, and his hands tightened on her shoulders. Not to a painful point, but a feeling that made her calm in an instant.

"That so?" he asked.

"I know this isn't happening the way we talked about it, and—"

"Nothing is ever as I plan, Siena."

"Are you happy?"

"And terrified," he admitted. "But so happy."

So happy.

That was all she needed to know. The rest, they could deal with. Just like everything else in their life.

They faced it together.

Head-on.

Unafraid.

Unashamed.

Unbroken.

• • •

Four months later ...

"Your turn," Siena whispered to John.

He laughed, but she heard the stress in the sound. He smiled for their gathered, waiting family, but she saw the tension in his shoulders.

The further along in her pregnancy she became, the more changes she saw in John. Never toward her, but just him in general. She recognized his lack of sleeping, and his up and down moods. She saw his methodical cleaning, planning, and organizing even when he tried to hide it.

She wished he wouldn't hide it.

It was so much harder to settle him back when he hid it.

Leonard would be at their house when they got back—waiting for John, as the man always did. Twice a week, and sometimes more if John felt it was needed, his therapist came for an in-home session.

They never opened up discussion about John's mental health to anyone who asked. They didn't talk about his meds, his therapy, or anything.

Their choice.

John's choice.

Leonard, however, would be there tonight because Siena had made a call and asked for him to come, not John. Sometimes, she needed to do that. Sometimes, she had to be the voice when John was not letting his come through loud enough.

John took the one cupcake Siena offered to him—the only one left. Everyone else around them already had one, and now they were just waiting on him, too.

"My turn," John echoed.

Siena nodded, and smiled. "I love you, John."

"I know you do."

She always would.

"Everybody at the same time," Siena said, directing her comment at the room, yet never looking away from John. "Okay?"

"You got it, babe."

"Now."

Everybody bit into their cupcake, and blue frosting colored up the middle of the sweet cake. John stared at the sweet in his hand for a long while, and Siena reached over to wipe a bit of blue frosting from his bottom lip while cheers lit up the room.

"It's a boy!"

"A boy!"

John barely blinked as his father crossed the room to clap his son on the shoulders, and congratulate them. Jordyn followed behind Lucian, and did the same. Siena and John took a moment to take the congratulations, and the ones that followed from everyone else.

But soon, the room settled, their family faded as John looked at Siena, and it was just them once more. No one else.

He had wanted this gender reveal.

For his family.

To allow them *in*.

Sometimes, he still found it hard to let them in.

The pregnancy was one thing he continued to try to open up for them, but especially for his mother and father.

"Luciano, then," John said.

Siena smile wider. "Luciano Johnathan Marcello. And he will be perfect, John."

So perfect.

Just like his father.

• • •

Luciano Johnathan made his way into the world loudly. He made damn sure his mother felt every pain, and he didn't let her rest in the labor for even a single second.

Siena didn't mind.

Once that hazy-eyed, dark-haired baby that looked so much like his father was placed in her arms, the rest was forgotten. Nothing mattered but little Luciano.

And then his father got a hold of him, Luciano's eyes opened wide and found John's. Siena knew in that moment, she was probably never going to get him back.

Not entirely.

"Oh, my God," John murmured. "Look at this boy, Siena."

She had.

And in those few seconds, she memorized him.

"He looks just like you," she said.

He chuckled. "And you."

But not nearly as much as Luciano took after his father. Siena didn't mind.

John's finger traced the line of the baby's nose. Soft, gentle, and sweet.

"Everybody's waiting to meet you, Lucky," John said.

Everybody could wait, too.

The baby blinked, and his tiny little fingers instinctively curled around his father's thumb.

John smiled. "Yeah, I'm your daddy, *bambino*."

At the same time he spoke to their son, he reached for her. His palm cupped her cheek, and his thumb stoked her skin.

Even while falling in love with his child, he never forgot about her.

He still loved her.

Their forever was now.

And it was beautiful.

ACKNOWLEDGMENTS

I'm not going to use this space to discuss mental health again as I did that in the first book of the *John + Siena* duet. But I do hope that if you haven't read that note from me in *Loyalty*, then maybe you will go back and do that now. Especially if the subject matter in these books touched you on any level with a sense of compassion—mental illness needs a voice, please help it to become louder so that more people can get the help they need.

Thank you to every reader who messaged me about John, who thanked me for writing him, who admitted secrets to me about their life because John made them feel bolder, or because they felt they had something in common with my life ... thank you for sharing the beauty of yourself with me— every part of it, even if you feel like it's not the best part of you. It doesn't matter. Every part that makes you who you are is exactly what you are. It's *you*. And you are more than welcome to keep the messages coming.

To every reader who felt like they had to say they had never read books like this before ... I wish there were far more, and then maybe this wouldn't feel so eye-opening, or misunderstood. Please find compassion and care for those who are struggling—you never truly understand what someone is going through in their life, or the battles they fight just to survive.

To my editing girl, Eli, thank you for making the words shine! To Sasha, for helping me behind the scenes. Tracy, all my love to you for proofing and getting these books earlier than everybody else. London for letting me be the petty queen at least once a day, haha. And thank you to Mignon for the beautiful covers that captured this duet so perfectly. Sometimes, life and love feels like standing knee- or throat-deep in water that's about to drown you, doesn't it?

And to my hubby and boys … I always seem to thank you last in every one of these, don't I? Saving the best for last, I guess. Thank you for loving me just the way I am. Every obsessive, overreactive, difficult, broken, and honest part of me. Not all are so lucky.

Bethany-Kris

ABOUT THE AUTHOR

Bethany-Kris is a Canadian author, lover of much, and mother to four young sons, one cat, and three dogs. A small town in Eastern Canada where she was born and raised is where she has always called home. With her boys under her feet, a snuggling cat, barking dogs, and a spouse calling over his shoulder, she is nearly always writing something ... when she can find the time.

Find Bethany-Kris at her:
WEBSITE: www.bethanykris.com
BLOG: www.bethanykris.blogspot.ca
FACEBOOK www.facebook.com/bethanykriswrites
TWITTER: www.twitter.com/bethanykris
INSTAGRAM: www.instagram.com/bethany.kris

Sign up to Bethany-Kris's New Release Newsletter here:
http://eepurl.com/bf9lzD.

OTHER BOOKS

John + Siena

Loyalty
Disgrace

Cross + Catherine

Always
Revere
Unruly

Guzzi Duet

Unraveled, Book One
Entangled, Book Two

DeLuca Duet

Waste of Worth: Part One
Worth of Waste: Part Two

Standalone Titles

Effortless
Inflict

Donati Bloodlines

Thin Lies
Thin Lines
Thin Lives
Behind the Bloodlines
The Complete Trilogy

Filthy Marcellos

Antony
Lucian
Giovanni
Dante
Legacy
A Very Marcello Christmas
The Complete Collection

Seasons of Betrayal

Where the Sun Hides
Where the Snow Falls
Where the Wind Whispers

Gun Moll Trilogy

Gun Moll
Gangster Moll
Madame Moll

The Chicago War

Deathless & Divided
Reckless & Ruined
Scarless & Sacred
Breathless & Bloodstained
The Complete Series

The Russian Guns

The Arrangement
The Life
The Score
Demyan & Ana
Shattered
The Jersey Vignettes

Find more on Bethany-Kris's website at www.bethanykris.com.

www.ingramcontent.com/pod-product-compliance
Lightning Source LLC
Chambersburg PA
CBHW072350020726
47506CB00004B/1085